SACRED GROUND

What Reviewers Say About
Missouri Vaun's Work

Slow Burn

"This is the first book by Missouri Vaun that I've ever read and I wasn't sure how that was going to go. I'm pleased to say that I was not disappointed at all. In fact, I was hooked right at the first chapter and still had my undivided attention throughout the rest."—*Lesbian Review*

"This book is like a breath of fresh air after a hard day. In fact, this is the kind of book I would grab to read after a bad day, or after reading something very intense. ...This is a charming and tender romance with great characters, a wonderful setting, moments of excitement and lots of love. I really enjoyed this book, and I think you will too."—*Rainbow Reflections*

The Mandolin Lunch

"Two timid school teachers find love in this cozy lesbian contemporary from Vaun. The result is touching..."—*Publishers Weekly*

"*The Mandolin Lunch* was a very pleasant surprise. The characters are very lovable, the story is sweet but what I really enjoyed above all are the descriptions of Garet's work as an artist. Vaun knows what she's writing about and the details of the process from blank page to illustration, the journey of the drawing feels authentic and fascinating"—*Jude in the Stars*

The Sea Within

"This is an amazing book. *The Sea Within* by Missouri Vaun is an exciting dystopian adventure and romance that will have you reading on the edge of your seat."—*Rainbow Reflections*

Chasing Sunset

"A road trip romance with good characters that had some nice chemistry."—Kat Adams, Bookseller (QBD Books, Australia)

"*Chasing Sunset* is a fun and enjoyable ride off into the sunset. Colorful characters, laughs and a sweet romance blend together to make a tasty read."—*Aspen Tree Book Reviews*

"This is a lovely summer romance. It has all the elements that you want in this type of novel: beautiful characters, great chemistry, lovely settings, and best of all, a nostalgic road trip across the country."—*Rainbow Reflections*

"I really liked this one! I found both Finn and Iris to be well fleshed out characters. Both women are trying to figure out their next steps, and that makes them both insecure about where their relationship is going. They have some major communication issues, but I found that, too, realistic. This was a low key read but very enjoyable. Recommended!"—Rebekah Miller, Librarian (University of Pittsburgh)

"The love story was tender and emotional and the sex was steamy and told so much about how intense their relationship was. I really enjoyed this story. Missouri Vaun has become one of my favourite authors and I'm never disappointed."—*Kitty Kat's Book Review Blog*

Spencer's Cove

"Just when I thought I knew where this story was going and who everyone was, Missouri Vaun took me on a ride that totally exceeded my expectations. ...It was a magical tale and I absolutely adored it. Highly recommended."—*Kitty Kat's Book Reviews*

"The book is great fun. The chemistry between Abby and Foster is practically tangible. ...Anyone who has seen and enjoyed the series *Charmed*, is going to be completely charmed by this rollicking romance."—*reviewer@large*

"Missouri Vaun has this way of taking me into the world she has created and does not let me out until I've finished the book."
—*Les Rêveur*

"I was 100% all in after the first couple of pages and I wanted to call in sick, so I could stay home from work to immerse myself in this story. I've always enjoyed Missouri Vaun's books and I'm impressed with how she moves between genres with such ease. As paranormal stories go, this one left me thinking, 'Hmm, I wish I was part of that world,' and I've never read a book featuring vampires or weres that left me with that feeling. To sum it up, witches rock and Vaun made me a believer."—*Lesbian Review*

Take My Hand

"The chemistry between River and Clay is off the charts and their sex scenes were just plain hot!"—*Les Rêveur*

"The small town charms of *Take My Hand* evoke the heady perfume of pine needles and undergrowth, birdsong, and summer cocktails with friends."—*Omnivore Bibliosaur*

"I have a weakness for butch/femme couples so the Clay/River pairing worked for me, even if their names made me laugh. I like the way Missouri Vaun writes and felt like I got to know the folks in Pine Cone in just a few short scenes. The southern charm is front and center in *Take My Hand* and as River Hemsworth discovers, the locals are warm and welcoming."—*Late Night Lesbian Reviews*

Love at Cooper's Creek

"*Blown away...how have I not read a book by Missouri Vaun before.* What a beautiful love story which, honestly, I wasn't ready to finish. Kate and Shaw's chemistry was instantaneous and as the reader I could feel it radiating off the page."—*Les Reveur*

"*Love at Cooper's Creek* is a gentle, warm hug of a book."—*Lesbian Review*

"As always another well written book from Missouri Vaun—sweet romance with very little angst, well developed and likeable lead characters and a little family drama to spice things up."—Melina Bickard, Librarian, Waterloo Library (UK)

Crossing the Wide Forever

"*Crossing the Wide Forever* is a near-heroic love story set in an epic time, told with almost lyrical prose. Words on the page will carry the reader, along with the main characters, back into history and into adventure. It's a tale that's easy to read, with enchanting main characters, despicable villains, and supportive friendships, producing a fascinating account of passion and adventure."—*Lambda Literary Review*

Birthright

"The author develops a world that has a medieval feeling, complete with monasteries and vassal farmers, while also being a place and time where a lesbian relationship is just as legitimate and open as a heterosexual one. This kept pleasantly surprising me throughout my reading of the book. The adventure part of the story was fun, including traveling across kingdoms, on "wind-ships" across deserts, and plenty of sword fighting. …This book is worth reading for its fantasy world alone. In our world, where those in the LGBTQ communities still often face derision, prejudice, and danger for living and loving openly, being immersed in a world where the Queen can openly love another woman is a refreshing break from reality."—Amanda Chapman, Librarian, Davisville Free Library (RI)

"*Birthright* by Missouri Vaun is one of the smoothest reads I've had my hands on in a long time."—*Lesbian Review*

The Time Before Now

"[*The Time Before Now*] is just so good. Vaun's character work in this novel is flawless. She told a compelling story about a person so real you could just about reach out and touch her."—*Lesbian Review*

Proxima Five

"A fascinating Sci-Fi adventure! If you love sci-fi already this book will have everything you want, and if you are new to sci-fi this would be a great story to introduce yourself to the genre. I highly recommend this story and, as this was my first Missouri Vaun story I am excited to read more!"—*LESBIreviewed*

The Ground Beneath

"One of my favourite things about Missouri Vaun's writing is her ability to write the attraction between two women. Somehow she manages to get that twinkle in the stomach just right and she makes me feel as if I am falling in love with my wife all over again."
—*Lesbian Review*

All Things Rise

"The futuristic world that author Missouri Vaun has brought to life is as interesting as it is plausible. The sci-fi aspect, though, is not hard-core which makes for easy reading and understanding of the technology prevalent in the cloud cities. …[T]he focus was really on the dynamics of the characters especially Cole, Ava and Audrey—whether they were interacting on the ground or above the clouds. From the first page to the last, the writing was just perfect."—*AoBibliosphere*

"This is a lovely little Sci-Fi romance, well worth a read for anyone looking for something different. I will be keeping an eye out for future works by Missouri Vaun."—*Lesbian Review*

"Simply put, this book is easy to love. Everything about it makes for a wonderful read and re-read. I was able to go on a journey with these characters, an emotional, internal journey where I was able to take a look at the fact that while society and technology can change vastly until almost nothing remains the same, there are some fundamentals that never change, like hope, the raw emotion of human nature, and the far reaching search for the person who is able to soothe the fire in our souls with the love in theirs."—*Roses and Whimsy*

Writing as Paige Braddock

Jane's World and the Case of the Mail Order Bride

"This is such a quirky, sweet novel with a cast of memorable characters. It has laugh out loud moments and will leave you feeling charmed."—*Lesbian Review*

Visit us at www.boldstrokesbooks.com

By the Author

All Things Rise
The Time Before Now
The Ground Beneath
Whiskey Sunrise
Valley of Fire
Death By Cocktail Straw
One More Reason To Leave Orlando
Smothered and Covered
Privacy Glass
Birthright
Crossing The Wide Forever
Love At Cooper's Creek
Take My Hand
Proxima Five
Spencer's Cove
Chasing Sunset
The Sea Within
The Mandolin Lunch
Slow Burn
The Lonely Hearts Rescue
Forever's Promise
Sacred Ground

Writing as Paige Braddock:
Jane's World The Case of the Mail Order Bride

SACRED GROUND

by

Missouri Vaun

2024

SACRED GROUND
© 2024 By Missouri Vaun. All Rights Reserved.

ISBN 13: 978-1-63679-485-3

This Trade Paperback Original Is Published By
Bold Strokes Books, Inc.
P.O. Box 249
Valley Falls, NY 12185

First Edition: June 2024

Credits
Editor: Cindy Cresap
Production Design: Susan Ramundo
Cover Design By Inkspiral Design

Acknowledgments

The idea for this story came about during a brainstorming session with VK Powell and D. Jackson Leigh way back in 2016. They probably don't remember it because this was the same brainstorming session that launched the small-town romance trilogy set in the fictional town of Pine Cone, Georgia. We were all pitching ideas for feedback and the concept for *Sacred Ground* was a story I'd been thinking of for a few months prior to their visit. The basic outline for *Sacred Ground* stayed in a notebook until now. Sometimes a story has to ferment for a time. I'm so happy to finally share these characters with you.

I'd also like to thank a few people. First, Celina for sharing her experiences as a ghost writer. And then I'd like to say a special thank you to my beta readers, Alena, Jenny, and Kate. I really appreciate all of your notes and suggestions.

Thank you to all the folks at BSB who support this whole process, my editor, Cindy; Sandy; Ruth; and Rad. I continue to be so grateful to be part of the BSB family. I'd also like to say thank you to my readers. I appreciate all of your support and encouragement.

Dedication

To Mom, I miss you so much

CHAPTER ONE

The coffee shop softly hummed with activity—murmured conversations, the intermittent hiss, and bright clinking noise from the industrial-sized espresso machine. It was an occupational practice for Jordan Price to survey her environment. She paid close attention to the details. Jordan was a hunter, and everyone left tracks—everyone. People, human and non-human, marked the world with paths, signs of passage. In the modern world of concrete and asphalt, passages were subtle, but they were still there, and she was particularly good at reading the signs.

Vampires were the easiest to notice. They were just a little too perfect. It was harder to spot the average, everyday demon. More and more these days, they tended to blend in with the human population. Humans honestly weren't looking that great. Almost everyone was overworked and underpaid and just generally stressed out. You could see it in the faces of all the patrons currently in this café.

She stirred a bit of raw sugar into her coffee as she studied those seated at tables around her. Typical of this San Francisco neighborhood, almost everyone was on some sort of electronic device, lost in their own world, looking for escape. They had no idea what easy targets they were. The basic urbanite was pretty damn clueless in her opinion.

Jordan liked this locally owned coffee shop. The decor was light industrial with a touch of Boho shabby chic, with cushions on the sofa and two upholstered chairs on the far side of the space. There was an outdoor patio bounded by bamboo in planter boxes, but she preferred to sit inside with her back against the concrete wall.

"Something on your mind?" Sterling Eli asked as she sipped her latte.

"Why do you ask?"

"You just seem more serious than usual."

Jordan had always referred to Sterling by her last name, short and easy, and honestly, it suited her better. Eli just seemed like a better fit. Sterling seemed too flashy for someone who preferred more of a supporting role in life. Eli always wanted to help everyone, to literally save the world, one church mission trip at a time. Her most recent mission to Brazil for Habitat for Humanity had left her with bruises and a large, half-moon scar over her left ear. It wouldn't have been noticeable except that her hair was in a crew cut. And the bruise along her jaw had faded to the point of being almost unnoticeable against her brown skin.

"Are you sure you're okay?" Jordan asked, ignoring Eli's original question.

"I'm fine, seriously." Eli smiled over the top of her drink. "I got mugged and they stole my phone...I'm okay. Don't make a big deal about it."

"I keep telling you if you had one of these no one would bother you." Jordan pulled a flip phone from her pocket and wiggled it in the air.

"Well, if I was a hundred years old like you then maybe I'd have a flip phone." Eli slurped her latte loudly for effect.

"I'm not a hundred...yet."

"Speaking of birthdays, don't you have one later this week?"

"Yes, the big four-two." She frowned. Forty-two—how had that happened?

"Will you be in the city or up at the cabin? We should have pizza or something to celebrate."

Jordan nodded. She hated parties, but if she just agreed with Eli now and then canceled later there'd be a lot less fuss. She canvased the room again. People came and went through a large opening that was basically a retractable garage door.

"I lost you again, where did you just go?"

"Sorry, I was thinking about how most people are so unaware of what's going on." Jordan sipped her coffee and didn't look at Eli as she spoke. "They are just lost, scrolling their phones for hours." She didn't want to tell Eli what she was really thinking about because then Eli would worry more than usual.

"I've actually enjoyed not having mine for a few days." Eli checked her watch. "That reminds me. I've gotta swing by the Apple store on the way north and buy a new one."

"Okay, I'll see you later."

Eli picked up her messenger bag and waved to Jordan as she exited. In seconds she was swallowed up by pedestrian traffic. Jordan relaxed in her chair and finished her coffee.

Her phone vibrated in her pocket and she checked the screen. It was an encrypted text from Sorcha Loftus summoning her to Guild headquarters. Jordan frowned and shoved her phone back in her coat pocket.

She wasn't that far from the Guild offices. Maybe today was the day she should make her departure from the Guild official. She'd been wrestling with the idea for months, but somehow facing down the ripe age of forty-two seemed like the right time. Besides, in her opinion, the Guild was off track. They'd lost their way in the last decade. She'd stuck with them because she rationalized that she wasn't in the fight for Sorcha or the council, she was in the fight for the greater good. But ten years was a long time to be in constant disagreement with the leadership. The stress of it all was wearing her down.

Jordan was opposed to the way the Guild courted demons when it suited them and shut things down when it didn't. If a vampire had money or any sort of political power then the Guild basically gave them a pass. That was all far too subjective for Jordan's liking. This job was much simpler when the world was black and white, good and evil, and humans didn't mix with demons. The lines had always seemed very clear to her. She didn't agree with the Guild on most things now and they could probably sense that even though she tried to keep her political feelings mostly to herself.

Jordan dropped her coffee mug in the plastic bin near the exit. She walked briskly from the coffee shop in the SOMA neighborhood over to Market Street where she hopped on one of the vintage trolley cars headed for the financial district of downtown. Jordan figured if she had more time, she'd have walked, but the trolley was so convenient.

It always struck her as odd that the Guild's headquarters were in the financial district. Their concern was supposed to be with the balance of forces, good and evil, not money. Although, money carried its own sort of evil, so maybe the location in the financial district made sense. She probably stood out amongst the tailored suits and office wear in her long dark coat, faded jeans, and boots.

She was just about to push through the double glass doors when a hooded figure bumped her shoulder as they exited. Jordan glanced over, but she couldn't see the person's face. She assumed it was a woman from her slight build and height, but she couldn't be sure. Either way, the person who'd bumped her gave off a definite vampire vibe.

Jordan hesitated. Should she bail on this meeting with Sorcha and follow?

"Hi, Jordan Price, right?" A man's voice cut through her thoughts. "It's Miller Diggs, remember? We met at—"

"Did you see that person just now? The one in the hoodie?" Jordan asked. He held his hand out in greeting, but she ignored it. She vaguely remembered meeting Miller recently on a job, or after a job was completed.

"The person who just bumped into you?"

"Yeah, that one."

"Want me to go kick their ass?"

Miller looked like any other average thirtysomething cis straight guy. He wasn't bad looking, he wasn't good looking, he was just average. Which wasn't a bad thing in this line of work. The last thing a hunter needed was to be memorable. Jordan tried her best not to be seen at all. She frequently dressed in black, never wearing anything with bright color. Demons loved bright colors, especially vampires. Miller was wearing a royal blue shirt and she'd considered mentioning something to him, but then she'd decided to let it go. She wasn't his keeper or his nursemaid. He'd figure things out soon or suffer the consequences. Life was the most effective teacher.

"Maybe just follow them and see what's up." Jordan strained to see the person who was getting farther away the longer they chatted. "I'd go, but I have a meeting with Sorcha."

"Don't worry." He was all business now. "I'm on it."

She stood and watched him jog down the sidewalk for a moment before entering the building. The Guild offices were on the top floor of the sleek, glass and steel high-rise. She walked past the first set of elevators to the express elevator and waited for the lift to arrive. Jordan hated these meetings almost as much as she hated elevators. She was the one in the field, not the suits. It was annoying to have to fill them in on things they clearly didn't understand. They were literally hiding out in this glass tower, above it all, above everyone. Well, this would be her last check-in, so at least she could be happy about that. As she rode the lift she wondered if Eli would have tried to talk her out of quitting if she'd known that was Jordan's plan. Eli was always one for staying in the fight, even if the *good guys* were sorely outnumbered.

Sorcha Loftus was the head of the board of trustees, a circle of elders that made up the governing body of the Guild. At one time the Guild had been part of the early Church in Rome. Set up to monitor and keep the dark forces of the underworld at bay. But at some point, for reasons she didn't fully understand, there had been an irrevocable break with the Church that had never been repaired. Many of the articles of exorcism from Scripture and the Church were still used in practice, but without the oversight of a priest. The Catholic Church still strongly believed that exorcism could only be performed by a priest or bishop, but she'd seen it done and even done it herself. More important than ordination was the belief that the Creator held dominion over evil. The bottom line was that to beat back a demon you had to be a true believer.

So many of the common perceptions of exorcism were shaped by Hollywood. And in Jordan's experience they weren't always as scary or filled with pea soup as movies made them seem. Even still, she preferred a good old-fashioned demon hunt to an exorcism every time. She was a hunter at heart. Although, lately, she'd lost some of her zeal for ousting individuals identified by the Guild as demons because her faith in the Guild's decisionmaking had seriously waned. The targets they chose to eliminate or ignore seemed weighted in the wrong direction. Society had fallen so far from its ancient origins that demons now operated openly in politics and business, in fact, they thrived. Jordan wasn't a fan of allowing a demon to exist, regardless of their financial or political station. These days, the Guild didn't necessarily agree with her.

The elevator doors swished open on the top floor, and she turned toward Sorcha's office. She took a chair in the empty seating area and waited to be summoned. It was late in the afternoon and the sinking sun flamed red through the tinted windows. Sunset, that's when things got interesting in her line of work.

The door to Sorcha's office opened electronically. It was one of those modern-type doors, with no discernable handle so that when it was closed it appeared to just be part of the wall. This was the only invitation she would receive to enter. It was all so annoyingly controlled to give the appearance of power or strength. The elitist trappings of the Guild offices had really begun to annoy Jordan.

The foyer outside Sorcha's office was dark when the door behind her closed except for the red light from the security scanner. She stood for a few seconds in the small space while she was scanned for weapons, then the next door opened. Jordan hated this office. The whole entry experience was nothing more than a power play designed to keep hunters in their place.

Sorcha's office was bigger than Jordan's entire apartment. The shiny metal surfaced desk, which was the size of a small car, was as far from the door as possible. Sorcha looked like a tiny queen on a throne. There was recessed lighting just above her that gave the impression that she was in a spotlight on stage. The corners of the office were dark. Not for the first time, Jordan wondered how old Sorcha was. She seemed to strangely defy the aging process.

Sorcha didn't speak as Jordan crossed the room, but Jordan knew the drill. She stood for a moment when she reached the desk, and when Sorcha didn't look up, she took a seat in one of the very stiff leather chairs. The overhead light was too bright. She glanced up at it and saw spots.

"Good afternoon, Ms. Price." Sorcha rested her entwined fingers on the desk as she studied Jordan. Her gray hair was in a severe cut that came to a sharp point at her jawline. Her dark red lipstick was perfect. Otherwise she looked as if she wasn't wearing makeup of any kind, but that had to be impossible because her face had a smooth, ageless quality. Jordan suspected that Sorcha was a least twenty years her senior. Whatever health regime Sorcha practiced, it was working for her.

"I just passed a vampire exiting the lobby of this building." She wondered if Sorcha ever came down out of the tower long enough to notice what was happening at ground level.

"An informant." Sorcha's response was dismissive.

"Since when did we start using vamps as informants?" This was part of the new gray world order that she really didn't care for. The barrier between the upper and lower worlds was thin. These days an act of betrayal was enough to breach it. If the boundary between humans and demons wasn't firmly maintained, then who would decide good from bad? Everything would be open to opinion. Who could be the judge in that world?

"Sometimes it's necessary to work *with* the underworld in order to understand it."

She didn't buy that explanation for a minute. Jordan decided to keep her opinion to herself and not mention that she'd sent Miller after the vamp in question. The only good vampire in her opinion was a dead one. But she realized hers wasn't the popular opinion, especially in a time of *anything goes*. Perhaps it was better to get out of this gig sooner rather than later, before things became so muddy you couldn't tell up from down.

"I sense disapproval from you." Sorcha's gaze bore into her.

"No." She lied.

As if on cue, a figure stepped into the light from one of the darkened corners behind the desk. Jordan sensed immediately that this man was a vampire. He was dressed in an elegant suit. His hair was combed back perfectly, and his dark brown skin seemed ageless.

"What the f—" Jordan lurched to her feet.

The vampire stood at the edge of the desk with his hands behind his back as if he felt completely at ease and was in no way threatened by her presence.

"Mr. Vega is my guest and you will treat him with respect." Sorcha's statement wasn't a request. It was an order. "Take your seat."

"No." Sometimes, with the Guild leadership, it was best to just roll over and show them your soft underbelly, show them you weren't trying to be the alpha. But this wasn't one of those times and Jordan's patience with Sorcha was way beyond over.

Sorcha slipped one hand under the desk, where there was no doubt an alarm button, and within seconds two security guards entered the room. They flanked Jordan but didn't engage.

"Do we have a problem, Ms. Price?" Sorcha asked.

As if that was a question Jordan could answer honestly. Yes, there was a problem. The slender vampire at Sorcha's elbow had a smug expression which made her want to lunge across the desk and punch him in the face.

"I'm here to serve the Guild." Jordan answered Sorcha in the most neutral fashion she could muster. She wasn't there to serve Sorcha, not today. "However, I am now officially offering you my resignation. Today, this meeting, will be my last."

She'd clearly caught Sorcha by surprise. Sorcha's face showed very little emotion as she stared at her from the other side of the oversized desk. A few moments of awkward silence passed between them. Jordan did not break eye contact.

"I see." Sorcha looked down at her hands on the sleek surface as if she were trying to regain her composure, as if she'd ever lost it in the first place. Jordan could feel Sorcha's displeasure from the other side of the desk.

Not exactly a ringing endorsement for her to stay. Perhaps Sorcha was as ready to be rid of her as she was to be rid of Sorcha. Jordan didn't really know of any hunter who'd actually walked away. Most were killed in the line of duty. Even her grandfather, also a hunter, hadn't lived long enough to enjoy old age.

"This is highly irregular, and I will have to consult the council in this matter."

Consult all you want. I'm getting off this crazy ride. Jordan wanted to leave while she was still at the top of her game. She definitely didn't trust the Guild any longer to watch her back. Jordan was on high alert, flanked on both sides by Sorcha's goon squad *and* with a vampire in the mix. She was acutely aware of the fact that she was unarmed.

Jordan didn't respond. She wasn't going to argue. It wasn't Sorcha's call to make.

"May I task you with one last job before you depart?"

Hmm, a request this time rather than an order.

"As you wish." Jordan figured she owed the Guild that much.

"All the information you need is here." Sorcha took an envelope from her desk and slid it across the sleek surface to Jordan.

Jordan accepted the medium-sized manila envelope with a nod.

"You may leave now." Sorcha's statement was completely without emotion.

Not that she'd expected any sort of heartfelt good-bye. She glared at the two security guards, heavyset guys with sidearms and combat clothing. She didn't really want to turn her back on any of them.

"And, Ms. Price..."

She turned to Sorcha and waited.

"Remember that being a hunter requires one to overcome the desire for self alone."

Jordan frowned as she walked toward the door. What the fuck did Sorcha mean by that? As if devoting your life to serving the Guild wasn't a selfless act? She'd had no life of her own because of this job. The work was all she had, and it was long past time for that to change.

The two guards stopped on either side of the door as she made her exit. Jordan glared again at them as she passed. She wasn't in the mood to be intimidated.

CHAPTER TWO

Grace Jameson scanned the departure screen for her flight. Delayed. A three-hour delay made it hardly worth it to leave and go home. With workday Atlanta traffic, it would take forty-five minutes to get to her apartment and probably an hour to get back with rush hour. She let out a sigh and scanned the terminal for a place to camp for a little while. She could kill a little time in the bookstore and then find a spot to do some work on her laptop. As a freelance writer, Grace always had a project in progress. And if she consumed enough sugar and caffeine she just might get some writing done.

There was a huge line at Starbucks, but she had plenty of time so she ordered with the app and after taking a quick turn through the magazine section of the bookstore, circled back to retrieve her Americano with a dash of honey. It took a moment to find a perch where she could set up her mobile workstation. Finally, a table opened up across from the crowded coffee spot and she snagged it.

Grace sipped her drink as she scrolled through email on her phone. Nothing seemed urgent, so she stowed the device in her bag and opened up her laptop. She had notes from the first interview with her client, Michael Lucas. With three hours to kill she could at least get an initial outline written that she could share with him when she arrived in San Francisco. That way he could approve or give notes so that she could course correct before the manuscript got too far along. She'd planned to use the audio from the in-person interview to flesh things out. Audio wasn't always chronological. People tended to jump around as they talked, so she'd have to work up an outline to organize the timeline before she began to write in earnest.

She usually tried to craft around two thousand words to give clients an idea of voice for the book. Ghostwriting memoirs had turned out to be something Grace enjoyed more than she'd expected to. She found people endlessly interesting, even the annoying ones. Grace tried to remain as neutral in the process as possible and just listen.

Sometimes people forgot they were speaking to her, a writer. They almost forgot why she was there, and the longer she listened, the more they'd reveal. Grace considered it part of her job to tell the truth. But the truth was relative sometimes wasn't it? Every child in a family had a different view of their parents. Everyone had their own truth. Sometimes, in order to tell your truth, you couldn't avoid hurting someone else's feelings.

Grace's initial job out of college was at the *Daily News* in Atlanta. She spent the first year doing supportive research, casually referred to as *leg work*. Which meant she'd show up at a fire, a trial, a murder scene, then scurry back to file notes in the newsroom. The next morning, she'd open the paper and see those notes under someone else's byline.

Grace really wanted to have her own byline under those headlines, so she tried to be patient. It was hard to break in as a green reporter at a major metro daily. In hindsight, maybe she should have started at a smaller paper and worked her way up. At least she'd have had clips in her portfolio.

The ghostwriting gig started as a side hustle, a fun way to make extra cash. But then layoffs started happening at the paper, the news staff shrank, and what was left of the *Daily News* moved away from downtown to the suburbs.

The side hustle became her main focus. She still thought about those days in the newsroom. The adrenaline rush as deadline approached, the frantic energy during a big news day, and the great personalities that populated the news desk. But that industry had changed forever and there was no going back.

Her phone rang and she checked the screen before answering.

"Hey, where are you?" asked Natalie.

She and Natalie had been friends since college. They'd been roommates at the University of Georgia and even shared an apartment for a while when they first moved to Atlanta to find jobs. They had even dated once, for about twenty-four hours, until they realized their relationship worked much better as a friendship, *without* benefits. Honestly, they were too much alike to date. They would have ultimately become the lesbian cliché—a couple that begins to look like twins. Grace wanted a partner who didn't look anything like her and who would never want to borrow her clothes. Someone like Rachel Maddow—cute, masculine-of-center, smart, successful, and politically aware. That seemed like a reasonable expectation. Although Natalie was always telling her that she was way too picky. Maybe, but maybe not. She'd rather be single than settle for less than she wanted.

"I'm at the airport. My flight got delayed."

"Do you want me to come get you?"

"No, but thanks." Grace closed her laptop so she could focus on the conversation. "The minute I got home I'd have to turn around and come back. If the flight ends up getting canceled I'll call you."

"Okay, I'll be around."

"What? No big plans tonight?"

"Please, after that last disaster which I'm now referring to as *no-parking-girl*." Natalie snorted.

"How have I not heard this story?" Grace smiled.

"I met this woman at the fundraiser last week. I told you about her."

"Oh, yeah, right." It was hard to keep up with Natalie's dating life, although Grace did her best.

"And I thought there was potential…"

"Until?" Grace prompted her.

"Until we drove down to Midtown for dinner, and she completely balked at paying for parking." Natalie paused for effect. "I had to pay for parking."

Grace laughed. "I thought you were going to tell me some horrible tale…you really got that upset over parking?" She was trying to be a supportive friend, but she couldn't stop laughing.

"It's not funny." Natalie huffed. "If you ask a woman out you should be prepared to pay for dinner *and* parking."

A booming announcement blared over the speaker nearby.

"Sorry. It's so loud here."

"Anyway, I'm not going to get involved with someone who doesn't think enough of me to pay for parking. I mean, seriously."

"I hear you." Grace watched the sea of travelers shuffle through the terminal.

"Hey, maybe you'll meet someone interesting in San Francisco."

"Dare to dream."

"I'm serious, Grace. A fling would do you good. You're such a workaholic these days."

"I pay for my own parking and I like it that way."

Natalie laughed.

She knew there was probably some truth in Natalie's assessment, but as a freelancer she just didn't feel like she could say no to work. It was feast or famine and currently she was on the *feast* side of the fence, which is where she wanted to stay.

"Plus, I'm only staying there for one full day and two nights. That's not going to leave me much time for the club scene." She paused. "I'm not sure there is a club scene in San Francisco. I read the last lesbian bar closed a few months ago."

"Sad. But listen, lesbians also go to regular clubs."

"Thanks for the tip." Grace smiled.

"You're so old-fashioned sometimes. Everyone goes everywhere now. It's not like it was back when we were in college."

"Now you're making me feel old." Grace was about to leave her thirties behind, but still felt she had a lot to figure out about the world.

"You're not old, you're hot. And don't you forget it." Natalie's statement was playful. "Don't forget, we hooked up once, and my standards are very high."

Grace laughed and shook her head.

"One beer-induced sleepover and you'll never let me forget it."

"What are friends for?"

Grace heard voices in the background on Natalie's end of the phone.

"Okay, hon, I've gotta run. Be safe. And text me when you land."

"I will. Bye for now."

Grace stowed her phone. When she looked back up someone had taken the other empty chair at her table. The woman's sudden appearance caught her by surprise.

"Do you mind if I sit here?"

"Not at all." She smiled. What was Grace going to say? Considering the woman was already sitting down.

The first thought that struck Grace was that the woman seated across from her seemed of a different era. Not that she looked old, but her clothing and her manner seemed out of place or out of date. The woman had sharp features and a long face. Her nose was elegant and her blue eyes shadowed. Her hair was pulled back into what looked like a painfully tight bun and her dress looked like something Laura Ingalls Wilder would have worn. Grace must have been staring without realizing it because the woman turned and looked at her.

"Are you a believer?"

"Excuse me?" Grace wasn't sure she'd heard correctly. And if she had then that was the creepiest entry point for a conversation she'd ever heard, especially with a total stranger.

"Do you believe?"

Yep, she'd heard correctly.

"I'm sorry, but I have to go find my gate." Grace smiled thinly as she packed up her laptop.

"Not believing makes it no less real." The creepy lady from the land of the lost smiled at Grace. She hadn't changed her position in the chair. She sat stiffly, clutching a small purse in front of her. She wore a dress that looked as if it had been purchased in a vintage thrift store.

"Okay, thank you for letting me know." Grace didn't feel threatened by the woman as much as just seriously unnerved by her.

"You have power, it is your inheritance, remember to call upon it." The woman abruptly stood and walked away.

Grace stared at the willowy figure of the woman as she was swallowed up by pedestrians with rolling luggage. After a minute or two, when she could no longer see the woman, she dropped back to her seat. She sipped her coffee and stared off into space. *What was that all about?* She would have chalked it up to the rantings of a random delusional person, but somehow the encounter felt different, intentional. What did the stranger mean by inheritance?

She got an alert on her phone that her gate had changed and that the flight departure had moved up. *Good.* Grace only had another hour to kill before takeoff. Maybe she could still get a little work done.

Before setting up her laptop again, she got up and moved the now vacant, extra chair to a neighboring table. This was now a table for one. Life was so much simpler that way.

CHAPTER THREE

Jordan stood near her apartment window, but not directly in front of it. She'd trained herself to avoid being an easy target. Outside on the sidewalk a woman walked a small, scruffy dog. But otherwise, the street was quiet.

Jordan had tried to sleep for a half hour after her unsettling meeting with Sorcha, but every time she closed her eyes the dreams would come. Describing them as dreams wasn't completely accurate. These visions were unnervingly real, almost like memories, but someone else's memories. A lot of the dreams involved flying, but in a context she couldn't recognize. There were storms too that she saw from above, and a raging sea, and words spoken in a language she couldn't understand.

Her meeting with Sorcha hadn't gone well, but that had become the norm. Jordan couldn't help feeling like the Guild had some other agenda she wasn't aware of, which inspired a definite lack of trust on her part. The thought nagged at her insides like hunger pains. Even more reason to make her exit.

Someone knocked at the door as she was pouring a cup of coffee from the insulated French press. She sampled the hot beverage as she crossed the room.

"Hi there, Owen." The six-year-old kid who lived down the hall stood in front of her door. She glanced down the hallway. No one else was around. "Don't you have homework or something?" It always worried her that his parents never seemed to be around.

"I finished it already." Owen had long blond hair and big blue eyes. He was dressed in dinosaur pajamas head to toe. "I was supposed to bring this to you." He held an envelope up to her.

Mail was frequently misdelivered in this building. She never seemed to get anything but junk mail so she wasn't that concerned with the problem.

"Thank you." She took the envelope. At first glance, it didn't seem like junk mail, it looked like an actual letter.

"You shouldn't drink coffee at night. It will keep you awake."

"I work nights, remember?" She winked at him as she took a sip.

"Oh yeah…" He fidgeted, shifting his weight from one foot to the other shyly. "I forgot."

Jordan smiled. "Thank you for this." She held up the letter for emphasis.

"Okay." He grinned and then whipped around and ran down the hall.

Jordan watched from the doorway until she knew that he was safe inside. She sighed and closed the door. Working nights was no way to have a life.

She drank the last swig of coffee and set the cup on the counter. She reached for her long overcoat and double-checked the contents of the interior pockets: two vials of holy water, a crucifix, a travel-sized King James Bible, and her grandfather's flask.

Jordan dropped to the sofa facing the window. The sky outside had transitioned from orange to pink and now almost purple. It would be nightfall very soon and her work would begin. But for the moment all she could do was wait.

The envelope she'd received from Sorcha had contained an address and the tip that some sort of ritual offering was to take place. That was a bit vague so she'd done her best to prepare for anything. She had weapons on hand but decided not to take anything beyond the spiritual defenses she might require. Bullets were mostly no good, except the silver variety for the occasional lycanthrope encounter. Yeah, werewolves were easy, if you could track one.

A ritual offering implied the calling forth of a demon, so she figured tonight's event would require an exorcism. She had a fair amount of experience with rituals and exorcisms. Hell, she'd been doing this a long time. She'd seen more than her share of shit that defied rational explanation.

The word exorcism was an ecclesiastical term that came from the Greek exorkizo, meaning "to bind with an oath," or to demand strongly. During an exorcism, a demon was commanded in the name of God to stop their activity within a particular person or place.

Exorcism had become a lost art. Most people, even within the church, nowadays saw it as a superstitious relic from back when illnesses like epilepsy and schizophrenia were considered "devils" to be cast out. People just couldn't tolerate the truth in Jordan's opinion.

People wanted to believe that up was up and down was down. But what resided below was always trying to find a doorway. She'd seen furniture move on its own, objects levitate, and other even more unsettling paranormal occurrences. Encountering someone under the influence of a demon was something you never forgot. The person would lose consciousness, their personality withdrawn to make way for another self. Another mind took possession of the person, of the entire individual, their nerves, muscles, voice, and eyes.

Jordan knew without a doubt that the things humans feared most were actually true. They existed somewhere deep inside the world, buried beneath medicine, science, and psychology.

The only light in the room came through the window from the streetlight. She'd lost herself in thought without remembering what she'd been thinking about. In addition to the dreams that had been happening lately she'd been losing time. It was unsettling to suddenly realize you'd lost an hour and had no idea to what. Maybe she was getting old. It was good that she was going to get out while she still had most of her wits intact.

The small hairs at the back of her neck tingled. As she stood in the center of the room, she decided to rethink weapons.

There were two wooden stakes mounted to levers that she could strap to each forearm. Jordan took a moment to slide each one on and then adjust the leather straps to hold them in place. She checked each release with a sharp flick of her wrist and then reset the spring. When not deployed they were easy to hide underneath her sleeves.

She tugged on the long coat. She didn't turn on a light as she crossed the room to the door. She didn't want to illuminate the space so that she could be seen from outside. A healthy dose of paranoia was helpful in her line of work. Yes, she hunted demons, but sometimes they hunted her and she didn't want to make herself an easy target.

On the cabinet beside the door were a few more talismans she needed before departure. She felt across the cool surface of the metal cabinet for a long chain that bore a silver cross. She slipped it over her head and let it fall inside the collar of her shirt. The metal was cool against her skin. There was also a small leather pouch about the size of a rabbit's foot made for her by a shaman. It was stitched with horsehair and contained soil from Ireland, an eagle's feather, black magic, and Celtic medicine. A long strand of leather was attached to one end of the object, and she wrapped the strand around the leather pouch so that with each stroke she pushed outward. The idea was that this would keep evil away from her. She held the soft, bound leather in her hand for a moment before putting it in the front pocket of her jeans.

The hallway was eerily empty when she exited her apartment. She walked to the landing to take the stairs. Jordan never took the elevator, which was old and confining and reminded her too much of a coffin. As she stepped outdoors onto the landing a flurry of wings swept overhead in the utter darkness. She couldn't see anything, but she could hear them. Jordan turned the collar of her coat up and started down the three flights of stairs.

She reached ground level at the rear of the building and took the sidewalk toward where she'd parked her car. As she rounded the corner of the building, she saw the figure of a man standing in the street looking up at her building. He was backlit by the streetlight so she couldn't make out his features. But she got the distinct impression that he was waiting for her.

CHAPTER FOUR

The client's address was in Pacific Heights. As the Uber driver turned and drove up the incredibly steep, narrow street, Grace couldn't help but think of all the movies she'd seen set in Pacific Heights. This particular neighborhood was truly breathtaking, definitely San Francisco's star neighborhood.

The streets were lined with a collection of French Chateau and Spanish-style mansions. She also spotted quite a few restored Victorian homes that looked like they dated back to the 1800s. As she climbed out of the car, she turned and took in the view of the bay. At this elevation she could see the marina, Alcatraz, and all the way to the Golden Gate bridge while simply standing on the sidewalk.

Wow, amazing view.

Grace had known that this particular client was wealthy, or well-off. But standing on this street, she was feeling a bit intimidated. When the publisher had contacted her to ask if she was interested in the project, the trip to San Francisco alone had been appealing. She'd taken the job mostly based on the location. When the questionnaire came back from the client he'd sounded so completely full of himself she'd almost declined the project. Maybe he sounded worse on paper than he would in person. No wonder he wanted someone to write his life story. He'd obviously done something worthwhile to end up living here.

Normally, Grace didn't make house calls. When first getting started as a ghostwriter she'd taken whatever she could get and had initially been willing to travel to wherever the story took her. But now that she was more established she didn't usually meet clients at their private residences any longer. But this guy had insisted, and the fee he'd offered seemed worth the effort.

It was interesting how much clients expected from the memoir process. People wanted the world to know them, to know that they were amazing, and most of all smart. But memoir wasn't a linear life story. It was a narrative carved from your life, a collection of chosen events that would be meaningful to the greatest number of people.

It was part of a ghostwriter's job to manage expectations and help people see themselves clearly. A ghostwriter was sort of like a coach. Grace had to push and demand that her clients dig deeper, otherwise she was nothing more than a glorified stenographer. Churning out some sort of shallow retelling of events from someone's life was a disservice to the subject and the audience.

Mostly, Grace listened. And then after a while, after the client had initially talked themselves out, she would begin to ask questions. Most importantly, a ghostwriter had to make sure to leave themselves out of the story. This, whatever this turned out to be, was not her story.

The sun had sunk just below the horizon. It would be dark soon. Grace had tried to get an earlier flight, but weather delays due to a chain of thunderstorms in the Midwest had stalled the departure from Atlanta. She'd expected her client to ask to postpone until the next day because her arrival was so late, but he insisted that they keep their appointment, saying he was quite a night owl.

She glanced at the address on her phone and realized she was standing in front of the wrong house. Grace walked up to the crest of the hill and rotated to study the mansion with the Beaux arts facade.

Holy shit.

There were mansions in Atlanta, but not like this, and certainly not with this view. As she stood staring up at the ornate facade she chastised herself for not asking for a higher fee because this guy could clearly afford it.

Grace took a deep breath and climbed the marble stairs to the front door and rang the bell.

After a moment, the door was opened by an elegant looking man. He was tall, thin, with perfectly quaffed, short gray hair, and he was wearing a tailored suit. The suit fit him like a glove.

"Hello, I'm Michael Lucas. You must be Grace." He motioned for her to enter. "Please come in." He remained in the shadow of the huge door as he ushered her inside.

"It's very nice to meet you, Mr. Lucas." Grace couldn't help glancing around the vaulted foyer. "You have a beautiful home."

While the exterior had all the intricate architectural details of the early 1900s, the interior space had been reimagined and reconstructed, including an elliptical grand staircase with a bronze banister.

"I'd be happy to give you a tour. The house has almost nine thousand square feet of interior living space. The top floor terrace even has an infinity pool." He sounded like a kid showing off his favorite toys, but in a non-annoying sort of way. "The terrace has an amazing view of the city at night." Michael was supposedly in his late fifties, but he had the energy of someone in their thirties. His exuberance was contagious.

Grace couldn't help smiling. "I'd love a tour."

As they made their way from floor to floor, through the five bedrooms and six bathrooms, Grace marveled at Michael's art collection. She stopped to admire particular pieces and he was quick to provide backstory for each. It was obvious that he liked to talk about himself and he was clearly well-traveled. He had collected pieces from all over the world. The entire house had the feel of a high-end art gallery, it was impressive, but certainly not homey in any way. None of the rooms looked lived in, not like her messy apartment for sure.

Every window seemed to take full advantage of the unobstructed views of the bay and the Golden Gate Bridge, which honestly, Grace never tired of looking at.

"Shall we sit here to begin the interview?" Michael stood behind a narrow leather armchair. There were two matching chairs with a small table in between.

"Sure." Grace removed a small tape recorder from her purse. "Do you mind if I record our discussion?"

"Not at all." Michael motioned for her to sit and then he turned toward a nearby cabinet and poured himself a drink. "Would you care for something?"

It was best if she didn't drink while she was working, so Grace declined. Michael took a seat across from her with his tumbler of red wine.

"Where should we begin?" He smiled over the rim of his glass.

Grace fought the urge to say *at the beginning*. He already gave off the vibe that he enjoyed talking about himself so if she hoped to keep this interview to a reasonable timeframe she needed to direct the conversation.

"Why don't we start with the first thing you remember from your childhood?" Grace set the recorder on the table between them and relaxed into the chair. Her body was on East Coast time so in her mind, it was already late. This was going to be a long night.

CHAPTER FIVE

"Why are you here?" On some other occasion this might have been an existential question, but this was just Thursday, and Jordan was standing on the sidewalk near her apartment. It was late, fully dark, and she was glad Miller hadn't seen her exit her apartment because Jordan didn't really want him to know exactly where she lived. Jordan had picked this nondescript location for a reason. It was easy to forget.

"What are you doing here?" Jordan rephrased the question and made no attempt to hide her annoyance.

"The Guild sent me." He scrunched his manicured eyebrows as if doing so made him seem more intimidating. It didn't.

At five feet, ten inches, they were exactly the same height. She glared at him, making direct eye contact until he averted his gaze.

"What's your name again?" She remembered, but wanted to mess with him a little. She'd actually met him a few times. The first time was in a dark graveyard. She'd just taken out one vampire and two undead assholes single-handedly. Miller had shown up with Guild bean counters after the action was over to do damage control. As it turned out, there wasn't any damage control to do. Jordan did her job and she didn't involve civilians if she could avoid it. Then she'd seen him again today, outside the Guild offices.

"Miller Diggs." He angled his chin up in a proud stance, trying his best to act tough.

"Yeah, that's right." She paused. "Hey, any luck with that vamp earlier today?"

"Uh, no, I lost her on Mission Boulevard."

"That's too bad."

"It wasn't my fault. There was this whole thing that happened—"

"Listen, I can handle this assignment alone." She cut him off with a wave of her hand. The streetlight overhead flickered as a creature with wings flew in front of it, momentarily blocking the light. She pulled her long coat tighter although she didn't button it so she still had access to interior pockets in case she needed to reach something quickly.

"I think the Guild feels this is a two-person job. You may need backup."

Did Miller know something she didn't? Jordan studied him. Was someone on the Guild high council his uncle or something? Fine, if they wanted to send a human shield what did she care. She doubted Miller had what it took to survive any sort of real encounter, but far be it from her to tell the suits how to run things.

"You drive." She wanted to be able to keep an eye on him.

"Okay, sure." He was way too eager.

They crossed the street to his black SUV. The light flickered again. She heard the wings but didn't look up. Probably just bats. Hopefully bats. A gust of chilly wind disturbed her hair, and she brushed it off her forehead. The breeze had dislodged a beer can from the curb, and it bounced noisily down the deserted street. If she didn't know better she'd have thought someone or something was trying to get her attention.

Jordan paused beside the open passenger door and slowly surveyed the street. Something caught her eye, movement in her peripheral vision, but when she looked again it was gone. She glanced over at Miller as he started the engine. He seemed oblivious. There was a tiny, microscopic twinge in the pit of her stomach that suggested she should leave Miller and go it alone, or send Miller and not go at all.

You always think you know exactly how things are going to go. At least that's what Jordan thought. But on this particular night she was feeling just a little unsettled. If you did a thing for long enough, or some might say, too long, you got comfortable. Maybe comfortable was the wrong word, but you definitely got casual, too relaxed, too sure of yourself. That's when things could go sideways. And in Jordan's line of work, a mistake could be deadly, in this life and the next.

Maybe she was just tired. She'd been doing this kind of work for a little more than two decades. But it was a hard job to quit. Demon hunting was a calling, a sacred calling. The sort of call you had to answer. Even if she stopped working with the Guild she wasn't sure she'd ever truly be off the clock. Once she could see such creatures in the world, she wasn't sure how to stop seeing them.

Jordan shook off the feeling of unease and climbed into the passenger seat. Miller drove slowly down the darkened neighborhood street until he reached the intersection, then turned left toward the marina. She hadn't mentioned the address so obviously he'd gotten the details from someone else regarding the location. Perhaps he was informed after all.

"Are you a believer?" Miller asked.

Jordan had been absently staring out the window as they passed the rowhouses along nineteenth. Miller seemed to be taking the scenic route.

"What?" She continued to stare out the window.

"Are you religious? I mean, do you really believe in all this stuff?"

"Stop the car."

"Don't get mad." He seemed puzzled by her response. "I was just making conversation."

"If you don't believe any of it, why are you here?"

"I didn't say I didn't believe it. I was asking you what you believed."

"What do you really want to know?" Jordan was fairly certain there was a legitimate question behind the stupid query he'd led with.

Miller was quiet for a minute. Then he glanced over at her with a serious expression.

"How did it all start?"

"What do you mean by *it*?"

"You know, this…all of this…good and evil." Miller seemed to struggle with finding the right words. He made a sweeping motion with his hand "God and humans and the world. How did it all start?"

Was he serious? Jordan knew it was Guild policy for more experienced hunters to pass down knowledge to hopefuls, but she wasn't exactly the teaching sort. In fact, she was fairly sure she didn't have a knack for it. She was impatient and annoyed by all the questions. Didn't anyone ever read a book anymore?

"Do you really want to know?" She'd try to give Miller the benefit of the doubt. This was going to be her last run for the Guild, she might as well help him out.

"Yeah, I do." He glanced at her and then turned back to the road as the world outside the SUV transitioned from neighborhood to industrial warehouses. She could smell the salt and seaweed of the bay through the air vents of the car. It was always strongest near the old part of the shipyard. This whole area had been bustling at one time. Now it was just the skeletal ruins of a bygone era.

"At first there was nothing, just endless space." Jordan knew that she probably sounded exasperated, but she hadn't asked for a sidekick and this guy certainly wouldn't have been her first choice even if she had. He was way too green, and something about his manner rubbed her the wrong way. He was too eager and his eagerness hung around him like a cloud of bad cologne.

"What do you mean by endless space?" Miller eased the vehicle into a spot along the empty, dark alley.

Jordan wasn't sure if Miller simply didn't care about the finer points of the trade, hell—*any* points of the trade. Or if he was just dim in general.

"Don't they teach you *trainees* anything these days?"

"Don't use the word trainee. That makes me sound like a chump." Miller frowned at her as he got out of the driver's seat.

Technically, he was what the Guild called a "hopeful," but he acted more like a trainee at a fast food joint. Jordan wasn't sure if having Miller along for this last call was going to be helpful or a hindrance. And she wanted to know who on the leadership council had suggested he join her.

"How can there just be nothing?" He stopped in front of the parked car and lit a cigarette. The flash of the match illuminated his face for a few seconds.

She watched him take a long drag of his cigarette.

"I mean, even nothing is something, isn't it?" He wasn't looking at her as he spoke.

Jordan exhaled and shoved her hands in the pockets of her overcoat.

"There was no beginning and no end, no time, no shape, and no life—just an immeasurable void." He took another drag of the cigarette which glowed brightly. He squinted at her as if he was actually listening. He should be listening. She was dropping serious wisdom on Miller right now and if he was smart he'd soak it up.

"Then perhaps God felt lonely." Jordan continued.

"God can feel lonely?"

"Maybe." She shrugged. Some of this was her own personal theory, more of a gut feeling. "So, the infinite created the finite."

"You mean, like humans and animals and trees?" He sounded like a toddler.

Jordon frowned at him for several seconds.

"I'm done talking to you about this." She turned and started walking toward the row of empty warehouses. She could hear Miller's quick footsteps behind her, but she didn't stop or turn around.

"Hey, I want to know this stuff, seriously. I didn't mean to piss you off."

"Put that cigarette out and keep your voice down."

He fell in step beside her. Miller might be the same height as Jordan, but he was beefier than she was. Jordan figured she could still take him if she had to. That was one of her little mental games. She liked to size people up in every way she could think of. Mostly because she didn't like surprises. It was actually sad how often she was *not* surprised. People were assholes. She'd been doing this work a long time, and she was beginning to think there was no such thing as clear black and white. These days it seemed everything was painted with an ashy shade of gray. It hung in the air and on her clothes. She hated the gray zone.

Good and evil had been an item since before the world was the world. But the day Lucifer fell to Earth, that was the day the game changed forever. What had been for eternity an uncomfortable balance of shadow and light became real for mankind. No more Garden of

Eden, no more blissful unconsciousness, no more getting cradled by the Creator. Yeah, the dark angel ruined it for everyone.

Thanks for nothing.

The origins of evil were planted deep within every person. It fed on the same flesh and breathed the same air. But it wasn't the same. Jordan knew that from firsthand experience. She had the psychic scars to prove it. And some physical ones too.

"What's our plan?" Miller asked.

"Our plan?" Jordan stopped walking and looked at him.

They were way beyond the reach of the lone, flickering streetlight. The moon was nearly full, but a thick marine layer shadowed it. The glow of the moon bathed in fog gave the entire scene a damp, eerie ambiance. A flurry of wings flew erratically overhead. A small swarm of bats dipped and swerved above them. She could hear and feel them more than see them. What next? A howling dog?

In the distance she heard a siren. She looked back at Miller. He seemed too calm, even for someone as dumb and inexperienced as he was.

Jordan reached for a small flask she kept in her inside coat pocket. It was a flat, rectangular flask that had belonged to her grandfather. The Celtic symbol for the Trinity was engraved on the front of it. He used to carry holy water in it, but recently she preferred bourbon. She glanced sideways at Miller as she took a swig. The liquor warmed her insides as it snaked through her system.

"Hey, can I have a hit of that?"

"No." She screwed on the cap and returned it to her pocket.

"Whatever." He tried to act like he didn't care as they started walking again.

Jordan slowed her steps as they approached the warehouse. A microburst of cold air cut through her coat. A rapid shift in air temperature meant they were getting close. She could see that the street they were on dead-ended near the water. These buildings had probably once been a hub of commerce from ships coming through the Golden Gate. The weathered brick and broken glass in the dark windows were like details on an aging face. The air was thick with the scent of the ocean and…something else. There was just a hint of something that smelled a little bit like sulfur. She held her hand out as a signal for Miller to stop.

The expression on his face told her that he was about to ask more questions. She put the forefinger of her other hand in front of her lips as a signal for him to keep quiet. Then she tapped the edge of her ear. He needed to learn to see and hear. He needed to notice subtle signs.

Someone was in the building to their right. She took slow, quiet strides toward the nearest window. Just the faintest orange glow could be seen. This wasn't electric light. The light undulated and she guessed it was a candle or a small torch of some kind. It was hard to tell how far into the building they'd have to go to find the source. But this was why they'd come. She crossed the threshold and stepped inside.

CHAPTER SIX

G race climbed out of the dark, four-door sedan onto the steep sidewalk in front of the hotel. Michael had insisted that his car service deliver Grace to her hotel along Union Square and now she was grateful for the small convenience. As the car pulled away from the curb, a biting wind whipped her hair around her face. She shook her head, facing into the breeze, and then gathered her hair in her fingers in an attempt to tame it until she was indoors.

Fog was rolling in from the bay. The air temperature had dropped at least twenty degrees, and she was feeling smart that she'd kept her jacket and scarf with her for the initial interview. Grace was just about to climb the stairs to the elegant turn-of-the-century hotel when she noticed another entrance to her right. Perhaps she'd have a glass of something before calling it a night.

Warm air swooshed past as she opened the door to the below-ground establishment. Grace took a seat and braced her elbows on the glossy wooden bar. She rested her chin in her hands and took a deep breath, then exhaled slowly. This had been the longest day on record, and she was mentally exhausted. The interview for the memoir had gone as well as could be expected since she was dealing with a complete narcissist. He was charming, but a narcissist just the same. She really needed to start having each client fill out a personality profile prior to signing a contract with them.

After such a tiring day, she was happy to discover that the hotel had a very nice bar. Shelves of liquor and wine greeted her view. Grace would be able to have a drink without leaving the premises.

On the drive to the hotel she'd seen a lot of unhoused people, most of them gathered around tents on the sidewalk. Through the car window, some of them seemed harmless but a few of them gave off a vibe of hostile unpredictability. The thought of having to use Uber at this hour, alone and in a strange city, was not appealing.

She surveyed the room. The place was styled after a vintage speakeasy, with an entrance below street level and a sitting room that doubled as a foyer. The thick mahogany bar was well worn from a thousand patrons, but gleamed from no doubt endless polishing. Low lighting from what looked like antique fixtures ringed the room. The glass over each bulb was etched with a decorative pattern of swirls and leaves, or was that supposed to be waves of water? Grace couldn't quite decide. There were booths with burgundy leather seats along one wall with a few patrons and tables in the center of the space, but mostly it seemed like a quiet night. If there'd been a crowd, she'd missed it.

"What can I get for you?" A handsome bartender whose bodybuilder arms strained to break free from his shirtsleeves set a square white napkin on the bar in front of her. His disinterest was almost palpable. Perhaps he found her completely uninteresting or perhaps he'd had an awful day too.

"Um, I think I'll have an old-fashioned. Thanks." That sounded strong. A strong drink was definitely in order. It was well past midnight in her time zone, and this would be just the ticket to usher in the new day, or help her forget this one, whichever came first. She internally set her limit at one drink. Actually, she probably wouldn't even finish the first drink. But half a drink would be just the ticket to calm her nervous system so that she could rest. Then she'd head up to her room and tuck herself in and sleep.

"I wouldn't have pegged you for an old-fashioned." An elegant looking woman slid onto the stool next to her just as she was sampling her drink.

Grace smiled thinly but didn't respond. She didn't want to seem rude, but she wasn't really up for small talk. On another night, maybe, but she was talked out.

"Are you in the city for work or pleasure?" The woman didn't get the hint. She wasn't unattractive, in fact, the more Grace looked at her the more attractive she seemed to become. That was a strange thing to notice. She had straight black hair that didn't quite touch her shoulders, an olive complexion, and perfect red nails. The color of her eyes seemed to undulate from brown to black in the low light. Grace adjusted her glasses for a better look.

"Work." Something about this woman made Grace want to leave, or stay. Honestly, she couldn't decide.

"I'm here for work also." The woman glanced around the room. "This bar is really dead tonight."

She seemed to place particular emphasis on the word *dead*. A shiver traveled up the small hairs along Grace's arm.

"I'm Thea Shaw." Thea extended her slender manicured hand.

"Grace Jameson." Thea's hand was ice cold.

"Cold hands, warm heart." Thea seemed to sense her silent observation.

"It is surprising how cold it gets here at night when the marine layer rolls in." Grace thought talking about the singularly unique San Francisco climate seemed like a safe topic. She was about to leave her drink and be on her way to a good night's sleep and was currently at her limit for cordial small talk.

"So, what sort of work do you do?"

"I'm a writer." Grace didn't feel like revealing too much detail, but that much seemed harmless.

"A writer, wow." Thea smiled over the rim of her wine glass. "That sounds like a great way to make a living."

"Sometimes," Grace muttered into her glass.

"Let me buy you another one." Thea's gaze was intense.

"Um—" Grace wanted to politely refuse but found herself nodding in agreement instead. *What the hell was that? And when had she finished her first drink?* Ice cubes were all that remained in the bottom of the glass in front of her.

She watched Thea walk to the far end of the bar to speak to the bartender. The charcoal dress she wore was like a second skin, hugging every curve of her svelte body. Grace was annoyed with herself for noticing, but it was as if she couldn't help herself. Her phone buzzed in her bag, and she shook her head as she searched for it. She had way too much stuff in her purse. Who would be calling this late? Everyone in the eastern time zone was probably asleep. She glanced at the screen. A spam call from a strange number that consisted of only the number six in successive groupings of three. Who would keep that phone number? Super creepy. Thea appeared suddenly while she'd been distracted with her phone.

"Here you go." Thea smiled. "That bartender is pretty hot, don't you think?" She glanced over her shoulder in his direction.

"I hadn't noticed." Grace twirled the glass once between her fingers. Was Thea trying to figure out what her sexual preference was? "Thanks." She raised the glass in Thea's direction.

Thea smiled as she sipped her red wine.

Grace took a few sips of the fresh drink in front of her. It seemed stronger than the first one, or perhaps she was just feeling it because she was tired. She was in a strange city, in the wrong time zone, and she'd had a very long, frustrating day.

"I probably won't be able to finish this, but thank you anyway." She tried to sound gracious and mean it. She took a few more sips. Fatigue seemed to be catching up with her quickly. Her head felt foggy all of a sudden and she was feeling a bit tipsy.

Grace stood up and braced her hands on the bar. This was why she should only have had one drink. She reasoned that she was too tired for the second drink not to have a strong effect.

"It was nice to meet you, Thea." She let go of the bar but swayed a little and had to regrip the edge. That's when she noticed the six empty glasses in front of her. She set her bag on the bar and searched for her phone. The screen read two o'clock.

She frowned. Somehow two hours had passed. She had no recollection of its passing or of having finished a six-pack of old-fashioneds.

"Are you alright?" Thea stood also. Her wine glass was empty too.

Were all those empty glasses hers? If she'd been sitting here for two hours, why didn't she remember it?

"I'm just tired." Grace brushed her off. Something weird was happening and it frightened her a little. "I'm going to go up to my room now."

"I'll walk with you." Thea looped her arm through Grace's. "Us girls have to stick together." She patted Grace's arm as they crossed the ornately patterned carpet toward the elevator. Grace felt very unstable on her feet. If Thea hadn't been with her she feared she'd have toppled.

"Do you have your room key for the elevator?" Thea asked.

Grace fumbled in her bag for the card key. She held it out to Thea.

"What floor?"

"Six, I think." Was the number a coincidence?

"We're on the same floor." Thea smiled.

Grace slumped into the back corner of the elevator and braced against the handrail. She didn't feel well at all and was afraid she might actually throw up before she reached her room. The doors swished open in slow motion and Thea took her arm again as they made their way down the long hallway. The floor seemed to tilt away from her, making her feel unbalanced. Was the pattern in the wallpaper moving?

"I don't feel so well. I never drink that much."

"Let me help you inside." Thea pushed the door open and then assisted Grace into the room.

Grace tumbled sideways onto the bed like a rag doll. She sensed Thea lift her useless legs and feet onto the bed. Her lack of awareness and control scared her. She tried to reach for her phone in her bag, but Thea moved it out of her reach to a nearby chair. Thea returned to sit on the edge of the bed and stroked Grace's hair.

"Everything is going to be okay." Thea leaned closer and Grace could have sworn that the dark irises in Thea's eyes glowed red. She sensed Thea's mouth very close to hers and then the tip of Thea's tongue lightly trailing down her neck. Somehow her scarf was gone and the collar of her blouse was open.

"Leave me alone." Grace attempted to roll away from Thea.

"Don't worry, Grace. It will all be over soon."

Grace braced her palms against Thea's arms, but her limbs were worthless. Thea hovered above her. She cocked her head and smiled down at Grace. She had the strangest sensation that someone else was in the room, but she couldn't be sure. Was she even still in the hotel?

Grace was outside herself, somewhere, in a dark surging sea with no horizon. And then later, but she had no idea how much later, she sensed her body in motion. A glimpse of naked tree limbs in front of the moon like dark spiderwebs. Was she outside? She was unsure and couldn't bring her mind into focus. Shadows at the edge of her vision closed in.

Beyond that point was darkness and loss. She'd have been terrified if she hadn't felt so adrift. She was lost.

CHAPTER SEVEN

Miller fumbled in the dark behind Jordan. She motioned for him to hang back and give her some space. His footfalls on the old floorboards were too clumsy and loud. The ancient wood creaked under his weight with every step. Whoever or whatever lay ahead of them would surely hear them coming. She wanted to salvage some element of surprise if that was at all possible.

Details from their earlier conversation looped through her brain.

Yes, humans had free will. Ever since Eve handed Adam the apple. So, it was true that evil was a choice—sometimes—but with so many disguises how could anyone recognize true evil when they saw it?

This was the question Jordan should have been asking herself as they entered the abandoned warehouse. She was so certain she'd recognize evil at first glance. But maybe she shouldn't have been so sure. The signs had been shifting lately and something seemed to lurk in the shadows just beyond her recognition. Her gut instincts had always been what saved her, but lately, her gut was all in knots. It was as if some horrible thing loomed, and she couldn't quite make out the shape of it.

Jordan could see the doorway just ahead, at the end of the narrow hallway. The light seemed brighter beyond that threshold. She held her hand up, a signal for Miller to wait. She peered around the doorframe into the room. Thick candles sat in a circle on the floor, each in a puddle of melted wax. In the center of the circle was some sort of crude altar that looked as if it had been constructed out of wooden packing crates. Something, nestled in a blanket, moved on top of the altar. Jordan stepped closer, afraid of what she'd find, but figuring she already knew. A tiny hand reached for her finger as she pulled the blanket aside.

Someone was moments away from sacrificing an innocent. This was bad. This was black magic for sure. She'd been so certain they'd find a coven of vampires, but this was something else. Jordan lifted the child into her arms, blanket and all, and cradled him against her chest. He cooed softly. The candles gave every indication of having been lit for a while, wax pooled around each, but he was so calm that Jordan reasoned the child had not been alone for very long. She held him at arm's length to examine him for injury but saw none. She drew him close again, pulled her coat around him, and was just about to pivot for the exit when a sharp pain pierced her side and stabbed the infant's foot with the same strike. The baby shrieked in pain.

Jordan shifted the terrified child to her right arm and pressed her left hand to her lower abdomen. When she looked down at her palm it was covered with blood. She swung around to find Miller trying to disarm the hooded person she'd seen earlier. The assailant wielded a knife that resembled an ice pick, except the point was uneven as if it had been formed by hand—an ancient spike roughly hewn.

"What the fuck?" Her side hurt like hell. The wound radiated heat.

Miller was losing the fight. He was outmatched. Despite her smaller size, the vampire was clearly a better technical fighter than he was. She was like a whirling kickboxer, all hands and feet, and Miller staggered and fell backward with a thump, his face bloodied.

Jordan faltered, but she caught herself. She wanted to put the hooded attacker in a chokehold but that was impossible to do with only one hand, plus she had the infant to think of. Getting the child to safety was her first priority.

"Here! Take the kid." Jordan shouted to Miller as he got to his feet.

He stumbled in her direction. He accepted the infant and cradled the baby in his arms. Blood from his seeping temple got smeared on the blanket.

"Stay behind me." Jordan stepped in front of Miller, wedging him between where she stood and the altar. The assailant paced in front of Jordan with the bloody weapon in her hand waiting for another opportunity to strike.

The vampire swept the hood back and Jordan thought perhaps she'd seen her before. She wracked her brain to bring forth the details, but her head was a little foggy. She had long, straight black hair and a thin face. She was probably in her late twenties, and based on her display with Miller, she was well trained as a fighter. Probably someone's bodyguard. The vampire lunged, quick like the strike of a snake, but Jordan caught her wrist and in one strong motion brought the woman's arm down to meet her raised knee, which dislodged the knife. It clattered loudly to the floor. While still holding the vampire's wrist, Jordan landed a solid punch with her right fist. That move caused Jordan as much pain as it did the vampire.

"Get the kid out of here!" She motioned for Miller to go while keeping her eye on the vampire.

"I'm not leaving you," he shouted.

"That baby is all that matters…Go!"

She glanced quickly at Miller as he ran for the door. The infant's cries echoed through the abandoned building. The woman circled Jordan. She made no move to follow Miller. Good, it was Jordan she was after and Jordan liked these odds. She mirrored the woman's movements and kept her stance ready for the vampire's next move. The woman tried to reach the weapon on the floor, but Jordan kicked it aside. That pissed the vampire off. She scowled at Jordan and then took a swing at her. She missed but managed to advance again. The vampire was so fast, she grabbed the front of Jordan's coat with both hands, and shoved Jordan backwards at the same time. They toppled the makeshift altar of packing crates. Shards of flimsy and aging wood shattered beneath them on the floor. The debris toppled a few of the candles, one of them rolled toward some scraps of newspaper in a corner and caught fire.

Jordan couldn't dislodge herself from her attacker. She felt as if the wound in her side was making her strangely weak and disoriented. Under normal conditions she'd have easily bested this vamp. Now the woman was on top of her. She punched Jordan. But since the woman was only braced on one arm, using her other to pummel Jordan, she was able to break the hold and toss the vampire off. But the vamp rebounded and lunged for Jordan again. She rolled aside just as the vampire landed a blow to the floor with her fist.

Jordan lurched to her feet and backed away, circling the vampire. With a flick of her right wrist, she deployed the wooden spike hidden in her sleeve. In the mostly dark space she was able to hide it from view with the side of her coat. When the vampire flew across the space, Jordan was ready. She fell backward with the woman on top of her, but just for an instant. Recognition registered on the vampire's face before the wooden spike through her chest relegated her to dust.

Ashes to ashes, dust to dust.

Jordan laid on the floor for several minutes. She was winded. She got to her feet slowly, she had her head down with her hands braced on her knees. Once her pounding head stopped spinning, she remembered the runaway candle. She crossed to the wall and kicked the singed bits of paper and debris away from the wall and stomped out the remaining embers. It was when she returned to the center of the room that she heard the familiar sound of wings, lots of wings. A flurry of dark-winged shapes invaded the space. They swarmed her position, circling around her all the way to the ceiling, before taking form in front of her. A woman in an elegant black suit stood before her, and the woman wasn't alone.

The woman, the vampire, in the form-fitting suit used a cloth to pick the weapon up from the floor. She wrapped the thick leather rag around the blade without touching it and turned to look at Jordan. She handed the weapon to one of her companions without taking her eyes off Jordan.

"Should I follow him?" A male voice came from somewhere behind her.

"No, we have no interest in him or the child," the woman in the dark suit answered.

Jordan took a breath and blinked a few times trying to clear her vision. Something was wrong. She'd been stabbed before. She'd even been shot a few times. This felt very different. Her head was swimming and she wasn't sure she'd be able to walk or even stand in a few more minutes.

"You've been poisoned." The woman was standing inches from her face and Jordan hadn't even seen her move. It was as if she'd read

Jordan's mind. The woman looked like a Scandinavian supermodel. She was tall, willowy, pale, and beautiful with short blond hair and irises that pulsed between green and red. Why wasn't this woman killing her? That's what vampires did. That was their whole fucking mission statement. "Remove the weapons from her arms."

She was flanked by two darkly clad fellows that she assumed were either familiars or vampires under this woman's thrall. They unfastened the mechanisms from her forearms. Jordan didn't even try to resist. She hated the feeling of weakness that had turned her body against her when she needed it most. Sure, she was completely outnumbered, but she'd been outnumbered before. Jordan swayed on her feet. Strong hands righted her.

"I kill your kind." Jordan was defiant despite her diminished condition.

"I'm sorry I wasn't here to witness that myself. I was delayed by another task." The woman was so close that Jordan would have felt her breath on her skin if she'd had any. But the undead didn't need air.

"Have you been following me?" Jordan coughed, which caused her to wince. She'd been aware of winged creatures dogging her steps lately. She hoped like hell that Miller had gotten out with the kid. She wasn't sure if she'd expressed the concern verbally or only inside her head.

"The child is safe now, but you are not." The vampire said something to the others that Jordan didn't understand. Something in a strange language.

Jordan became aware that there were at least six or perhaps ten others in the room with them. There was a scuffling commotion in the background somewhere beyond her view. "Take her to the van. We leave now."

That last part she understood.

"Where are we going?" Jordan was fading but doing her best to hang on.

No one answered her question. Her feet uselessly dragged along the floor as she was roughly ushered back out to the street. Jordan sensed herself being lifted off the ground as she was hoisted into a van with no windows along the sides. The interior was empty and the cool steel floor of the vehicle was hard against her back. A few of the others climbed in and knelt around her on the floorboard of the van. The woman invaded her vision again. The woman's hands were on her, searching the interior pockets of her long coat until she found what she was looking for. Two small vials of holy water. She ripped open Jordan's shirt and directed one of her minions to remove the vials. There was no way a vampire could handle it without injury.

"This is going to hurt." She spoke to Jordan and then nodded to her companion.

The holy water sizzled like peroxide on an infected wound. Jordan writhed, but strong hands held her in place.

"Again." The woman's command was firm.

The second vial was emptied onto her wounded side.

A burning sensation like hot coals pierced her insides and ignited every nerve ending. Jordan gritted her teeth, refusing to cry out. As the pain subsided, the woman invaded her field of vision once again.

"Remember this night." She paused and drew closer. "Remember the night when a demon saved your life."

Jordan tried to speak, but darkness tugged at her. She could feel her body moving through space and time, but had no sense of where.

"Who are you?" Jordan's question came out raspy. Instinctively, she reached for the woman's hand and the woman took it. The moment their palms touched and the vampire's cool fingers closed around hers, a sequence of images flashed through her mind, like someone shuffling a deck of cards. Were the mental images a sequence of visions that seemed like memories? Or were they actual memories? In them, she was a child and the vampire was there.

"Rest." The vampire squeezed Jordan's hand. "You will need all your strength now."

The woman backed out of the van and the two men who stood on either side of her closed the doors.

Jordan's head lolled from side to side with the motion of the drive along the winding road. She fought to stay awake, but eventually the shadow of injury sapped her strength and pulled her under. She drifted off fully expecting never to wake again.

CHAPTER EIGHT

Jordan squinted up at the bedside lamp feeling confused. She made a move to raise up, but the pain in her side reminded her that she shouldn't.

"Don't try to sit up." She recognized the familiar voice of her friend Sterling Eli. Eli returned to the chair near the bed and placed her palm on Jordan's forehead.

"Am I dead?" Jordan's question was barely more than a whisper.

"If you're dead then so am I, and if that's the case, I'm feeling very disappointed about the afterlife." Eli surveyed the rustic interior of the room. "I was hoping heaven would be a lot less like your old cabin in the woods."

Jordan started to laugh but coughed instead.

"Hey, careful." Eli held a glass of water up to Jordan's lips. "Take small sips. I think you've had a rough night." Eli waited for her to take a drink. "I don't know if you're aware of this, but someone stabbed you."

"No shit." Jordan glared at nothing in particular. She allowed her eyes to lose focus for a moment.

"When I left you at the coffee shop everything was fine. What happened?"

"It was a vampire." She took a deep breath. "How did I get here? I don't remember anything after the…attack."

Eli relaxed in the chair. She'd taken her jacket off and it hung on the back of the seat.

"I'm not completely sure how you got here." Eli helped Jordan sip a little more water. "I wasn't sure when you'd be up here next, so I stopped by to shore up the boundary and check for wildlife on the stoop." She paused. "But when I arrived you were the only wildlife sleeping on the porch. I guess whoever dropped you off didn't have the courtesy to carry you inside."

"Vampires can't come in if they aren't invited."

"Oh yeah, right." Eli had an expression of worry. "Are you sure it was vampires?"

"Very. At least some of them were anyway." Jordan realized she was still wearing the bloodied shirt, although it was half unbuttoned and a large white bandage covered the puncture wound on her side.

"Why would a vampire stab you? Why didn't they just bite you? Or kill you for that matter."

"I have no idea." Jordan shifted on the pillow. "There's another thing." She tried to lift the corner of the bandage for a better look. "I think the blade was poisoned."

"Here, let me." Eli lifted the covering so that Jordan could see it. Black tendrils extended from the entry point like a spiderweb.

"The vamp doused the wound with holy water twice after they dragged me out. It burned like hell." Jordan dropped back to the pillow.

"You need to go to the hospital, or at the very least, see a doctor." Eli replaced the bandage. "It looks like you were stabbed with an ice pick."

"I didn't get a close look. You know, since I was bleeding and surrounded by vampires and all." Jordan paused for emphasis and then switched off the sarcasm. "But it looked like it could have been the spike of Caiaphas."

Eli didn't respond. Jordan knew that Eli was as familiar with the stories of the Christian relic as she was. Caiaphas was the Jewish high priest that condemned Jesus and sent him to the Romans to die. Two nails from the crucifixion were discovered by archaeologists in Caiaphas's burial cave. The nails went missing shortly after they were discovered, but rumors in the underworld said the iron spikes had been fashioned into a weapon.

"There was a baby too," Jordan said.

"A baby what?"

"An infant…a human."

"An innocent." Eli grew even more serious if that was possible.

"Yes, and I'm pretty certain the spike went through me into the kid's foot." Jordan tried to recall the details of the encounter. "So our blood would have mingled."

"What else can you remember?"

"Like what?" Jordan was fatigued and not at her best. She felt her energy level sink.

"Any patterns drawn on the floor?"

Jordan was quiet for a moment, trying to visualize the scene again.

"I think there was something." She'd have to give it more thought, and at the moment her head was pounding. "I can't quite think…" She sank heavily onto the pillow. "I don't feel so good."

"You need to rest." Eli stood and tugged her plaid fleece jacket on. "I have to go take care of something. I'll be back soon." She paused at the bedroom door. "I'll call Sam from the car. At the moment, I think you need a doctor more than anything else."

Jordan nodded. It was good to have a doctor on speed dial when you needed one. Come to think of it, it was good to have someone like Eli in your inner circle as well. Eli had always come through for her, now and all the times before now.

"Thank you."

"Get some rest," Eli called from the next room.

She heard the door close and tried to relax. Unfortunately, her mind had other ideas. She couldn't stop replaying what had happened. Hardly any of it made sense, except the part where it was confirmed that vampires were back-stabbing assholes. And Miller hadn't exactly backed her up, but he hadn't been a complete waste of space either. If he hadn't been there then there was no way she'd have been able to get the kid to safety. She wondered if he'd made it. It seemed like the vampires had very little interest in chasing him. She hoped she was right about that.

She didn't know Miller well enough to trust him completely. Trust was something that had to be earned and tested over time. Those who existed within the circle of trust for Jordan were few and could literally be counted on one hand with fingers left over.

The bigger question was who was the vampire who had saved her? Jordan had never seen the woman before. And since when did vampires save anyone? The world was upside down at the moment and Jordan's exhausted brain couldn't make sense of it.

❖

Grace jerked awake, flailing her arms as if she were trying to fight off a phantom attacker. She realized after a few seconds that she was utterly alone and it was very dark. It was so dark in fact that her eyes had trouble finding focus. She sat up, dusted dirt from her face, and adjusted her glasses, which were completely askew. Then she braced her arms behind her. Grace sank her fingers into the loose soil. Why was she lying on the ground? The silhouetted shapes of trees began to take shape against the deep purple of the nighttime sky. If there was still a moon, it was hidden behind fog or clouds or the horizon.

Her heart began to beat wildly in her chest as she searched her surroundings for some point of reference. Where was she and how did she get here? What was the last thing she remembered? She couldn't recall anything—nothing. Her mind was a blank. A wave of nausea threatened to capsize her. She covered her mouth with her hand.

Breathe, just breathe.

Was she injured? No, she didn't feel any pain or discomfort, except that she was cold. Her thin blouse wasn't enough of a barrier against the chilly, sea-scented air. If she listened carefully she could hear the sound of the crashing surf, or was that just her heart pounding in her ears? She realized the fabric of her pants was damp from lying on the grass. The grass was tall and felt brittle and scratchy against her skin, but the fog had dampened the slender stalks just like a heavy dew.

She slowly managed to get to her feet, pausing once upright to make sure she wasn't going to get dizzy. Her brain was a jumble of random thoughts, none of which made sense. She swept her fingers through her hair to brush it away from her face. A few leaves that had been caught in her hair pulled free. *Lovely.*

Now that she was off the ground she surveyed the darkness for clues. Through the trees, not too distant, she saw a small square of soft light. A window? Where there was a lit window there must be a house. She needed help in some way but wasn't even sure what that meant. Her nervous system hummed with a general feeling of dread from some unknown source.

The heel of her pump sank in the soft earth as she walked. She stopped to work it free so as not to step out of it and lose her shoe in the dark. Stumbling forward again, Grace held her hands in front of her face as she pushed through scratchy limbs, making her way toward the small beacon of light in the otherwise completely deserted landscape. Finally, Grace stepped from the woods into a small clearing that surrounded a rustic cabin. She walked around the cabin until ambient light from another window lit the front porch of the dwelling.

She paused at the door with her hand poised to knock and considered that perhaps she'd woken up right in the middle of an overused movie trope. Didn't every horror movie she'd ever seen feature some hapless urbanite knocking on the door of a secluded cabin? And now she knew why they always knocked, against their better judgment—because they were desperate.

Grace took a deep breath and rapped lightly. After waiting a minute, she knocked again, this time a little louder.

CHAPTER NINE

A loud knock at the front door woke Jordan. She hadn't even remembered dozing off. She had a fuzzy memory of Eli saying she was going to call Sam. But Sam usually let herself in. Maybe the door was locked.

"Damn." Jordan cautiously swung her feet over the side of the bed and waited for the room to stop spinning. Her throbbing head felt as if it weighed fifty pounds. Her neck ached from trying to hold the weight of it.

Another series of rapid knocks.

"I'm coming," she muttered under her breath.

Jordan stood and then after taking several steps, braced against the doorframe of the bedroom. She rested there for a few seconds, and then made the rest of the long journey across the room between the bedroom and the front door.

She opened the door to find a stranger, a woman standing on the porch. They stared at each other. Neither of them spoke for what seemed like a long time but might have only been a few seconds. Jordan's sense of time was seriously screwed up at the moment.

The woman met Jordan's gaze directly for the first time. Her eyes were green. She regarded Jordan with a slightly wide-eyed expression. She had a pleasing round face, fair complexion, and chestnut hair that fell past her shoulders in loose waves. She was wearing an ivory silk blouse and dark dress pants. The woman was probably in her mid or late thirties. Wearing fashionably heavy frames, she looked like Clark Kent's little sister. Or a sexy librarian lost in the wild. Jordan couldn't quite decide which.

"How did you get here?" Jordan asked the first question that ran through her mind.

"Most people lead with hello."

"Sorry, hello." Jordan didn't invite the woman in, but she obviously wasn't of the undead variety or she'd never have made it past the barrier in the first place. That was the great thing about consecrated ground. It kept the demons at bay. "Can I help you?"

Jordan asked the question even though she had very little physical reserve at the moment to offer any assistance to anyone.

"I…I don't know where I am. I'm lost." The woman clasped her hands in front of her chest and nervously looked over her shoulder. "I just woke up in the woods and I don't know how I got there."

Jordan studied the woman. Her hair was disheveled and there was plant debris on her clothing. A smudge of dirt on her cheek. Jordan's internal system was suddenly on high alert. First, a group of vampire minions drove her out here in an unmarked van from the city and now a stranger had woken up on her property and had no memory of how she got there. *What the fuck?*

"May I come in?"

Her brain wanted to say no, but other parts of her body couldn't refuse such a polite request from a beautiful woman. Her brain lost the argument.

"You're welcome to come in for—"

She brushed past Jordan while the unfinished statement hung in the air. Jordan had been on the verge of saying that this woman could come in *for now*. Because Jordan had her own crises to sort out at the moment. The woman stood in the living room. She wasn't really looking at Jordan as she rotated to take in the room.

Jordan glanced outside. She didn't see a car or anyone else about. She closed the door and took a few steps closer to the woman.

"What's your name?"

"Grace…Grace Jameson." She looked frustrated as she shook her head. "I'm honestly having a very hard time remembering anything at the moment. Which I know probably sounds odd, but I swear I'm not a bad person…at least I don't think I am." Grace paused in her survey of the room to push her glasses back up her nose with her index finger. "I'm sorry, I didn't catch your name."

She hadn't given it, had she? Jordan was having this weird, between spaces sensation—here but not here at the same time.

"Jordan Price."

Grace's demeanor was intelligent and confident despite her situation. Everything about Grace gave off that all-American, likeable, girl-next-door vibe. Jordan could easily picture Grace as the charming, brave, loyal heroine of her own story, the kind of woman who would easily engage your heart and your mind with the same intensity. The sort of fearless and compassionate woman that you'd root for until the end.

That seemed like an odd observation to make, but it was as if the essence of Grace came to her all at once, as if they'd met before or known each other in a previous life. Except that Jordan didn't believe in reincarnation so the fact that she'd thought of it now made no sense. She was definitely not herself at the moment.

"I'm not sure what happened to my things." Grace hugged herself. "It's rather chilly outdoors so it stands to reason that I'd have had a jacket or something."

Without responding, Jordan tugged a throw from the sofa and gently draped it around Grace's shoulders. Grace drew the fleece blanket around herself more tightly. Jordan was strangely at ease with Grace considering they were complete strangers. Grace seemed equally relaxed in Jordan's space.

"You're hurt." Grace looked down at Jordan's exposed midsection.

Jordan had gotten out of bed assuming she'd find Sam at the door. She'd forgotten about her own appearance once Grace entered the house. Instinctively, she covered the bandage with her hand.

"It's nothing."

Grace had been so overwhelmed by her own situation and so grateful to discover in her hour of need that the cabin wasn't deserted that she was only just now taking in details about its occupant. Jordan was not who she'd expected to find on the other side of the weathered front door.

Jordan was a few inches taller than she was, androgynous, with thoughtful blue-gray eyes and a tangle of short dark hair that fell alluringly at her right temple. Jordan's hair was longer in front and cut more closely at the back and around her ears. Grace's first thought was that Jordan was definitely her type—tall, elegant features, with a strong jawline. She had to remind herself that she was probably not in a position to give a very good first impression. But then she redirected her thoughts as she focused on Jordan's blood-stained dress shirt which was unbuttoned at the bottom to reveal a large white bandage at her side. The open shirt also revealed a teasing glimpse of Jordan's sculpted abdomen. Overall, Jordan had the leanly muscled physique of an elite athlete. She was probably in her forties. It was hard to gauge Jordan's age given how fit she was. She was wearing perfectly broken-in jeans but was barefoot.

Jordan exuded strength but at the same time had a striking vulnerability that made Grace want to draw her into a hug. There was something else about Jordan, an air that told Grace she didn't reveal much, but what she did reveal was intentional. She had the strongest desire to ask what Jordan stood for, or what she believed in. She envisioned holding Jordan in her arms and whispering the question into her hair. She could see the moment as clearly as a memory, her body even remembered the weight of Jordan's head as it rested against her chest.

That was so strange. She tried to dislodge the image.

"I'm sorry, you're hurt and I've just shown up on your doorstep and—"

"It's alright." Jordan sounded as if she meant that. "Maybe you should sit down."

"I'm not sure who's more in need of a chair...you or me." It seemed they were both at the end of a very bad day. Even though she couldn't remember hers it couldn't have been very good if she'd woken up lying in the dark woods with no memory of how she got there. She didn't feel injured, but she didn't feel quite herself either. Actually, given the fact that she couldn't remember anything how did she really know if she was herself or not? That was an unsettling thought.

"Would you like a glass of water?"

"Yes, thank you." Grace dropped in a nearby chair.

Just as Jordan returned with a glass of water there was a light tap at the door. Whoever was on the other side pushed the door open without waiting. Grace jumped. Perhaps she was more unnerved than she realized.

"It's okay. That's Sam Litten. She's a doctor." Jordan held the glass out to her.

"Oh, sorry, I didn't know you had company." Sam hesitated in the open door.

Sam looked like she was around Grace's age, probably mid-thirties. She had a girlish figure and was a few inches shorter than Jordan. Her straight, light brown hair with streaks of blond was pulled loosely into a knot at the back of her neck. Sam looked like a surfer in a well-worn T-shirt under a light denim jacket with khaki trousers. Her clothing was neutral, but her persona was decidedly femme. In her hand she held what appeared to be a large medical kit. She'd have described it as a large white toolbox except for the blocky red cross on the front of it.

"Come in, Sam." Jordan took a few steps toward the door but allowed Sam to close it instead. "This is Grace. She...um...she..."

"I only just arrived." Grace wasn't sure what else to say. "I'm not feeling very well. I don't want to impose, but I think I might need to lie down." The water wasn't really helping and she was suddenly lightheaded.

"Here, let me help you." Seeing that Jordan was injured, Sam jumped into action.

She set the med kit on the floor and took the glass from Grace just in time. Her hand had begun to shake and she would probably have dropped it.

"I can settle her into the spare room." Sam looked at Jordan for confirmation.

Jordan nodded but didn't say anything. Jordan had a strange expression on her face that Grace couldn't decipher. Was she scared, or surprised, or confused? Or perhaps Grace was projecting because she was feeling all of those things herself.

Sam supported her as she got to her feet and then Sam ushered her to a nearby room, just off the main living space. Sam flicked the light switch, and a lamp with a low-wattage bulb came to life on the bedside table. The room had a double bed, a dresser with three drawers, an upholstered chair in the corner of the room, and a bedside table. The floor was bare except for an oval throw rug near the side of the bed. The walls were slatted wood, painted white. She felt like she'd entered some time warp, traveling back to 1940. The whole place seemed stuck in some previous era, moving at its own pace, cozy but not extravagant or showy.

"Just take it easy." Sam guided her onto the bed. She had a very soothing bedside manner. It occurred to her that Sam and Jordan might be a couple, but she hadn't really picked up a romantic vibe from them. She thought perhaps it was just her habit to study people and notice the small details. Was her memory beginning to return?

"Let me get my med kit and I'll be right back."

She nodded. The bed was comfy and she allowed her muscles to relax.

Jordan was still standing in the main room when Sam returned.

"How about you? Eli said you were injured." Sam studied her.

"Yeah, but you can take care of her first." Jordan tipped her head toward the spare room. "This will keep."

Sam held the front of Jordan's shirt open with her fingertips to examine the bandage. The wound was seeping a bit. No doubt because Jordan kept moving around when she should probably go lie down.

"What's the story with Grace? She's very pretty and totally your type." Sam kept her voice down so that only Jordan could hear the comment.

"I hadn't noticed." Jordan lied.

"You're definitely not feeling well if you didn't notice *that*." Sam pointed in the direction of the spare room and arched her eyebrows. "She's beautiful and clearly in need of rescue."

"Shut up." Jordan winced as she adjusted her stance. "You know as much as I do about her. She just showed up, confused and lost."

"That seems odd."

"Yeah." Jordan scowled. "This has been a really weird day."

"Well, you need to be in bed." Sam put her arm around Jordan's waist, careful to avoid the site of injury. "I'll see what I can find out about your mystery guest."

"Do you think she's a plant?" asked Jordan. "You know, seeing as how she's my type and all."

"So, you did notice."

"I'm injured, I'm not dead…yet."

Sam was holding Jordan's arm across her shoulder, with her arm still around Jordan's waist for support as they turned toward the bedroom. Sam paused and looked up at her face.

"But a plant by whom?"

"I'm not sure." Her brain was too foggy to sort anything out. And after what had happened earlier she wasn't feeling particularly trusting. But Grace didn't seem to present an imminent threat. "Either way, Grace doesn't seem like someone who would cause serious harm. She seems more like an innocent bystander. See what you can do for her and let's get her on her way to wherever she came from as soon as possible."

"I'll do my best." Sam nodded. "Want me to get her phone number for you too?" Sam smiled at her own joke.

"You're hilarious." Jordan winced.

"Although, I suppose you don't really need her number since she's already in your bed." Sam paused for effect. "I mean, not in your actual bedroom, but bedroom adjacent—"

"Please stop…it hurts to laugh."

Sam assisted Jordan as she eased back onto the bed, trying to put as little strain on her aching side as possible. Sam stood by the bed for a moment and studied her.

"Jordan, what's going on?" Sam grew more serious and hovered above her.

"What do you mean?"

"You seem different and I'm worried about you." Sam stroked her forehead.

"Different how?" Sam knew her better than almost anyone.

"I'm not sure yet." She kissed Jordan's forehead and let her lips linger. "I'll be back to check on you."

Jordan nodded and allowed herself to sink into the pillow. She let out a long slow breath and tried not to let her thoughts run away from her. Her mind was full of questions.

CHAPTER TEN

S am's palm on her forehead caused Grace to flinch. She didn't think she'd fallen asleep, but perhaps she had. She hadn't heard Sam come back into the room.

"I'm sorry. I didn't mean to surprise you." Sam seemed sincere.

Grace had placed her glasses on the bedside table. She reached for them.

"I don't feel right." Grace didn't know exactly how to describe what was going on.

"Are you injured anywhere? Do you have pain?" Sam was seated at the edge of the bed. She pressed her fingers to the pulse point at Grace's wrist. "Your heart rate is definitely elevated, and you feel like you might have a bit of a fever."

"I simply don't remember anything. How can that be?" Grace took a shuddering breath. "You're really pretty, you know that?" She covered her mouth with her hand, but it was too late. She'd already divulged the unfiltered thought. She sounded drunk, was she drunk? It wasn't like Sam was her type or anything, but when a woman was as naturally gorgeous as Sam, it was worth mentioning. "I'm sorry, I shouldn't have just blurted that out."

Sam smiled and focused on Grace, but didn't speak for a moment or so. Her blue eyes were soft and thoughtful. Sam tucked an errant strand of sun-bleached hair behind her ear.

"Is Sam short for Samantha?"

Sam nodded.

"Did you take something or maybe have too much to drink?" Sam gently asked. Those seemed like sensible questions.

"Wait…drinks. I did have drinks with someone." Grace blinked rapidly and tried to force her mind to remember the details.

"Have you ever blacked out before?" Sam must have sensed her rising panic. "I'm not trying to frighten you. I just want to try and help you figure out what happened."

"You can't scare me more than I already am."

"Are you allergic to any meds?" Sam asked as she searched her medical kit.

"I don't think so." She honestly couldn't remember.

"Okay, I'm going to give you some Tylenol and I'll get you another glass of water. Maybe if you just rest for a little while things will start to come back to you."

Tears gathered along her lashes and one slid down her cheek.

"Hey, you're okay." Sam touched her arm. "You're safe now."

Grace nodded and took a deep breath. She did feel utterly spent. Perhaps if she could just rest for a little while then her mind would reorient itself. She accepted the tablets and the glass from Sam. And then dropped back to the pillow. Even sitting up to drink water was exhausting.

"Where am I?" She couldn't remember if she'd asked Jordan.

"You're in Elk Grove." Sam closed the latch on the oversized medical box. "Elk Grove is near Manchester, about two hours north of San Francisco."

Grace tried to synthesize that bit of new information. She was two hours away from the last place she remembered. With no idea of how she got here.

"Thank you."

"You're welcome." Sam smiled at her as she stood up. "Get some rest."

Luckily, Jordan had been wearing her coat during the attack, which draped enough from the back that it made her a more difficult target. The weapon had barely pierced the side of her abdomen. If the point of entry had been closer to the center of her stomach she'd be in the hospital right now. Jordan tried to relax, but the wound in her side radiated heat. And no matter how she adjusted on the mattress she couldn't get comfortable. Frustrated, she exhaled loudly and pounded the bed with her fist a couple of times. She was pissed but there was nothing she could do about it at the moment.

Sam had put a fresh dressing on the wound and drawn a blood sample. Sam was worried about the dark striation that now stretched about six inches across Jordan's stomach from the puncture site. If it was poison then it was some sort of slow-moving poison because Jordan wasn't feeling any effects right now, other than from the actual site of injury. It had probably only been an hour since Sam's departure, but sleep just wasn't possible. It had been a very long night and now the sun would be awake soon too.

Jordan walked out onto the front porch, which faced north. To her right she could see the faintest hint of pink on the horizon to the east. To the west the Pacific Ocean churned and crashed against the rocky shore. She couldn't see it in the pre-dawn darkness, but she could hear it and she could feel it. The cool air was damp with mist and fog and the scent of the ocean hung in the air. It smelled of brine, salt, and seaweed, especially eelgrass. The rough surf seemed to churn everything into the mist that now drifted all around her. She loved this place.

In January the rivers and seasonal creeks made their presence known along with the winter storms, creating fingers of muddy water in the Pacific Ocean. Waterfalls cascaded off coastal bluffs, spectacular big waves crashed against the rocks, and between storms, the horizon was often clear enough to give you the chance to see the green flash at sunset. From the western side of the property you could sometimes see gray whales on their southward migration.

But it was June now and the first heat wave had arrived, quickly followed by fog. The Pacific micro-climate meant that when it was hot inland it was cool at the coast.

The grasses were high, dry, and golden. If she hiked down to the beach she was sure she'd find Starfish at low tide clinging to the big rocks. Leopard lilies bloomed near the water and coast lilies graced the world with their short-lived glory. There was so much to appreciate about the rugged beauty of the northern California coast.

Jordan spent a lot of time in the city. That's where most of her work was. But she was most at home in this remote spot near the sea.

Even without GPS it would be nearly impossible to get lost on Highway 1. The Shoreline Highway followed the Pacific coast and if the ocean was on your left then you knew you were headed north. But the side roads were a different story. The feeder roads were frequently narrow and steep. A four-wheel drive vehicle was preferred. The dirt road to Jordan's cabin passed through farm country and along the saddle of a ridge, which offered a great view of the eastern mountains and the ocean before dipping down toward the property boundary. She'd inherited one hundred acres of coastal land and the cabin from her grandfather and she hadn't been visiting often enough lately. And this time it hadn't even been under her own steam.

Someone had delivered Jordan to this sacred ground. Had they done it to keep her safe? And if so, safe from what or from whom?

Everything that had happened the previous evening still puzzled her. She had lots of questions and very few answers. Jordan was more than a little worried that her mystery vampire savior had taken the weapon. The last thing she wanted was to think of the religious relic in the hands of a demon. Was that what the entire thing had been about? Getting the weapon? Perhaps she was inconsequential in the entire affair. How had the vampire who'd stabbed her come to have the weapon in her possession in the first place?

Too many questions. Jordan was getting a headache.

Maybe what she needed was coffee. She'd carefully slipped into a sweatshirt and sweatpants, mindful of her injury, but was still barefoot. The boards of the porch were cool and damp beneath her feet. She retreated into the warmth of the cabin. It had been quite a while since she'd spent any time up here so she didn't know what supplies she had on hand, but she was sure that she had a stash of coffee in the freezer for emergencies. Jordan was happy to discover that there was also a loaf of bread in there too. It was double bagged to keep it from getting freezer burn. That was likely Sam's handiwork. If she was lucky, Sam would bring some additional groceries when she came back because Jordan's car was still in the city, parked near her apartment building, right where she'd left it.

Jordan opened the bag and scooped a few heaping spoons of ground coffee into the French press. She preferred to grind the beans fresh, but this was a desperate situation that called for desperate measures. She filled the kettle, put it on to boil, and then decided to check on her houseguest. The sky outside the kitchen window had transitioned from deep purple to pink, but it was still very early.

She braced her shoulder against the doorframe with her arms crossed and watched Grace sleep. Her hair fanned out a bit on the pillow. Jordan stood there until she heard the faint whistle of the kettle. She removed it from the burner before it got too loud. She had just placed the lid back on the French press when Grace spoke behind her.

"I heard something whistle." Grace's hair was tousled and she tried to tame it with her fingers. She'd slept in her clothes and her shirt was slightly askew. The throw from the previous night was draped over her shoulders like a shawl.

"Sorry, I was making coffee." Jordan leaned against the edge of the counter.

"There is a God," Grace muttered as she shuffled toward the table and sat down.

"I didn't mean to wake you up."

"It's fine." Grace adjusted her glasses as she focused on Jordan. "I didn't sleep well anyway." She paused. "I meant to thank you last night for allowing me to stay."

"No problem." Jordan decided that Sam was right. Grace was completely her type. "Maybe when the sun is up we can retrace your steps and locate your things."

"What things?"

"Well, you mentioned last night that you were fairly certain you had a jacket and—"

"And my bag, my purse, and my phone." Grace braced an elbow on the edge of the table. "It seems very unlikely that I wouldn't have had my phone with me." Grace was staring at a spot on the floor as if her brain was idling while she searched her memory for clues.

"Would you like a piece of toast?" Jordan held the bag of frozen whole grain bread in front of her. Leave it to Sam to buy the healthiest bread possible. "I'm afraid until I get some groceries this is our only real breakfast option."

"Toast sounds good." Grace focused on her for a moment. "How are you feeling this morning?"

"A bit sore, but fine." Jordan had her back to Grace as she pried two pieces of frozen bread apart with a butter knife. She dropped them into the toaster.

"Do you mind if I ask what happened?"

"Um, just an accident at work." There was no way she would tell Grace she'd been stabbed by a vampire. Civilians were better off in the dark about those things.

"What sort of work do you do?"

"Freelance mostly."

Grace watched Jordan lower the handle on the French press and then pour coffee into two mugs. Jordan's answers were far too vague for Grace's liking. But if Jordan thought she'd give up that easily, with such an obvious brush-off, then she was in for a surprise. Grace was a journalist at heart, and she always got to the heart of a story.

"I only have sugar, no cream on hand." Jordan held a mug up in her direction.

"I don't need anything in it. Thanks."

The slices of bread popped up, but after inspection, Jordan set the toaster again. She turned to face Grace, braced one hand on the counter, rested her weight against the edge, and sipped her coffee. Under Jordan's intense gaze, she felt a bit like a crime suspect brought in for questioning.

"Are you a cop?" Jordan gave off a real law-and-order vibe, but something told Grace she wasn't with the police.

"No, why would you ask that?"

Grace shrugged. Two could play at this game of vague responses.

"Private detective?" She took another guess.

"Sort of."

"Are you in the witness protection program or something?"

Jordan laughed and shook her head. "You ask a lot of questions for someone who just woke up."

"I'm a journalist." She sipped her coffee. "I can't help myself." Grace thought perhaps if she revealed a personal detail then maybe Jordan would too.

The toaster dinged and Jordan brought both pieces to the table, each on a separate small plate. She offered butter to Grace.

"Thanks."

"So, you're a journalist." It wasn't really a question. "What kind of stories do you write?"

"Mostly memoirs." She scooped out more butter than she probably needed. "I ghostwrite memoirs."

"I didn't even know that was a thing." Jordan rested her elbows on the table. After the butter melted, she took a bite.

She studied Grace as if she were under a microscope. It didn't really make her nervous, but Grace couldn't help but notice the scrutiny. If Jordan wasn't a cop then she was definitely in a related field. It was obvious to her that Jordan was someone who didn't trust easily.

Well, guess what? After drinks with Thea Shaw, Grace didn't trust easily either. Flashes of her time with Thea at the bar had come back to her during her fitful night of no sleep. Unfortunately, she still couldn't remember what had happened after Thea escorted her to her room in the hotel. Maybe in time, those details would come back to her as well.

"I could loan you a clean shirt if you'd like to take a shower."

"Is that a hint?" Grace figured that Jordan's offer was well intentioned but she couldn't help giving her a hard time.

"No, I mean, I just thought—"

"I was joking."

"Okay, good to know."

Maybe she should tone down the sarcasm a little. Jordan seemed a wee bit on edge, and it wasn't as if they knew each other very well or anything. It wasn't as if this was a normal situation of morning-after toast and coffee. Grace had to remind herself to be guarded despite how safe she felt with Jordan.

"I would appreciate a clean shirt and a shower." She held up her mug. "And maybe even a little more of this."

"Say no more." Jordan set the kettle on to boil again and prepped the French press.

Grace wondered if Jordan was aware of how often she touched her side. She wanted to ask more about the injury but didn't want to pry. At least not before a second cup of coffee and a shower.

CHAPTER ELEVEN

Alone in the bathroom, Grace braced her hands on the pedestal sink, stared into the mirror, and took stock. She looked like someone who'd been living in the woods for a week. No wonder Jordan kept staring at her. She exhaled loudly and then splashed cold water on her face.

Step one, get yourself cleaned up. Then she'd begin the task of figuring out how to get back to her life from this remote outpost. As cozy as it might be, and as intriguing as Jordan seemed, this was not where she was supposed to be.

There wasn't really a shower in the modern sense. The bathroom featured a large claw-foot tub with one of those showerhead hose things and a shower curtain that could be drawn to turn it into a shower. The fixtures on the tub seemed newer. While she waited for the tub to fill with hot water, she opened the medicine cabinet. You could tell a lot about a person from what you found in their bathroom. At the moment, this little investigation wasn't revealing very much.

There were no prescription meds in the cabinet. A couple of toothbrushes, still in packaging. She'd definitely borrow one of those. The shelves were otherwise fairly sparse. There was a box of Band-Aids, a roll of gauze, a bottle of peroxide, and aspirin. As the tub continued to fill, she rotated in the room. There were no knickknacks on shelves, no potted plants, no decorative soaps or towels. In fact, the entire space, while comfortable, was without decoration.

Grace slipped out of her clothing and held onto the edge as she climbed into the deep soaking tub. She lowered herself slowly and went all the way under for a few seconds. The hot bath felt like a tropical vacation. She might just stay forever.

Grace shampooed her hair and sank under the surface again to rinse it. Then she took the bar of soap and lathered it between her hands. Every inch of her body ached from fatigue and lack of sleep, and worry. But the warm soak was helping wash all of it away. As she swept her hand across her skin with suds, she felt something on her shoulder that she hadn't noticed before. It wasn't sore, but she could feel some sort of indent in the skin in two spots just at the back of her shoulder near the base of her neck. She had a mental image of Thea Shaw like a flashbulb, there and gone.

Grace sat up in the tub. Her palm still rested over the injury to her shoulder.

What was the last thing Thea said to her? Something like, it will all be over soon? What the hell had she meant by that?

The soothing effect of the hot bath couldn't override her nervous system so she climbed out of the tub and began to towel off. She needed a better look at the spot at the base of her neck. The mirror over the sink was all fogged up from the steamy bath. She swiped at it with her hand first, but all that did was make it worse. She used the edge of her towel to dry a large enough opening so that she could see herself. She half turned and leaned closer. The spot on her shoulder was hard to see, but it looked like two small punctures in her skin.

Was it a spider bite? What else could have made those marks? They didn't look infected or anything, just red, so she figured that they would heal and that would be the end of it. But the fact that she couldn't remember how she'd gotten them was a bit unsettling. How many hours was she blacked out? Maybe something bit her while she was on the ground. The punctures seemed too far apart for a snake bite, and surely if she'd been bitten by a snake she'd have gotten sick right away.

Grace reached for the flannel shirt Jordan had loaned her. Unfortunately, her hips wouldn't fit into Jordan's slim cut jeans, so she was relegated to sweatpants. This look wasn't going to be her best, but at least she was clean, and now smelled of vanilla shampoo and sandalwood soap—a vast improvement.

She gathered her discarded clothing in hopes that Jordan had a washer she could use. She finger combed her hair as she exited the bathroom. Droplets dampened the shoulders of her shirt.

❖

Jordan had planned to get cleaned up later, after Sam returned to take a look at her bandage. She wanted to get the *all clear* from Sam before getting the wound wet. It was chilly out since it was still early, so she'd gotten a down vest for herself and a jacket for Grace. She was sitting at the table in deep thought when Grace appeared fresh from the bath.

Seeing Grace in her borrowed flannel shirt conjured images in her head of what might have been, what could be. If things were different. Grace filled out the well-worn flannel in a way that Jordan never did. Grace made plaid flannel sexy as hell. Jordan was sure she was staring and redirected her gaze.

"I feel so much better. Thank you for the clothes." Grace smoothed the front of the shirt which only accentuated the curve of her breasts further.

"I'm glad." Jordan tried not to stare. "I thought these might fit and be better for our excursion than your dress shoes." She handed a pair of waterproof, slip-on boots to Grace.

Grace tugged the boots on over heavy socks and tucked the sweatpants into the boots.

"They're a little loose, but I think these will work nicely." She shifted her weight from side to side.

"It's still chilly out so I have a jacket for you too."

"Thank you." Grace accepted the fleece-lined denim coat. "I'm feeling a bit like a lumberjack right now." Grace looked down at her clothing and laughed.

"You may feel like a lumberjack, but you certainly don't look like one."

"Is that so?" Grace quirked her eyebrow and smiled at Jordan.

Jordan cleared her throat. "Sorry, I didn't mean anything by that."

"Don't panic, it will take more than one well-placed compliment to get me into bed." Grace clapped her hands over her mouth the moment the words left her lips and regarded Jordan with wide eyes. "I am so sorry, I don't know why I said that. It just came out…like I was someone else…"

"It's okay." Jordan tried to brush it off.

"I mean, not that getting into bed with you is a terrible idea…I mean, not that I wouldn't want to if you wanted to." Grace squeezed her eyes shut and braced her hands on her hips. "I am making this so much worse."

"For the record, I don't panic that easily." Jordan held the door open for Grace. "I just didn't want you to feel uncomfortable because of my comment."

"I'm glad we sorted that out." Grace stepped onto the porch.

Jordan wasn't sure they had sorted it out. Grace seemed a wee bit erratic. Since Jordan didn't know Grace, she wasn't sure if that was normal or abnormal behavior.

Grace stepped off the porch into the tall grass and Jordan followed. The marine layer was thick above them. It had an eerie lavender gray color. Sometimes Jordan imagined the fog being the underside of water. A sea that hovered above the material world. That was a strange thought.

The sun was up, but the fog hid it completely. When she turned toward the woods she realized that Grace had been watching her as she looked up at the fog.

"Do you remember which way you approached the cabin?" The toes of Jordan's boots were wet from the heavy dew.

"I came from the back." Grace studied the tree line. "Somewhere through there because I remember fighting my way through these branches."

"There's a deer trail over here." Jordan motioned to the right. "Let's follow it and then once we're past the thicket we can cut back toward the way you walked."

Grace nodded and followed Jordan's lead.

"Is all of this your property?"

Jordan was walking in front and didn't turn around when she answered.

"Yes. It originally belonged to my grandparents."

"So, you grew up here?"

"Not exactly." She didn't really feel like sharing at the moment. Jordan was trying very hard to keep a cordial distance from Grace, but it wasn't easy. Something about Grace churned her insides in a good way, in a way that she hadn't felt in a long time.

"Are you okay walking?"

"What do you mean?" Jordan stopped and turned.

"With your injured side." Grace motioned toward Jordan's midsection.

"Oh, yeah…I keep forgetting about it." She turned and started walking again. "Let's cut through right here."

She angled east, through the trees toward the natural meadow. When they reached the edge of the clearing, Grace stopped.

"This seems familiar." Grace surveyed the grassy opening. "I remember waking up in what I thought was a field. But I was able to feel dirt, so there must have been a place without grass."

Jordan walked slowly, zigzagging so that she didn't miss anything, until she found a space in the tall vegetation where the ground had been disturbed. She knelt beside the dark earth and looked for signs.

"Is this where I woke up?" Grace asked, as if Jordan would know.

She looked up at Grace from her crouched position. After a minute or so, she stood up. Whoever brought Grace here, they'd taken the time to dig a shallow trench in the earth.

"Were they trying to bury me?" The pitch of Grace's voice went up. "Assholes." She mumbled.

"I'm not sure what they were trying to do." Jordan scanned the surrounding tree line. They were far from the boundary of the property. Someone had carried Grace for quite a distance. There were no tracks in the grass and no beat-down trail from off-road tires. No one had driven to this spot.

"My bag!" Grace held up her purse as if she'd just struck gold. She started to inspect the contents. "It looks like everything is here, except my phone." She held the bag at her side and continued to search the tall grass. "Do you think there's any chance my phone is here somewhere?"

"I doubt it." Whoever dumped Grace probably didn't want her location to be tracked. They would certainly have tossed her phone and her laptop.

They searched in the tall grass until they found her jacket, her scarf, and even her rolling bag which someone had had the courtesy to pack but not the courtesy to place it where Grace could locate it in the dark.

"Check your luggage for your laptop."

Grace did as Jordan suggested.

"It's not here either." Grace zipped the large front pocket of her suitcase. "Damn."

Jordan was suspicious of the location and the way in which Grace had been laid in what almost appeared to be a shallow grave. Although, she didn't mention that last part to Grace. That seemed far too morbid for a civilian. For a hunter, that sort of discovery was just another day at the office.

Grace looked over at Jordan, who had a curious expression. Did Jordan know something she didn't? Or did she suspect something sinister? Whatever the case, Jordan wasn't sharing her thoughts at the moment. Either way, Grace was feeling happy that at least she'd found some of her belongings. She could go back to the cabin, change into her own clothes, and figure out how to get back to the city. She'd obviously missed her flight to Atlanta so she needed to call home and let someone know where she was. At the very least, her friend Natalie would probably be wondering what happened and why she wasn't home.

Jordan was kind enough to carry her suitcase, despite her injury. Grace tried to dissuade her but eventually gave up. Jordan was stubbornly chivalrous. Once again, she followed Jordan back down the path through the tall grass. She studied Jordan as they walked in silence, noticing her broad shoulders and long strides. Jordan had an easy confidence that made Grace feel calm in this unknown environment.

This coastal northern California landscape was so different from Georgia. This time of year in Atlanta the temperature and the humidity climbed and everything was lushly green. Not like here, where the grass was more like straw, brittle and brown. Ancient cypress trees bent by the wind from the sea grew in an arc with their limbs almost touching the ground. Trees close together having grown in this manner created tunnels of branches in some places. With the heavy fog, it almost felt as if she was in an Irish wonderland and that passage through any of these woven natural tunnels would open upon an undiscovered country.

When they cleared the trees and rounded the side of the cabin, Sam was seated on the steps with a cup of coffee.

"Good morning." Sam was holding the steaming mug in both hands. "Out for a walk so early?"

"We retrieved Grace's things from the meadow." Jordan set the bag down at the foot of the aged wooden steps.

"I picked up a few groceries for you and I wanted to see how you were feeling." Sam stood and held the door open for them.

"If you'll excuse me for a moment, I'm going to change." Grace was grateful for the flannel shirt Jordan had loaned her, but she'd begin to feel more like herself if she was able to wear her own clothes.

As before, Sam was dressed in casual attire that somehow made her look like a fashion magazine spread for a surfer girl on holiday. She glanced back at Jordan and Sam once more before she closed the bedroom door to undress.

Jordan tossed her puffy vest onto a chair and poured herself another cup of coffee. She offered more to Sam.

"I've had my quota, thanks."

Jordan leaned against the counter edge and took a sip of coffee.

"Did you find any clues when you located Grace's things?"

Jordan shook her head. "Not really." She did have some thoughts, but nothing she wanted to share at the moment.

"Does that worry you?"

"A little."

"Do you still think she's a plant?" Sam was standing very close when she asked the last question so there was no way anyone would hear but Jordan.

"I just don't know." Normally, Jordan had strong gut feelings about things. If she couldn't sort something out she'd usually rely on intuition. But where Grace was concerned she honestly couldn't get a solid read. Something told her that Grace was nothing more than an innocent bystander, but innocents could sometimes blindly wreak havoc without intending to.

"Can I take a look at your side?" Sam's fingers were already hovering near the hem of her sweatshirt.

"Sure." She held up the fabric so that Sam could gently pull one side of the gauze bandage away. The puncture wound looked as if it was nearly healed, which seemed oddly fast. And the dark spiderweb had spread further across her torso. She still worried that she'd been poisoned. Wasn't that what the vampire who'd rescued her had said? But she didn't feel sick, just a little stiff and sore.

"I got the results back on your blood work." Sam spoke without looking up. She replaced the bandage and then braced her hands on her hips. "The results were…unusual."

"What does that mean?"

"It's almost as if your blood is reacting to a virus, but unlike any virus I've ever seen." Sam smoothed down the front of Jordan's sweatshirt. "I sent it to a friend of mine at the CDC for a second opinion. It seems like the weapon was definitely laced with some sort of toxin, but I haven't been able to confirm what it was yet."

"I feel okay." Jordan took a swig of coffee.

"Let's keep it that way." Sam's expression was serious.

"Hey, have you talked to Eli?"

"Not today."

"I was hoping she'd give me a ride to the city."

"Um, I think she had to deal with something and won't be back until tomorrow." Sam averted her eyes. It wasn't like her to be vague, and she tried not to read into it. "You should probably at least take it easy for one more day anyway." Sam reached for her jacket.

"Did I hear something about a ride to the city?" Grace reappeared, wearing jeans and a cotton blouse, with a cardigan.

She'd thought Grace looked good in the flannel shirt, but she looked even better now, more herself. It was weird that Jordan had that thought since she didn't really know Grace. Maybe it was just that Grace seemed more comfortable in her own clothes.

"I'll give my friend Eli a call and see if she can give us a ride." Jordan set her empty mug in the sink.

"I'd offer, but I've got a full schedule today." Sam walked to the door and Jordan followed. "Like I said, not that you ever listen to me, but I think you should take it easy today." She looked at Grace. "You too." Sam gave Jordan a hug and then she was gone.

Jordan rotated to face Grace. They stood staring at each other for an awkward few seconds. Jordan wasn't used to having a stranger in her space, especially not in this place. The cabin was her retreat, her escape from the outside world. But this time, the outside world had followed her. She also wasn't in the mood to babysit a civilian who wasn't part of the world she lived in.

"I think I'm going to go for a walk." She needed space to think. Simply by her presence, Grace was creating too much noise for Jordan to get a clear read of her own feelings.

Grace watched Jordan tug on her vest. Jordan didn't look at her when she spoke. It was clear that this wasn't an invitation for Grace to join her. Fine. As a matter of fact, good. Grace hadn't had any time to herself and was happy to have a little time alone, even if it was in someone else's house.

Jordan closed the door without waiting for Grace to respond. She took a deep breath and let it out. Jordan seemed on edge. Maybe it would be good for her to walk off whatever was going on. It wasn't like Jordan was the only person inconvenienced by any of this. And it wasn't her fault that she'd ended up here, was it?

In any event, whatever bad mood Jordan was in was certainly not her fault.

The bag of groceries Sam brought was still sitting on the counter in the kitchen. She figured she might as well make herself useful. Grace took out things and placed them on a nearby pantry shelf and then put a few of the items in the fridge. She stood for a moment and rotated in the space, taking in the kitchen. Like the bathroom, the room was cozy, but sparse at the same time. The collection of dishware was small. It looked like there was only enough to handle no more than three people at a time. Jordan obviously didn't entertain guests here. Perhaps this cabin was more of a retreat. It did have that sort of vibe. Only the necessities and nothing more.

As she moved through the cabin she began to notice there were several crosses hanging on the walls—a Celtic cross, a Catholic crucifix, a Russian Orthodox cross, and even a plain wooden cross. There was literally a cross in every room. Grace also took note that where there were items arranged, like on a shelf or on the sofa, or photos on the wall, that they were always in groupings of three.

On the coffee table there were three different translations of the Bible. She sat on the sofa and picked up the Bible on top of the stack. She thumbed through the tissue thin pages until she came to a clump that was stuck together. When she gently separated the pages she discovered that some sort of red-brown smear was across the page. Was that blood? Grace quickly closed the book and dropped it onto the table.

There was something strange about this place and about Jordan. How had she not noticed any of this the previous night? Because she'd not quite been herself, that's why. She rubbed her fingers across the marks on her shoulder. They were slightly raised and they tingled.

Regardless of how intrigued she was by Jordan, and whatever her backstory was, the idea of spending another night out here on the edge of nowhere wasn't very appealing.

Grace rubbed her arms with her hands as if she was cold and trying to warm up. But she wasn't cold, she was simply unsettled. She crossed the room, and as she neared the window something caught her attention. When she glanced out the window she realized she was being watched. A striking looking woman stood just outside the gate. Grace had the thought that she'd met this woman before. But when? She was tall and elegantly dressed in a black suit. The woman was flanked by four other individuals, also dressed in black. One of them, an intimidating man who looked like a bouncer at a nightclub, was holding an umbrella for the woman.

Grace stood in front of the window. She knew she was unabashedly staring, but found herself unable to take her eyes off the stranger at the gate. She was inexplicably drawn to her. The heavy fog had not lifted and it swirled around the small darkly clad group just outside the rustic fence giving the impression that the figures were floating or not quite solid. Grace was afraid if she looked away they might disappear.

Chapter Twelve

Jordan's one-mile power walk hadn't eased the tension that radiated through her body. An unsettled sense of something she couldn't quite pinpoint caused her to turn and briskly walk back toward the cabin. The minute she exited the tree line near the house, she knew why. Standing just outside the property fence was the vampire who'd dragged her from the building and into the van.

She slowed her pace and scanned the perimeter. Jordan didn't sense anyone else was about except for the vampire and her small cadre of minions in matching black suits shielding her with a large umbrella.

"How did you find me?" Jordan stood a few feet away, keeping a safe distance. The vampire wouldn't be able to cross the barrier of consecration, but she wasn't sure about the others.

"I had you brought here, Jordan. Somewhere I knew you would be safe."

She and the woman studied each other for a moment and Jordan once again had the unsettling sense that they had met before.

"Are you expecting rain?" Jordan looked up at the sky.

"Funny." But the vampire didn't smile or laugh.

Jordan knew that if the marine layer lifted and the sun did decide to show itself the umbrella would be all that saved this woman from an unpleasant solar burn.

"You know my name, but I don't know yours."

"Kith."

The name sounded so strangely familiar.

"Do you understand what is happening?" Kith asked.

Jordan didn't respond. She actually had no idea what was happening but wasn't about to let Kith or any other blood sucker know that.

"You've felt the discordant vibration." It was a statement rather than a question.

She thought that was actually a pretty good description of what she'd been feeling lately. Weird, unsettling sensations that she couldn't give a name. Premonitions, dreams, worse than usual. And some of them didn't feel like dreams at all—they seemed far too real.

"Very soon, you will reach the age of forty-two." Kith continued. "In Japanese culture, the number forty-two is unlucky because the numerals when pronounced separately—*shi ni*, four two—sound like the word for *dying*."

Okay, that was a bit of cryptic numerology she didn't really need to hear. Sure, she'd been stabbed, but she wasn't dead yet.

"Did you come by to wish me a happy birthday?"

Kith ignored the question. Her gaze bore a hole right through Jordan's chest.

"In Christianity there are forty-two generations in the Gospel of Matthew's genealogy of Jesus." Kith paused for effect. "It is prophesied that for forty-two months the Beast will hold dominion over the Earth."

"And he opened his mouth in blasphemy against God...and them that dwell in heaven." Jordan had no patience for riddles. "Yeah, I can quote the Bible too. What are you trying to say?"

"The beast is a metaphor for the empire that killed the prophets. That's the subtext of the entire book of Revelation."

Jordan never took John's text literally, but she also wasn't a Bible scholar. As far as she was concerned it was all poetic conjecture, a fevered dream, not a prophesy of actual events that would unfold.

"St. John's *revelation* was directed against the rich, the powerful, and everything connected with the apparatus of the state."

Thoughts were beginning to gel in her mind. What was Kith trying to tell her?

"Are you talking about the Guild?" She genuinely wanted to know.

"I'm saying that things happened in the past the same way they do now. There never was a time when things were not in motion. Humans have tried to articulate the Truth through myth, religion, and philosophy, but these forces are sometimes too close and too large to see with accuracy from Earth."

From Earth? What the hell? She was obviously alluding to something larger than the Guild.

Kith's gaze and her confusing prediction or riddle or whatever this was, was making Jordan's head hurt. She took a step back and looked at the ground for a few seconds to clear her focus then returned her attention to Kith.

"There are angels of light and of shadow." Kith's voice was mesmerizing. As she spoke, her lips didn't move but Jordan heard the words inside her head. *"Angels existed long before us, and an angel escorted your soul at birth. You are beginning to remember, aren't you? You know I'm speaking the truth to you."* Kith paused and then began quoting Scripture again. *"And in those days, the sons of God lay with the daughters of men…"* The corner of her mouth turned up in a half smile.

Jordan reminded herself that Kith, despite being lethally gorgeous, was a vampire. But for the first time, Jordan considered that Kith *was* actually telling her the truth. Since when did the undead stand around and quote the Holy Bible? Who was this woman? She had an air about her that told her that Kith was much older than Jordan had originally assumed. But, like all vampires, her age was forever frozen at the time of her transition, which Jordan guessed was her late twenties.

"You are changing. The ritual was supposed to prevent the change. Because if you change, everything changes, and more than anything…they fear change." Still, Kith's lips were unmoving, her words only inside Jordan's head like an echo chamber.

"Who is they?" Kith had to be talking about the Guild.

Jordan heard the door behind her creak on its rusty hinges and she glanced over her shoulder. Grace's appearance on the porch broke the connection. She turned back to face Kith. This time, Kith spoke in an audible voice.

"Does she know yet?" asked Kith.

What was Kith talking about? What did Grace know or not know? Jordan glanced back at Grace standing on the porch hugging herself. When she turned again toward the gate, Kith was gone and the others with her. Nothing remained but the mist.

The ground seemed to shift beneath her feet with Kith's departure, Jordan staggered and fell backward. Although, she did not feel herself land. She lay on her back looking up at the sky as if resting on a cushion of air, hovering just above the ground. The fog thinned above her and the brightness of the sun caused her to blink, but she didn't look away.

"Are you alright?" Grace knelt beside her. As she bent to meet Jordan's gaze her face blocked the sun.

The light filtered through Grace's long hair like tiny shards of a star. Grace hovered above Jordan and Jordan found herself unable to speak or move.

"Jordan, what's wrong? Do you want me to call Sam?" Grace tucked her hair behind her ear, and when she did the sunlight struck her irises at just the right angle. For the briefest instant their color shifted from green to amber with flecks of red.

Grace was unsure of how best to help Jordan. Her body seemed rigid, frozen, but the expression in Jordan's eyes told her that she was aware and awake. Was she having a seizure? Had she fainted? Grace honestly couldn't figure out what had happened. One minute, Jordan had been talking to the small group at the gate, and then as if they'd literally evaporated into thin air, they were just gone. No sound, no visible transportation of any kind, just gone.

As if in slow motion, Jordan lifted her arm and lightly stroked Grace's cheek with her fingertips. The gesture surprised Grace, but she didn't pull away. Jordan had a far-off expression as if she was looking through Grace to something that lay beyond. The impression was so strong that Grace instinctively looked over her shoulder, but there was nothing there.

"Can you stand?" Grace looped her arm through Jordan's. "Let me help you."

"I'm fine." Jordan brushed her away.

Whatever the brief connection had been between them, it was gone now. Jordan seemed angry, or frustrated, or...It finally struck Grace that maybe what she was sensing from Jordan was fear. She backed away from Jordan to give her some space.

Jordan climbed the steps and went inside, leaving Grace standing in the front yard. After a few seconds, she followed. She found Jordan in the kitchen gulping a glass of water. She was breathing hard between gulps and as soon as she drained the glass she refilled it and drank again.

"Who was that woman?"

Jordan looked at her and then returned her gaze to the window over the sink.

"Hey, I know we don't know each other...that we're strangers to each other, but something is going on and you need to start talking to me about what that is." Grace stood next to Jordan, forcing Jordan to deal with both her presence and her question. "Something happened out there and I want to know what."

"It's personal." The muscle along Jordan's jaw line tensed.

Grace could see that the direct approach wasn't going to work. Fine, if Jordan wasn't ready to talk then she could wait. Apparently, she was stranded anyway, with no phone, no ride back to the city, and a splitting headache. Grace had nothing but time on her hands for the rest of the day at least. She pressed her fingers against her temples and left Jordan standing near the sink. She walked to the bedroom and closed the door.

Grace was tired and still not feeling quite right. The coffee and toast hadn't settled well in her stomach. She decided to lie down for a while and give Jordan some time to cool off, or whatever. Grace couldn't quite relax. Her mind hummed with questions and strange sensations, almost like a waking dream. She tossed and turned but could find little relief.

She wasn't sure how much time had passed when she heard a light tap at the bedroom door. She must have dozed off, because the angle of the light through the window seemed lower. Was that possible? The grogginess in her head told her it was. Luckily, her headache had subsided for the moment.

"Come in." Her voice was raspy, so she said it again a little louder. "Come in."

Jordan peered around the edge of the door with a cup and saucer in her hand.

"I thought you might like a cup of tea."

Grace smoothed her hair away from her face, reached for her glasses, and propped up against the pillow.

"Is that a peace offering?"

"I guess it is." Jordan stood in the center of the room for a few seconds before she set the drink on the bedside table. She didn't come closer, and the minute she set the teacup down she backed away to sit in a vintage upholstered chair in the corner of the room. It was a narrow chair with some sort of green and brown floral print. It didn't look like the sort of chair Jordan would own unless it had been handed down to her from her grandmother.

Jordan slouched in the chair with her long legs extended in front of her. To the casual observer she'd have seemed relaxed, but energy pulsed off of her lean frame. As if at any moment she would spring into action. What sort of action Grace had no idea. It was just the feeling she got.

"Who was that woman earlier? You two seemed to have some intense history. Is she an ex-girlfriend or something?"

Jordan actually laughed. That was the first time Grace had seen her laugh and it warmed her heart a little.

"Okay, not an ex-girlfriend." Grace sampled the tea. It tasted like chamomile, which made her happy.

"Earlier, you said something was going on and you wanted to know what it was." Jordan seemed to be carefully choosing her words, like she was on a witness stand or something. "What did you mean by that?"

"Oh, I don't know…I met some woman at a bar in San Francisco and the next thing I know I've blacked out and I wake up in the dirt, at the north end of nowhere in a cabin in the woods." Grace paused. "I mean, we've all seen that movie, right? It doesn't end well."

"I see what you mean." Jordan adjusted her position in the chair. She leaned forward, braced her elbows on her knees, and studied Grace. "You never mentioned meeting a woman at a bar."

"Didn't I?" Grace sipped her tea. "I think details about last night were slow to return to me."

"What did she look like?"

"Pretty…like, eerily pretty. Dark hair, slim…" Grace let the description trail off, because it wasn't what Thea had looked like that stayed with her, but what she felt when she was with her. Out of control, or more accurately unable to control herself. Loss of control was a horrible feeling. "I remember losing track of two hours at the bar and saying yes to more drinks even though I normally never drink more than one. And her eyes…honestly, I could have sworn they changed color as we talked."

Grace wasn't looking at Jordan as she relayed these details. She was staring at a spot on the wall, trying to remember things.

"Did you get her name?"

"Thea Shaw. Yes, that was her name." Grace looked at Jordan, who had a dark expression on her face. The moment of laughter had passed. "Do you know her?"

"No, that name doesn't sound familiar."

They were quiet for a moment. It was obvious that Jordan was trying to sort something out in her head. Grace sipped her tea and waited.

"What were you doing in San Francisco?" Jordan's question almost sounded accusatory.

"Are you sure you aren't a cop?"

"Sorry." Jordan took a deep breath and then softened her tone. "Do you mind if I ask what you were doing in San Francisco?"

Grace laughed. "Much better."

Jordan smiled, but her eyes remained laser focused on Grace.

"I was interviewing a client for a manuscript."

"Who was your client?"

"Okay, seriously, are you a private detective?"

Jordan frowned. "Listen, all I'm trying to do is help you figure out what happened."

Grace sensed something else was going on under the surface with Jordan but decided to play along.

"My client's name is Michael Lucas."

Jordan straightened in the chair as if the mention of Michael's name had struck a nerve.

"Do you know him?" Grace was sure she already knew the answer.

"He's a fucking vampire." Jordan sounded completely sincere about that statement.

"A what?"

"A vampire."

"Okay, this is the part where I tell you that vampires aren't real." Grace experienced a twinge of disappointment because she actually found Jordan kind of hot, but now she had no choice but to doubt Jordan's mental health. The cute ones always came with baggage of some kind. She sighed and sank back into the pillow.

"Just because you don't believe in them doesn't mean they don't exist." Jordan frowned.

"Uh, yes it does." Grace couldn't help the sarcasm. "You know Santa Claus isn't real either, right?"

"And why do you keep touching your neck?" Jordan ignored her attempt at humor.

Grace hadn't even realized she was doing it.

"Something bit me and the spot kind of tingles."

"Will you show me?"

"If you really want to see it." She wasn't completely in the mood to allow Jordan to have a look, but what could it hurt at this point?

Jordan was already on her feet and moved to the side of the bed as Grace unbuttoned the top buttons on her blouse so that she could free her shoulder without revealing too much. Jordan drew closer. She held the collar of Grace's shirt open with her fingers and bent forward for a better look.

It was obvious to Jordan the moment she saw the marks on Grace's shoulder that she'd been bitten by a vampire. She knew Michael Lucas was a vampire and it was highly likely that the woman Grace had encountered at the hotel bar was also a vampire. San Francisco was crawling with them.

Grace looked up at her with the most soulful expression. Jordan couldn't look away and their eyes locked. As she stared into Grace's eyes she lost herself a bit. Her brain waves shifted into a lower gear and idled.

Time slowed.

Even the air in the room grew utterly still.

As close as she was to Grace it was impossible not to notice the sensual curve of her breast just below the opening of the shirt. And the smooth, perfect skin along her neck and collar bone. Jordan's head began to swim. She slipped her finger beneath Grace's bra strap, pulled it aside, and pressed her lips to the place where it had been. Then she filled her fingers with Grace's hair at the back of her neck and tilted Grace's face up so that their lips met. She sensed Grace's fingers tease at the hem of her shirt. Grace broke the kiss and whispered against Jordan's cheek, "Save me."

Somewhere in the distance was a loud banging. The door. Someone was at the door. The continued knocking broke the thrall and Jordan half fell, half staggered backwards until she caught herself against the dresser.

Grace seemed frozen and Jordan couldn't tell by Grace's expression if she'd experienced the same dream-like trance Jordan had just experienced or not. She'd almost fallen victim to a vampire's thrall before, when she was younger and less experienced. This was something different, and besides, Grace wasn't a vampire…yet. And if Jordan could help it, she wouldn't become one. There was still time. The whispered plea echoed inside her head as she watched Grace from across the room.

Save me.

Jordan strode to the front door and swung it open to find Eli walking up the steps.

"Why were you banging on the door? Why didn't you just let yourself in?" She didn't mean for the questions to sound so terse, but she was a bit rattled.

"What are you talking about? I just got here." Eli paused on the top step.

"That wasn't you banging on the door just now?"

"No."

"Fuck." Jordan rotated and looked back toward the guest room. Grace was standing in the bedroom door. "I think I'm losing it."

"Okay, take a breath." Eli's hand was on her shoulder. "Why don't you sit down? You look a little shaken up."

Jordan nodded and allowed herself to be ushered to the kitchen. She sat at the table and covered her face with her hands.

CHAPTER THIRTEEN

G race heard voices and followed Jordan to the kitchen. Grace could see that Jordan was in some sort of distress. She pulled up short when the visitor greeted her.

"Hi, I'm Sterling Eli, a friend of Jordan's. My friends call me, Eli." Eli extended her hand to Grace.

"I'm Grace." She shook Eli's hand. "Am I dead?" Grace figured maybe now was the time to ask.

Eli smiled. "I'm fairly certain you're not dead."

"Okay, just checking. This has been a very strange day."

Eli was a stoic figure. She wasn't as tall as Jordan, but she had a solid, square build, a handsome face, and inquisitive dark eyes. She wore a gray dress shirt, combined with the casual flair of Levi's and a plaid, fleece-lined jacket.

Something had happened when Jordan looked at the injury on her neck and Grace wondered why. Jordan had bolted from the room as if she'd seen a ghost or as if Grace was a ghost. Which she was pretty sure she wasn't. Although, if she was actually dead and this was some sort of afterlife, or more aptly, purgatory, then everything that had happened would make more sense.

Right now, Jordan seemed equally annoyed by Eli for some reason.

"Where have you been? I've been trying to reach you." Jordan, seated at the kitchen table, glanced up at Eli.

"I'm sorry, I had to take care of something. It was an emergency."

Grace was still standing in the center of the room, not really sure what to do next. Should she go hide in the bedroom, should she sit down, should she eat something? She was unsure and she felt as if she was imposing on some sort of friend disagreement between Jordan and Eli.

"She's been bitten by a vampire." Jordan motioned in Grace's direction.

"What?" The pitch of Grace's voice went up a little.

"Sorry, I shouldn't have said anything without talking to you first, but Eli has experience with this sort of thing too. She might be able to help."

"When did this happen?" asked Eli.

"Last night at a hotel bar in San Francisco." Jordan was talking as if she was so confident of the details, as if Grace wasn't standing in the room perfectly capable of answering for herself.

"I didn't say I was bitten. I don't remember being bitten. And you're acting as if you know for sure what happened." She knew every statement sounded angrier than the one before, but Grace couldn't help herself.

"No one ever remembers being bitten." Jordan was completely serious. "It'll come back to you later."

"Okay…" Grace squeezed her eyes shut and held her hands up as if she was trying to stop the world from spinning, which in fact she was, because she wanted to get off this merry-go-round of delusion. "First, there is no such thing as vampires—"

"I'm afraid Jordan is right. Vampires do exist." Eli's statement was calm and matter-of-fact.

"Excuse me, but I can tell from all the crosses that you probably believe there's a God, some heavenly father with flowing hair and a white beard." She was looking at Jordan as she spoke. "You probably believe in angels too and that the world was made in seven days. So, of course you believe in vampires."

Jordan frowned, but Eli smiled. The knowing, annoying sort of smile that a parent bestows on a child who's being ridiculous.

"I'm not making that statement as a matter of faith. I've actually seen them." Eli pulled a chair out for her. "Why don't you sit down?"

Funny, Grace just now noticed there were only three chairs. What was with all the threes?

"Just because you've been bitten doesn't mean you'll become a vampire, we just need to find the creature that bit you and kill them."

Jordan turned to Eli who'd also taken a seat. "I have a name and a pretty good description—"

Eli held her hand up, cutting Jordan off. "I think Grace needs a moment to catch up."

Grace swept her fingers through her hair and then covered her face with her hands. *Catch up* was the understatement of the century.

"I know people like to look upon spiritual things as being intangible and ethereal, unconnected with real life, but not believing makes something no less real." Jordan paused; she was looking at Grace as she spoke. "The footprints of evil date back to the beginning of humankind. Was evil created or did we simply discover it? Who knows. Perhaps it was a consequence of free will." Jordan placed her palms on the table and sat back in her chair. "Evil is like a shadow that grows longer as the days pass."

"Isn't the entire notion of good and evil simply a human construct?" Grace enjoyed a good debate as much as anyone, but at the moment she was feeling very tired. "Can a tree be good or bad?"

Eli laughed. "Looks like you've finally met your match, Jordan."

"Evil is a construct if you only see evil as formless and without shape." Jordan shifted her position. She focused on Grace, with her elbows resting on the edge of the table. "Satan fell from heaven like lightning—"

"How art thou fallen from heaven, O Lucifer, son of the morning." Grace quoted a passage she'd heard in her father's sermons over and over, especially when he was trying to frighten her into being good. Which basically meant doing what *he* wanted her to do and being what *he* wanted her to be.

"Isaiah 14:12." Eli's eyebrows arched. "You know your scripture."

"And so, the war in heaven would be waged on Earth for the souls of humankind." Grace paused. "My father was a Baptist minister. He loved to rain down fire and brimstone from the pulpit every Sunday, but that still doesn't mean I believe any of it *or* that vampires are real."

"There is evil in the world." Jordan's gaze was intense. "It walks, it talks, it pays taxes, and it doesn't care who it hurts to get what it wants."

"You know, funny thing…I learned in my high school Latin class that *Lucifer* was formed out of two words, *lux*, which means light, and *ferre*, which means, to carry. So, Lucifer actually means *bringer of light*." Grace remembered when she'd dropped this bit of knowledge on her father and gotten herself promptly grounded for two weeks. Her current audience seemed equally receptive to her command of Latin.

"Is that a joke?" Jordan was not amused.

"We're just going to have to agree to disagree about this because I don't see the world quite as black and white as you apparently do." Grace glared at Jordan. She wasn't going to be bullied by a zealot.

No one spoke for a few moments.

"Can you give me a ride to the city to get my car?" Jordan finally broke the standoff. She was looking at Eli when she asked.

"Yeah, I can take you—"

"Tonight." Jordan cut Eli off.

"Tonight? Are you sure you're up to it?" Eli paused. "You seem a little off balance."

"That's why you're going with me." Jordan stood.

"If you're driving to the city, then I'm going too." Grace wanted to get out of this crazy house and back to the real world.

"That's not a good idea." Eli's comment was gentle but firm.

"Look, I appreciate your concern, but I need to get back to my life." It was going to be hard to catch up on all the email and texts that had probably piled up while she was in blackout mode.

"Go ahead." Jordan motioned toward the door. "No one is stopping you from leaving."

"Jordan—"

"Let her go." Jordan cut Eli off again. She made a sweeping gesture toward the door.

Grace was annoyed by Jordan's theatrics, as if she was daring Grace to leave. Grace crossed the room, walked through the door, and trotted down the front steps. The sunset was hidden by dense fog. A chilly wind tugged at her blouse and swept her hair across her face. She calmed her hair with her hands and reached for the front gate. Once on the gravel road she was reminded of how remote this place was. There were no houses in any direction, only eucalyptus trees along the roadway and oaks in the distance, and beyond that the blueish purple ridgeline of the coastal range.

She'd stormed from the house without her things, with an urgent need to be away from Jordan and the small confines of the cabin. As she looked toward the western horizon, a tingling sensation traveled up her arm to the small hairs at the back of her neck.

"I'm sorry."

Grace had no idea that Jordan was standing next to her until she spoke. Jordan's tone had softened. She wasn't looking at Grace as she spoke, but instead was staring out into the fog.

"I shouldn't have told you to leave."

"I don't understand what's happening." For all her bravado, Grace was suddenly afraid and thought she might burst into tears against her will.

"I can help if you'll let me." Jordan shoved her hands in her pockets. The breeze stirred her hair. "Someone brought you here for a reason. I'd like to find out why."

Jordan looked at her. There was honesty in Jordan's eyes, but still Grace's mind couldn't accept what Jordan was saying as truth.

"I know you don't believe what you haven't seen. But if you'll let me, I will help you get through this." Jordan placed her hand at Grace's elbow and turned her back toward the cabin. "This fence line marks a consecrated boundary. No demons can cross this barrier."

"You just said that I'm turning into a vampire." Which Grace still didn't believe, but she was inclined to test Jordan. "I crossed the barrier with no problem."

"You aren't a vampire yet." Jordan smiled thinly as they climbed the steps to the front porch. "I'd like to keep it that way. You'll be safe here until Eli and I get back."

Grace nodded but seriously wondered if that was actually true.

CHAPTER FOURTEEN

The drive to the city took two hours, even with light traffic. Jordan hadn't worn her long coat since the previous evening and had forgotten all about the envelope she'd shoved into the interior pocket as she was leaving her apartment.

She withdrew the now well-traveled letter and turned it over to examine both sides of the envelope. There was no postage and no postmark, and no return address. Her name and apartment number were written in perfect cursive letters on the front of the envelope and it was closed at the back with a wax seal. The design of the seal looked like wings. How had she not noticed that when Owen had given it to her?

"What's that?" Eli glanced over.

"A letter my neighbor's kid brought to me last night, before I left my apartment."

"Who's it from?"

"I'm not sure. There's no return address."

She shoved the envelope back in her pocket. Whatever it was, it would keep. The last thing she needed was one more cryptic message. Her head was hurting already.

"What do you think Kith meant when she talked about the sons of God getting together with the daughters of men?" Jordan had a vague memory of reading that in the Bible, but what did it really mean?

"It's from the book of Enoch." Eli was a student of theology. Religious studies had been her focus in college. Eli didn't take her eyes off the road as she spoke. "It basically means that the angels fathered children. At least, that's what I've always believed."

Jordan was quiet. Why was Kith talking to her about an angel myth? Kith had also said that she was *changing*. And that the ritual was supposed to prevent the change. What sort of change? Changing into what? She wasn't ready to share any of that with Eli just yet. She was still sorting out the encounter in her own head.

Having Grace around had been too much of a distraction and she was glad for a few hours away to figure some things out. She wanted to swing by her place first and then go back to the site where the attack took place to see if she could figure out what happened to Miller and the infant. She'd rest easier if she knew for sure that they'd made it out of harm's way. Jordan didn't like to leave loose ends, but she'd been in no condition to hang around. She'd literally blacked out once Kith deposited her into the back of the van.

They parked on the street in front of her apartment building. Her matte black, four-door Jeep was parked where she'd left it, much farther down the block.

"Wait here. I just need to grab a few things."

"Are you sure?" Eli rested an elbow on the console and spoke to her through the open passenger door.

"I just want to pick something up. There's no need for you to have to find parking." It was always hard to find open spaces after five o'clock. "I'll be right back."

She crossed the front lawn of the building and took the stairs to the third floor. Jordan had her keys in her hand and was about to unlock the door but could see that it was already ajar. She stepped back out of the direct line of the entryway and then gently pushed the door open with the toe of her boot.

Jordan peered around the doorframe. The living room was trashed, but empty. Every drawer had been upended, every cabinet in the kitchen vandalized. What the hell were they looking for? A rustling sound came from the bedroom. Someone was still inside.

She crossed the entry and hugged the wall as she approached the bedroom door. From her vantage point she could see that the mattress had been ripped open and lay askew, half on and half off the bed frame. Still, no one was visible in the dark apartment.

Jordan reached for the light switch and flicked it twice in rapid succession. That was all she needed to spot two figures near the closet. The flash of light had momentarily blinded them giving Jordan a brief advantage. One of the men swung about with his gun raised only to be met with a boot to his arm. The gun flew across the room, landing somewhere in the debris that was formerly the contents of her closet.

She lunged at him, catching him around the waist, digging her shoulder into his midsection, and shoving him into the woman standing a couple of feet behind him. The three of them toppled into the closet. Clothes were yanked from their hangers, the hangers themselves flinging off the rack into the chaos around the closet.

The man shoved Jordan off with both hands and tried to extricate himself from his partner and the tousled clothing. Before Jordan could regroup and fully get to her feet, he kicked her in the gut from his position on the floor. She stumbled backward, tripped over the exposed bed frame, and fell onto the mattress. Jordan somersaulted across the mattress and landed on her feet on the other side of the bed.

The woman, who was also armed, fired a shot in Jordan's direction. The silencer muffled the discharge, but Jordan saw the flash as the bullet was ejected, and a millisecond later, her bedside lamp was toast. The glass base of the lamp shattered with a loud crash. Jordan hoisted the mattress from the floor and rushed both assailants. Bullets passed through the mattress at odd angles as she pressed them against the wall. She was trying to count. Was that five shots or six? Either way, in her weakened state Jordan felt like she was outmatched which pissed her off.

Jordan scanned the room looking for a weapon. There was a baseball bat somewhere in the living room if only she could get to it. She hadn't had time to access her weapons stash hidden in the wall. *Fuck.*

She could hold them back no longer. The man worked his way around the edge of the mattress and tackled her, which allowed his partner to break free and reload. But Jordan was rolling around on the floor with him, which didn't give the woman a clear shot. Jordan reversed direction, while still holding onto the guy. As one jumble of punching fists, arms, and legs, they knocked the woman off her feet. As the woman scrambled to right herself Jordan managed to elbow the guy in the face, once, twice, and a third time in quick succession. His nose was broken for sure and blood streamed down his face. She shimmied out from under him as he struggled to regain his composure. He grabbed at her ankles as she crawled backward into the living room. She kicked him to break his grasp.

The moonlight that flooded through the large front window illuminated his face. Jordan knew this guy. Well, not exactly, but she'd seen him in Sorcha's office before. He worked for the Guild. What the literal hell was going on?

The woman entered the room from the bedroom. She had reloaded and took aim at Jordan. She grabbed a metal platter from the floor nearby just as the woman fired. The bullet ricocheted, catching the woman's partner in the shoulder.

"Stop fucking shooting if you can't actually hit her." He gripped his arm as he glared at the woman. Jordan took the opportunity to swing the platter in his direction, hitting him in the side of the head. She didn't knock him out, but he was wounded now, and stunned.

The woman rushed her position and kicked the platter out of Jordan's hand. Then stood over her, the handgun pointed at her chest.

"Why are you doing this?" Jordan had faced attackers before, plenty of them, but never from the Guild. "Aren't we on the same damn team?"

"No time for witty banter, Jordan." The corner of the woman's mouth turned up in a half smile. She was fierce, with short dark hair and a slim build. Her dark lipstick contrasted sharply with her fair complexion. "Consider your retirement from the Guild official."

"Go fuck yourself."

"Defiant to the end." The woman was overconfident. She never saw what was coming.

Eli swung the bat striking the woman in the arm. Her arm swung limply at her side and she staggered from the blow. Jordan struck again with her boot from the floor, buckling the woman's knee painfully. She dropped like an anchor, grasping her injured knee. Jordan wrestled the gun from the woman's grip. Off to her left she saw Eli swing again, but the man was able to duck, missing the blow.

Just as Jordan reached the gun, the woman was on top of her. She had Jordan in a choke hold. Jordan braced against the floor and rolled hard so that she was able to pin the woman beneath her, on her back. She drove her elbow into the woman's ribs.

Jordan could see that Eli was struggling with the man on the other side of the living room, but she couldn't shake her assailant to help.

Enough was enough. Jordan marshalled all her reserves and elbowed the woman again until she was able to break the hold and roll away. Jordan still had the gun and just as she was about to take aim, the woman launched onto Jordan. The bullet hit her in the chest at close range. Her limp body sank on top of Jordan.

She glanced over and saw Eli, pinned against the wall. The man's hands were around her neck. The bat was on the ground at her feet and Eli was pushing against him, but was losing.

Jordan shoved the woman's body aside and fired a shot at the man. His arms drooped, he sank to his knees, and then fell onto his side.

Adrenaline surged through her body. She got to her feet and rushed to Eli.

"Are you okay?"

Eli nodded. She rubbed her throat with her hand and coughed.

"I know you told me to wait, but I saw the light flash off and on and I worried something was wrong."

"This is one instance when I'm really glad you didn't listen to me." Jordan placed her hands on her hips and arched her back, which ached from rolling around on the floor getting punched by a guy who was way above her weight bracket.

Eli stumbled toward the kitchen, tripping on a cord from an overturned lamp along the way. She took a bag of frozen peas from the freezer and pressed them to her neck. She'd probably have bruises from the chokehold the man had on her. Jordan checked each body for a pulse, but found none.

"They're both gone." She shook her head in an attempt to clear her thoughts as she walked back to the front door. She was shaken and bruised, and not just her ego. The whole encounter could have gone a very different way if Eli hadn't shown up when she did.

"They were from the Guild."

"What?" Eli regarded her with wide eyes. "Are you sure?"

"Yeah."

"Jordan, what the hell is going on?"

"I wish I knew."

She kicked at debris on the floor. There wasn't really anything worth saving. Jordan trudged to the bathroom and took a few minutes to splash water on her face. They couldn't linger. She heard a siren in the distance. After a moment, she rejoined Eli.

"I think I'll just move rather than clean this up." She didn't keep much of value here anyway. It was a cheap apartment in a not so nice part of the city. She hadn't planned to stay long anyway.

"Say good-bye to your security deposit."

"Yeah." Jordan picked up a dark gray canvas duffel bag and walked toward a now empty bookcase in the living room. She felt along the top of the bookcase for the switch. When she toggled it, the left side of the doorframe between the living room and the bedroom shifted away from its position. Jordan reached for the edge of it and pulled it out of the wall like a hidden vertical drawer. Mounted on the hidden space were weapons. Jordan quickly freed each from its case and put it into the duffel bag. These weren't all of her weapons, just a few of her favorites, including a crossbow and a telescoping sword that she wanted for their little reconnaissance mission tonight.

"Here." She held a Glock 19 handgun out to Eli. This particular gun was highly reliable, simple to operate, with minimal recoil.

"I'm already packing." Eli pulled a small Bible and an ornate crucifix from her jacket pockets and held them up, one in each hand. "There's also this." She nudged the baseball bat with her foot.

"Leave it here." Jordan added the Glock to the rest of the collection in the duffel bag and zipped it with one sweep of her arm. The injury in her side registered the swivel motion. She winced and straightened.

"Maybe we should take a minute." Eli frowned. "We could come back tomorrow."

"No, we need to do this now, before the trail cools."

"So, you do like her." Eli's comment was playful.

"Who?"

"Grace."

"Oh, please." Jordan scowled. "I'd help anyone in the same situation."

Although, deep down somewhere inside, she knew Eli was right. There was something special about Grace that she couldn't quite ignore, no matter how hard she tried. There was something different about Grace. And because of that, Jordan knew she needed to be more cautious than usual.

"Whatever you say." Eli turned to leave, but as she drew close to the front door she stopped. She pushed the door closed to fully reveal the back of it.

There was text and a diagram in red paint that they hadn't noticed when they first entered the apartment.

"An apotropaic inscription?" Eli tilted her head as if that would help her translate the message. "What evil were they trying to keep from getting in…or out?"

"Another fucking riddle." Jordan tucked the sword, now in its compact, travel size, into her long coat. She'd found only one bottle of holy water in her stash, which she also dropped into an interior pocket. "What do you think it means?"

"The plot thickens." Eli studied the markings.

"Why do I bother hanging out with a religious scholar if you're not going to help me with this stuff?"

"Hey, it's not like I'm a walking textbook. I'll take a photo and figure this out when I get back to my place." Eli snapped a picture of the inscription with her phone. The flash went off unexpectedly and in that same instant, a flurry of dark winged creatures swept past the apartment window in mass.

The whirling, whooshing sound made Eli jump.

"That's been happening a lot lately." Jordan opened the door and stepped through it. "Come on, let's get out of here. I know it's my apartment, but it's giving me the creeps."

She closed the door and locked it.

Alone in the cabin, Grace began to question everything. Once again, she moved from room to room, looking for clues. At the back of the pantry, she discovered a set of narrow stairs that she hadn't noticed before. She decided to investigate.

The stairs led to an attic which ran the entire length of the cabin. At the top of the staircase was a single, naked bulb from which a bit of twine dangled from a short length of chain. Grace tugged the string and the bulb came to life, casting the corners of the room into shadow.

Head-height beams of oak braced the space. Each gable end had a small wood-framed window set into it. From this elevation, she could see a hint of the dusk gray sea in the distance, its surface salted with white caps.

Books stood in tall piles on the floor because the slanted walls wouldn't accommodate shelves. Some of the books weren't in English. Others looked quite old, their covers frayed at the corners, and the spines creased from use. She studied the books in hopes they would reveal more than she already knew about Jordan or about this place. There seemed to be lots of volumes on the occult. Some on mythical creatures, theology, and fables. Not the sort of light reading she'd choose if she was alone in a remote cabin. One slender book with an ornate gold foil pattern on the cover caught her eye. When she held it up to the light for closer inspection she could see that the pattern was actually wings. As Grace held the book it seemed to fall open of its own accord. She read the words on the page.

Angels facilitate the circulation of energy throughout the universe. For ages, the army of spirits have been receding farther from us. Banished by science and unbelief, the spirits have departed from their last stronghold in the sky. The glory of the celestial world forever hidden from mortal eyes.

She shivered, closed the book, and hugged herself. As she bent to return the book to its original place, it fell open again to a different section with a full-page illustration of a beautiful, winged figure. The image stirred a momentary feeling of familiarity. Grace studied the image. There was a caption beneath the illustration: Ariel, the lioness of God.

The light at the far end of the space flickered. Okay, now she was definitely a bit spooked. She chided herself as she descended the stairs to the kitchen.

Grace went to the bathroom and splashed cold water on her face.

She braced her hands on the edge of the pedestal sink and looked at her reflection in the mirror. Were the lenses of her glasses smudged?

Why did everything suddenly look out of focus. She lifted the frames and when she studied herself the image was clear. She lowered the glasses and everything became blurry again, as if someone had smeared something on the lenses. She removed the glasses and set them on the wide lip of the basin. How was it possible that she could see more clearly without her glasses than with them?

She splashed cold water on her face again, reached for a towel, and then decided she needed some fresh air. Cabin fever was setting in. She hadn't eaten anything since breakfast but realized she wasn't hungry, only restless, and very unsettled. She was sure she'd be unable to sit down so Grace decided to go for a walk. Grace retrieved the jacket that Jordan had loaned her earlier and trotted down the steps into the yard.

The sun was going down and she decided that perhaps she needed a flashlight. She went back into the house and looked around the kitchen until she found one and then began her trek again.

Grace walked around the corner of the cabin heading in the direction of the ocean. The crashing waves called to her and she decided to follow the sound of the surf. The arched coastal cypress tunnels she'd seen earlier were like an invitation.

The path ended at an overlook. When she reached the cliffside the blast of cold damp air was like an awakening. The mist sifted past, but in the midst of it were openings so that she could see the dark fathomless waters of the Pacific churning against the base of the rocky cliff. And then the fog would return and all would be hidden except for the deafening sound.

Grace's chest ached, like someone who longed to return to the sea but found themselves landlocked. She held her hands up, her skin shimmered like some fragile covering cast upon by the glowing white of the moon. She hardly recognized her feelings or herself. The strangest sensation overcame her, of the need to hold on to something solid, a deep fear of letting go. She closed her eyes and the details of the world seemed to drop away, all she could see was her path forward and standing on the path, was Jordan.

Grace blinked rapidly and backed away from the drop-off. She walked away from the overlook back toward the ancient cypress grove. She decided to walk toward the clearing where they'd found her things. She still held out hope that she might stumble across her cell phone somewhere in the tall grass.

Using the flashlight seemed unnecessary. After a while she realized that the darker it got the better she could see. She could almost see better without the flashlight than with it. As an experiment she turned the flashlight off for a minute and waited for her eyes to adjust. It was almost as if things had a slightly bluish luminous glow—the trees, the tall grass, and dust particles in the air. Something ahead of her moved. She suspected it was a deer, but quickly realized, based on its size and shape, that it was an elk. When she spotted the elk, the luminous glow, the shape of the animal was red. She could see herself reflected in the enormous reckoning eye of the animal.

They stood looking at each other for quite a while before she redirected her gaze. The minute she looked away the animal took flight. It was as if he'd been frozen in place by her stare. The entire encounter freaked her out a little.

The things Jordan and Eli had said earlier looped through her mind.

The vampire mythology that Grace knew was pretty much the product of Hollywood. Vampires had immortality, wealth, the power to enthrall creatures, including humans…the thoughts trailed off. Michael Lucas had all of those traits, didn't he? And Jordan seemed so certain that Michael was a vampire. But he'd been a perfect host during their meeting. She shook her head. She refused to believe it.

But then she amused herself considering the possibilities. Didn't vampires have some superhuman abilities? Yes, there were trade-offs, like no more sunbathing, but the not aging part was definitely appealing. Grace smiled, completely lost in thought. When she glanced up, she realized that she didn't know where she was.

She found herself in a clearing, surrounded by huge trees. She wondered if these were coastal redwoods because she'd never seen trees so large before. The trees created a circle around a grassy clearing, their limbs interconnected as if they were holding hands. Grace looked up. There was only a small bit of the purple night sky where the canopy of trees opened up. A shooting star streaked across the opening while she watched.

Grace considered that she should be afraid, alone in the woods as she was. But she was filled with wonder suddenly, as if she were experiencing the world for the first time. She became aware of an ethereal shape moving amongst the trees. Grace watched as the shape took form and emerged from the tree line into the clearing. Unlike the trees and the elk, the glow of the figure was white, and as the specter drew near, details began to emerge.

"Grandmother?" The ghostly figure resembled her grandmother, but a younger version, an image of her grandmother that she only recognized from old photographs.

"Hello, Grace."

"Is this real?" She couldn't stop the ridiculous question.

"What is *real*?"

Given recent events, that was a very fair question.

"I'm not sure I believe—"

"Living life means experiencing change." Her grandmother's soothing voice cut her off. "The faith you find in adulthood is in some ways, a faith in life itself."

Why did the question of belief keep coming up? Ever since the strange encounter with the woman in the airport Grace felt as if events were challenging her loss of faith. And now her grandmother was speaking to her from beyond the grave? She'd obviously slipped along the path, hit her head, and was dreaming.

The apparition she'd been so sure was her grandmother shifted and slowly began to resemble the illustration of Ariel Grace had seen in the book.

"Perhaps you don't remember your faith, but it remembers you." The ghostly woman smiled.

The smile and the serene expression on the woman's face sent a surge of warmth and calm through Grace's system. She closed her eyes and took a deep breath.

When she opened her eyes, the glowing figure was gone. Grace was alone.

Had she hallucinated the entire encounter? Grace stood motionless, unable to move. Her head ached with a thousand questions.

Something howled in the distance and she realized that while vampires might be kept at bay by the consecrated boundary, there were lots of other creatures who might not. As unsettled as Grace was, and unsure of whether she should wait for her grandmother to reappear, she decided it was best to return to the safety of the cabin. She took hesitant steps through the brittle grass, hoping she could remember the way.

❖

Jordan and Eli stopped at the warehouse first. She wanted to check for signs of who had created the altar and why. As expected, Jordan found nothing. Remnants of melted wax and wooden slats from destroyed pallets littered the floorboards, but the markings on the floor that she had seen were gone. Someone had removed any evidence of what had really taken place.

The moment she'd crossed the threshold into the abandoned space Jordan could still sense the presence of dark energy, but it was impossible to identify the source. She cautiously, slowly circled the spot where she'd been stabbed with the spike-like weapon. Eli waited quietly in the shadows while she allowed her feelings to search the air, but she found no clues. The site had been wiped clean by someone.

"I'm getting nothing here." Jordan frowned.

"What next?"

"Can I borrow your phone?"

Eli handed over the device. Having uncovered no evidence at the warehouse, Jordan's next goal was to find the infant. She searched on Eli's GPS for the nearest hospital, thinking that would be the most logical place to begin her search. For her own peace of mind, Jordan needed to know that the child was safe. They located the closest hospital, and within ten minutes they parked and walked toward the entrance.

A late-night urban emergency room wasn't a very pleasant place to be. Jordan scanned the waiting area as she followed Eli to the information desk. Every kind of person populated the uncomfortable plastic chairs—young, old, clearly infirmed, and quite a few that looked as if they were simply looking for shelter for the night. The ER was probably one of the few places that a person truly in need could find aid. Long ago, the Church had been that place, but the Church could no longer afford the care that folks falling through the cracks needed. Congregation sizes had been dwindling for decades, no one believed any longer. If people had seen the things Jordan had seen they'd be crowding the holy places, on their knees, praying for deliverance. But evangelism wasn't Jordan's concern. That problem was too big to solve. Plus, you'd have to get the populace to look up from their cell phones and actually see the world once in a while.

Jordan let Eli take the lead at the reception desk. She was a lot less threatening than a hunter any day of the week. Also, her face probably bore the marks of the attack at her apartment. She probably looked like she was in need of emergency care herself. Jordan hung back a few feet and tried not to be intimidating.

"Hello, I'm Sterling Eli, I'm with the North Bay Association of Ministers." That was sort of a stretch, but a harmless white lie was sometimes necessary. "I'm hoping you can help me with something."

"How can I be of assistance?" The woman, whose name tag read Simone was probably relieved to help someone who wasn't in dire need. She was in her thirties, and looked like someone who had had a desk job for a long time. She looked weary of dealing with the public. And perhaps a bit suspicious.

"An infant may have been brought to this hospital last night, possibly abandoned. I believe someone may have needed to find a place for their child and I wanted to confirm that the infant was safe."

"Let me check for you." Simone looked at her screen and started typing.

It took a couple of minutes before Simone returned her attention to Eli. Jordan hung back.

"There was an infant admitted last night with a foot injury." Simone stood behind the counter. "I could direct you to the viewing room if you'd like."

"Yes, thank you."

Simone gave them directions to the nursery on the second floor.

They reached the viewing room but quickly realized they didn't know which infant to look for. The nursery had at least twelve newborns, swaddled and mostly sleeping.

"You wait here. I'll go back down and get a name. I should have thought to ask." Eli turned to leave. "I'll take the elevator this time." She smiled.

Eli was not a fan of taking the stairs, but Jordan couldn't stand to be in the small box of an elevator, regardless of whether they were in a hurry or not. Jordan stood at the window with her hands in her pockets and waited. So many tiny souls, with no idea of the world they would live in. The lights in the room were dim, probably so as not to wake them. No one else was in the viewing area and Jordan allowed the stress in her shoulders to ease a bit. It was nice to have a few moments of quiet.

"Would you like to see him?" A woman in scrubs that featured a pattern of tiny pink rabbits stood next to her.

Jordan had been lost in thought and obviously hadn't heard her approach. Eli must have asked if they could see the kid.

"Yes, thank you." Jordan followed the nurse to the locked door. She entered a code on the keypad and held the door for Jordan to pass, then followed her inside.

As was her habit, Jordan checked the woman's ID for her name. The hospital tag looked different from Simone's, but that didn't give her pause. Perhaps each ward of the hospital had different tags. Her name was Catherine Greene. She was probably in her fifties. She had a very calm, pleasing manner. No wonder she worked in the nursery.

"He's right over here," Catherine whispered to Jordan.

Jordan rested her hands on the edge of the crib. She'd thought he was sleeping, but after a few seconds he turned and opened his eyes. As he'd done the night before, he reached out to her and she offered her finger. He grasped it firmly with his tiny hand.

"When someone leaves a child here without a name, we give them one." Catherine smiled down at him. "We named this little guy Hero."

"Hero." Jordan repeated his name softly.

"He came in with this injury." She touched his foot. "And he's been so brave that it just seemed as if the name fit."

"Hey, Hero, you're going to be okay now." Jordan lightly placed her palm over the crown of his head. What little fluffs of hair he had were feathery soft. "What will happen to him?"

Jordan wasn't completely sure of the process for infants without parents. She wondered where he'd come from and how he'd come into her world in such a scary way.

"A foster care agent from the city will evaluate him and try to find him placement in a home." Catherine didn't sound worried, but Jordan was. "After a waiting period, he'll be eligible for adoption."

Jordan didn't want to let go of his hand. She felt connected to him in some way.

"Excuse me, but you can't be in here." The command was polite, but terse.

"I'm sorry, Catherine said it would be okay—" Jordan straightened and then realized Catherine was no longer in the nursery with her.

"I'm the only staff member on the schedule for tonight." The older woman ushered her toward the exit. She issued her statements in a firm but hushed voice. "Who did you say you spoke with?"

"Her nametag said Catherine Greene."

They were standing just outside the closed door and the nurse's face blanched, as if Jordan had just told her the most terrible thing.

"That's impossible." The woman shook her head.

"Why?"

"Because Catherine Greene died three years ago in a car accident."

Jordan was speechless. She hadn't imagined Catherine's presence. She'd seen Catherine use the keypad for entry to the nursery. How was that possible?

"Sorry, that took longer than expected." Eli walked up just at that moment. "I have the infant's name."

"That's okay." Jordan held up her hand. "We can go." She looked at the nurse once more before she walked away. "I'm sorry to have bothered you."

The woman stood like a statue and watched them leave. She was clearly as shaken as Jordan was.

"I thought you wanted to see the baby." Eli was confused by Jordan's sudden need to leave.

"I did see the baby." Jordan pushed open the door to the stairwell. "I'll explain in the car."

Once outside the hospital, Jordan strode toward the car at a fast clip.

"Hey, wait up," Eli called after her.

Jordan reached the car first and turned to look at Eli. The parking lot was fairly full and puddles from an earlier shower reflected the moonlight and the clouds overhead. The asphalt around the wet patches was black, negative space reflecting nothing. Jordan seemed to be noticing clouds a lot lately.

"What happened back there?"

"A dead woman let me into the nursery, that's what." Jordan didn't mean to sound angry, but she was pretty sure she did. "I'm sorry. I'm not mad at you...I just don't understand what happened either."

"What do you mean by dead woman?"

"This nurse walked up right after you left and offered to let me in. I saw the little boy. They've nicknamed him Hero." Jordan braced her hands on her hips and took a breath. "Then the other nurse showed up and when I mentioned the woman who'd let me into the room I found out she'd been dead for three years."

Eli didn't respond right away.

"Okay, what do we do now?" Eli looked back toward the hospital.

"You don't have some insight into why I'm seeing dead people?" She was frustrated and feeling a bit strung out. Plus, her side was beginning to ache.

"I'm sorry, I don't understand either." Eli put her hand on Jordan's shoulder. "But I'm here with you, friend. We'll figure this out."

CHAPTER FIFTEEN

Grace realized she'd walked much farther than she'd thought. But this place was kind of magical and even more so after nightfall, ghostly messengers notwithstanding. She reasoned that she'd only imagined seeing her grandmother, turned ghostly angel. That the book had put the image in her head. Grace was out of her element and out of her head, nothing else made sense. As she walked, Grace redirected her focus to the beauty of the nighttime sky.

Atlanta was a huge urban dome of light. She never got to see so much of the sky at home. And it honestly seemed like the atmosphere was clearer as you moved away from the ocean's edge, beyond the reach of the marine layer. Maybe it was the lack of heavy Southern humidity.

Grace thought of Jordan as she walked. She held her hands out at her sides, palms down, and felt the tips of the dry grass stalks tickle her skin. How strange that she would find herself in such an odd predicament and after stumbling through the forest would end up knocking on Jordan's door. Their meeting felt like fate, except that she'd never believed in fate. She was so certain that people crafted their own path, by the choices they made and by the effort they put into their work. But what happened to her veered so far outside anything she would have chosen for herself. Yes, she'd agreed to take on this client in San Francisco. Was that enough to derail her life so completely? That seemed like a stretch.

And what about Jordan? What was her story for real?

She wasn't the most forthcoming with details. Grace had been sharing a very small space with Jordan for almost twenty-four hours and at this point didn't feel like she knew much more about Jordan than when she'd first arrived.

But she *wanted* to know Jordan. And that was an interesting thing to register.

Grace could have been more assertive about leaving. Sure, when she first arrived she was a bit under the weather, but today she was feeling better. She could have pressed Eli and Jordan to take her back to the city. That whole thing with the consecrated barrier was pretty weird and now, hours later, Grace was wondering if Jordan had been serious about it. But maybe part of her wanted to believe it because it meant she had a little more time with Jordan.

Was she that desperate for love that she'd put up with this whole crazy situation just because she thought Jordan was attractive? Attractive was such a polite word for how she'd been thinking about Jordan. If she allowed her thoughts to have free rein they went to very shockingly salacious places, sex-filled places, and Jordan had a starring role.

Snap out of it.

Grace couldn't help laughing at herself. Why was she so aroused? She'd been feeling that way all day. It was probably really good that Jordan left. Who knows what might have happened if they'd spent another night in close quarters. Grace honestly wasn't sure if she could be trusted.

What is happening to me?

As had been the case the first night she'd woken on the ground, Grace was able to use the light from a window as her guide back to the cabin. Once she could see the small square of yellow, warm light in the distance she knew she would be okay and she slowed her frantic march just a bit.

But then as she drew closer, she sensed movement outside the gated fence. Grace couldn't quite see what it was, but she could hear a heavy panting sound, like the sound dogs made, and there was definitely more than one.

Grace slowed her steps and tried to be as quiet as possible as she rounded the corner of the front porch. She could make out the dim outline of the creatures now. They were barely visible with a faint blue luminance along the fur of their backs. These creatures didn't pulse red like the elk. Did that mean these wolf-looking things were dead? Or perhaps they were only in her imagination, like the vision of her grandmother. She stopped at the bottom of the steps and flicked on the flashlight. As she moved the light along the fence the creatures disappeared, but in darkness they were clearly present. Okay, now Grace was really afraid.

She sprinted up the stairs, rushed through the door, then closed and locked it. After a few seconds she switched off the lamp so that the house was dark. Grace knew with the light on she was visible to whatever was outside so she wanted to disguise herself with darkness.

She paced for a few moments trying to figure out what to do.

Whatever these wolf-like animals were, they seemed unable to cross the barrier of consecration. Jordan had been telling her the truth.

Remember your faith. Grace heard her grandmother's voice as clear as if she was standing in the room.

Grace moved one of the kitchen chairs to the living room and placed it so that her back was against a solid wall. Then she drew her knees up, hugged them, and began to whisper the Twenty-third Psalm. When she got to the fourth verse of the Psalm she repeated it over and over and over.

Yea, though I walk through the valley of the shadow of death, I will fear no evil: for thou art with me.

For all her high talk of not believing, she ran toward the faith of her childhood in her hour of fear. She was reminded of the strange woman in the airport who'd asked her if she was a believer. She remembered the angelic figure's recent words. Maybe she was a believer after all.

❖

Eli had wisely insisted they get some food after visiting the hospital. That was a good call. Jordan had been so out of sorts she hadn't really eaten anything since breakfast. A burger and fries was probably not the healthiest choice, but she felt revived. In her refueled state, she convinced Eli to check out one more spot. A homeless encampment under the Highway 101 freeway. The place ran along the corridor known as Division Street. There were as many as three hundred people living in tents pitched along more than five city blocks in that location. It was like a mini city within the city and it was a frequent hunting ground for vampires.

The city had increased its spending on homeless services and the mayor restructured the administration of homelessness programs. But the new head of the Department of City Services was none other than Michael Lucas, Grace's client. His department was charged with reducing homelessness, but it was no surprise to Jordan that nothing had changed since he'd taken over. Nothing served the vampire agenda better than having easy access to a human population that almost everyone had given up on. There was no one to raise an alarm when someone went missing. Throw in the number of unhoused folks who suffered from mental illnesses and no one ever believed their stories when they complained about being stalked by the undead. Their complaints not only fell on deaf ears, they literally fell on dead ears.

Jordan walked deliberately through the tent city, careful not to get too close or trip on all the debris scattered about. Eli followed a few paces behind. She wasn't even sure what she was looking for. Maybe she'd run across someone who'd seen the woman that Grace described. Or maybe she'd discover something she wasn't even expecting. She honestly didn't know, but her gut told her that this place held clues.

She'd brought a bag full of hamburgers along with her. She shared the food with grateful hands as they wove through the encampment. It wasn't much, and a single bag of burgers didn't go very far, but it was something.

After making one pass through the disheveled tent city, Jordan decided she had to call it a night. Fatigue was catching up with her and she was a little concerned about leaving Grace alone for too long back at the cabin.

"I think I'm done for the night." She swept her fingers through her hair in frustration. At full strength it wasn't unusual for Jordan to stay out all night on a hunt. But at the moment, she was feeling about seventy-five percent herself, maybe less.

"I'll drive you back to your place so you can pick up your Jeep." Eli seemed fine with the decision to return. "We can come back another night."

Jordan nodded. Hell, she wasn't even sure what she was looking for. Just as they turned to leave, a familiar face appeared on the periphery.

"Hang on." She held her arm out to stop Eli. "I saw something."

Jordan walked toward a dark corner of the camp. Huddled next to one of the overpass pilons was Miller. He was wearing the same clothes he'd been in the day before, but they were rumpled and smudged with dirt, as was his face. She knelt in front of him.

"Miller!" Jordan grabbed the front of his jacket and tried to wake him up. His head lolled to one side, he seemed completely out of it.

"You know him?" Eli was at her side.

"This is the guy I was telling you about, Miller Diggs." She'd figured he was okay since they'd found the kid at the hospital. But he didn't look okay, and it certainly seemed like he'd been dumped here in hopes that something even worse might happen. "Miller... hey, snap out of it." She slapped him hard across the face. His eyes fluttered. She held his face in her hands forcing him to look at her. "Hey, man, it's me, Jordan."

Tears welled up in his eyes. His mouth moved, but no sound came out.

"I didn't know..." He mumbled.

"What?"

"I didn't know, I swear...and then they just left me...I had your back..."

"He's making no sense." Jordan looked up at Eli from her kneeling position. "We need to get him to the ER. He may have been drugged."

Jordan had a million questions for Miller, but he was in no condition to answer them.

"Help me get him up." Jordan hoisted him off the ground with Eli's help.

They half carried and half dragged him back to Eli's car.

A half hour later, Miller had been admitted to the hospital. They'd gotten lucky and caught the ER on a slow night. Jordan stood by as the nurse set an IV with fluids and then left the room. The light overhead flickered and then two of the three fluorescent bulbs went dark, which gave the room an eerie green glow.

Strange power surges had become the norm lately for Jordan. She stared up at the ceiling, but as usual, shrugged it off.

"I'm going to go get a coffee. Do you want one?" Eli asked. "It may take a little while before he's lucid."

"You go, I'm okay." Jordan sat down on the very uncomfortable vinyl chair. "I'll stay with him."

Eli nodded as she left. Jordan slid the chair closer to the bed. She really needed to know what Miller knew. She sat quietly waiting until he began to stir. The fluids seemed to be bringing him back. He blinked a few times as if trying to get his vision to focus. He seemed confused about where he was.

"You're in the hospital." She answered his silent question.

At the sound of her voice, he turned to look at her. It seemed to take a few seconds longer for his eyes to gain focus.

"You're going to be okay." She didn't know Miller very well, but she tried her best to soothe him.

"Jordan, I was trying to follow that vampire, but the Guild pulled me off." His voice was raspy. He coughed and swallowed before trying to talk again. "Then she showed up with the knife…"

"Do you know where the knife came from?"

"The Guild, I think." He paused. "That's why she was there… when you bumped into her."

That seemed crazy. That would mean the whole thing was a setup. And if that was the case, then why was Miller told to go with her?

"No offense meant by this comment, but why are you still alive?" she asked.

"I honestly don't know."

His response seemed sincere.

"Maybe you're not supposed to be."

"I feel like death warmed over." He coughed and squeezed his eyes shut.

"You'll feel better soon."

All Jordan could figure was that Miller had been dumped in the camp so that some vampire would do the dirty work of finishing him off. But who? And who was the hooded figure with the knife? She still wasn't sure even though she'd looked familiar.

"I checked on the kid at the hospital. He seems okay. But someone must have followed you there."

He nodded. She offered him a sip of water from the cup on the bedside table.

"Somebody jumped me in the parking lot after…I never got a look at them…" He sank into the pillows. He seemed truly spent.

Eli returned with coffee. She stood just inside the door and waited. Jordan nodded to her and got to her feet. They needed to get back up north. But then she had one more question.

"Hey, before the shit went down, did you get a good look at the vamp with the knife?"

He shook his head. "Sorry, no."

"Take care of yourself, Miller."

"You too." He grew serious. "Watch your back."

An hour later, Jordan was in her Jeep, heading north. She'd left instructions with the hospital to notify her the minute Miller was well enough to be released. She hoped he rebounded soon because there were too many pieces of this puzzle still missing. He had to have some of the answers; maybe he just didn't know it yet.

As it turned out, she had so much to think about that the two-hour drive from the city swept past in a blur. Jordan realized she was lost in thought for much of it, her ability to drive obviously based on muscle memory and her subconscious. That was a scary thought. At one point she sort of snapped out of her trance and didn't recognize where she was or how she'd gotten there. It wasn't that late and she hadn't even sampled the flask in her pocket.

She turned off the main ridge road onto the winding dirt lane that led to the cabin. It was utterly dark. She slowed because she could only see as far as the headlights and didn't want to hit an elk or deer or some other animal crossing the road.

Jordan expected to see the cabin lights. She was close enough that she should've been able to see them. It was late, perhaps Grace was asleep and had turned everything off. As the Jeep's headlights breached the crest of the road near the cabin, a flurry of dark figures scattered at the edge of the islands of light.

What the hell?

Her heart rate sped up. She yanked the steering wheel hard into the gravel driveway and screeched to a halt right next to the porch. She grabbed the duffel bag of weapons from the back seat and ran up the steps. She reached for the door, but it was locked. Jordan fumbled for her keys in the dark but finally got it open.

"Grace, where are you?" She dropped the duffel bag just inside the door and closed it swiftly behind her.

She heard a soft voice, not much more than a whisper, off to her left.

"Grace?" Jordan crossed the darkened room. Her eyes were adjusting to the moonlit room, so that now she could make out the shape of Grace sitting, huddled in one of the kitchen chairs next to the wall. "What's wrong? Are you hurt?"

She knelt in front of Grace, placing her hands on Grace's legs. Her touch broke some spell and Grace finally looked at her. She fell into Jordan, throwing her arms around Jordan's neck.

CHAPTER SIXTEEN

Jordan held Grace in her arms until she sensed Grace relax a little.

"Hey, it's okay, you're okay." Jordan swept her hand up Grace's back. "I've got you."

"There are things outside, I think they are some kind of wolves." Grace's words were muffled against Jordan's shoulder.

"They're gone now." She stood and pulled Grace along with her from the chair. "How long have you been sitting out here?"

"I don't know." Grace refused to let go. She rested her cheek on Jordan's shoulder.

"It's really late." She tried to get Grace to look at her. "Let me take you to bed."

"Yes, please."

"I'm sorry, that didn't sound exactly right. That's not what I meant—"

"I don't care what you meant." Grace pulled away and finally looked up at Jordan. "There's no way I'm sleeping alone with those... those things outside." Her expression was serious. She'd obviously been really scared.

Jordan could understand how she was feeling. She was unsettled herself. Surprising assassins in her apartment, finding Miller in the encampment, and having a conversation with a ghost were the last straws in a cup full of last straws from a very long day.

"Okay, I guess we're officially having a sleepover." She guided Grace toward the bedroom.

"Can we have popcorn?"

"Um, I don't think I have any."

"That's okay, I'm not really hungry anyway."

They walked into the bedroom arm in arm, and she released Grace only long enough to turn on the bedside lamp.

"What happened to your—" Grace didn't finish the question. She gently touched Jordan's face with her fingertips.

"I ran into a little trouble in the city." She figured her face was bruised. She definitely ached all over from the encounter.

"Let me get something for you." Grace left her for a few moments and then returned with a damp cloth from the bathroom.

Grace tenderly held the cool cloth against Jordan's cheek. It was nice to have someone who cared. Grace studied her as she pressed the cloth to the other side of her face. Jordan could have allowed Grace to pamper her for hours. Grace's touch was gentle and soothing.

"You know, in this long coat you look like a crime fighter or something. It's almost like a cape." Grace set the cloth aside and slipped her hands inside at the collar and began to push it off Jordan's shoulders. The intimate gesture warmed Jordan's insides.

"I guess you want me to take my coat off and stay awhile." She relaxed her arms and let the coat fall to the floor in a heap. But she knew that losing the coat would only raise more questions from Grace.

"What is that?" Grace gripped the retractable sword from Jordan's belt before she could stop her.

"Hey, careful with that." She shifted her arm out of the way just as Grace hit the release and the sword extended to its full length. The blade glistened in the lamplight.

Grace studied her for a moment without saying anything.

"Okay, what do you really do for a living?" Grace allowed Jordan to take the sword from her hand.

She leaned the sword into the corner between the bedside table and the wall. It seemed she wasn't going to be able to dodge Grace's questions any longer.

"I'm a demon hunter." She decided to just bluntly put it out there.

"Isn't a vampire a demon?"

"Yes." She was acutely aware of the fact that she'd declared earlier in the day that Grace had been bitten and would turn into a vampire if she was unable to find her sire.

"It's a good thing I'm not a vampire then, isn't it?"

Jordan wasn't sure if Grace was serious or just being sarcastic.

"Here, why don't you sit down and I'll get us a drink of something."

Grace nodded. She seemed really shaken up despite her attempt to make light of the situation. Hell, Jordan was shaken too. She probably needed a drink as badly as Grace did.

Grace watched Jordan as she crossed the bedroom and walked toward the kitchen. She turned her attention back to the sword, which honestly seemed to hum with some sort of mystic energy. She chided herself for even thinking that thought. She'd been out in the middle of the remote Pacific Northwest for less than twenty-four hours and she was thinking about mystic energy and vampires and creepy wolves. She'd even been visited briefly by someone, possibly her dead grandmother. Seriously, maybe she did need a drink, maybe more than one.

Jordan returned with two small glasses and a bottle of bourbon. She poured two fingers in each glass and handed one to Grace. She downed it like a shot and held the glass out to Jordan for more. Jordan arched her eyebrows, then downed hers and gave them both refills.

The liquor warmly snaked through her system and smoothed off a few frayed nerve endings. She kicked off her shoes then swiveled on the bed and slid over to the far side so that Jordan could join her. After the second glass was gone, Jordan refilled them again and they sat side by side, propped against the pillows, staring straight ahead but not talking.

Grace decided to sip the third glass, because she was beginning to feel the first two and she certainly didn't want a repeat of her night in San Francisco.

"What do you think those things were?" She sipped and allowed her gaze to lose focus. Only the lamp in the bedroom was on. The rest of the cabin was dark.

"Probably hellhounds."

Jordan's response was so matter-of-fact that Grace almost burst into laughter.

"Don't sugarcoat anything on my account." She couldn't help the sarcasm.

"They are called bearers of death because they were created by ancient demons to serve as the heralds of death."

"Seriously?" She turned and scowled at Jordan. "I just told you I was too scared to sleep alone and then you go ahead and tell me *that*?"

"Sorry, occupational hazard." Jordan shrugged.

"What, having no filter?"

Jordan laughed. "Well, you asked."

"Note to self, don't ask." She took another sip of her drink and scooted down on the pillow so that she could look up at the safe view of the ceiling rather than out into the darkness.

Jordan slid down too, mimicking her position.

"Whose death were they heralding?" Grace had to know now, despite the fact that she said she didn't want to. Had the wolves sensed the presence of her grandmother? Or were they heralding the death of someone who hadn't yet died? In the last twenty-four hours she'd managed to normalize an array of unsettling occurrences. What was happening to her sense of reality?

Jordan didn't answer right away.

"They may have been here for some other reason."

Grace didn't quite buy Jordan's vague response, but it was late and she was tired from her ordeal with the wolves, and the bourbon. Jordan downed the last of her drink and set the glass on the bedside table. Her hands were folded on top of her injured side. Grace wasn't sure if that was intentional, and in fact, she'd forgotten about Jordan's injury until just now.

Jordan's eyes were closed which allowed Grace to study her without discovery. She looked completely relaxed, like she might fall asleep at any moment. Grace took notice of her long, dark eyelashes against her cheek, and the way that sexy clump of hair fell across her forehead. And she noticed Jordan's hands. She had beautifully strong hands.

"I can feel you thinking." Jordan didn't open her eyes. "You can rationalize all you like, but in the end, you'll see that I'm telling you the truth."

"Maybe."

Jordan smiled, but didn't respond.

"You must be exhausted." Grace spoke softly as she sat up. "Why don't I help you with your boots so that you're more comfortable."

Jordan's eyelashes fluttered as if she'd dozed off.

Grace slid to the end of the bed and then, without waiting for a response, relieved Jordan of her boots. They were well worn and broken in so that once she loosened the leather laces they slipped off without too much effort. Grace climbed back up to the pillows and nestled in next to Jordan. Before getting too comfortable, she reached back for a blanket folded at the foot of the bed. She tugged it up over both of them and then relaxed against the pillows. She really was fatigued from her frightened, vigilant watch earlier in the evening.

Jordan turned off the lamp and darkness filled the room. Somehow, now that Jordan was at her side, she was no longer frightened. Her nervous system was almost back to normal, except for the tendrils of electricity that seemed to flow from Jordan's body to hers. That was a welcomed sensation, and one she hadn't genuinely felt in a long time. But Jordan had just revealed that she was a demon hunter.

Was that even a real thing? How did someone make a living doing a job like that? Talk of vampires, demons, and hellhounds made her worry that Jordan was a wee bit delusional. Grace had seen the wolves at the fence and when she'd tried to shine a light on them they'd disappeared. She hadn't imagined that, had she? Maybe she was the one who was delusional. She snuggled against Jordan's shoulder and tried not to panic.

CHAPTER SEVENTEEN

Jordan couldn't really relax. But it wasn't her fault. She was a hunter and she was literally in bed with a woman who would soon become a vampire if she didn't do something about it. Her body was at rest, but her mind was anything but.

The scariest thing was that Jordan actually liked lying next to Grace. In fact, she was having a difficult time not acting on the urge she felt every time Grace adjusted her position on the bed. Jordan's nervous system registered every movement, every brush of Grace's body against hers.

At one point, Grace slid her hand across Jordan's midsection and it was as if a match had been struck. Did Grace have any idea what she was doing? Or was she asleep and unaware of her actions? Jordan glanced over and she could see that Grace was definitely not asleep. Her eyes practically sparkled in the moonlight from the window.

"Grace—"

"Kiss me," Grace whispered as she placed her hand on Jordan's cheek.

She rolled onto her side and drew Grace into her arms and kissed her. She'd wanted to kiss Grace since the first moment she'd arrived, despite everything, despite all the alarms now sounding inside her head. Jordan was unable to stop herself. The kiss, which began as a languorous act of giving in, deepened and became more urgent, laced with need.

The soft press of Grace's body against hers raised the temperature of the room. She felt as if her chest, her entire body was in flames.

Grace's hands swept up her back under her shirt, her fingernails lightly trailing up her highly sensitive skin.

"Is this okay?" asked Grace.

"Yes." She'd said yes, but Jordan's brain was saying no.

She'd had a horrible, long day and every fiber of her being was fatigued, but being close to Grace made her want to forget all of it. The soft crush of Grace's breasts against hers made her want to relieve Grace of her shirt and the lacy bra that she could see at the opening of her blouse. Grace applied pressure with her hands on Jordan's ass, increasing the friction between them as they arched against each other.

She slid her palm down over the outside of Grace's breast down to the sensuous curve of her hip. She wanted Grace more than she'd wanted anything in a long time.

Somewhere, in the deep recesses of her brain, Jordan realized what was happening.

No. No. No. This couldn't happen. She couldn't let this happen. Jordan broke the kiss and pulled away from Grace. She had to be the strong one. If she couldn't stop Grace's transition then she'd be honor bound to…she could hardly form the words. She would be honor bound to kill the vampire that Grace would become, the demon that Grace would become. She absolutely could not allow herself to act on her attraction, regardless of how powerful it was.

"What's wrong?" Grace's face was flushed. She was propped up on her elbow. Her arm was still draped across Jordan, but she was half off the bed now.

"Nothing." Jordan couldn't look at Grace. She was miserable and wrought up. She wanted to make love to Grace more than anything, but she knew that was impossible.

"I don't believe you." Grace tugged at her arm. "Look at me."

Jordan rotated slowly to face Grace. "I'm sorry."

"Sorry for what?"

"I shouldn't have done that. We shouldn't be doing this." Jordan forced herself to get out of bed. "Not until we deal with—"

"Is this because you really think I'm going to turn into a vampire?" The pitch of Grace's voice went up.

"Look, I know you don't understand and probably still don't believe any of it, but this is what vampires do. They lure their victims with sex. You can't help it." Jordan paced at the side of the bed with her arms crossed. "Those random comments you made about getting me in bed. Those comments surprised even you because it's the vampire part of yourself talking."

"This is ridiculous—"

"And the terrible part is that I'm very attracted to you, which just makes everything worse."

"Wait…you're attracted to me, but you think the only reason I'm attracted to you is because you believe I was bitten by a vampire?" Grace sounded angry. "*You* are unbelievable!"

Grace climbed off the bed in a huff, dragged the blanket with her, and stormed toward the door in the dark, stubbing her toe on the bedframe as she went.

"Ow!" Graced hopped on one foot for a second and rubbed her injured toe with her hand.

Grace glanced back at Jordan, who stood frozen in the center of the room. Moonlight from the window softly lit the scene that had almost been romantic. She was infuriated that her angry exit had been marred by catching her toe painfully on the foot of the bed. *Damn, damn, damn.* But there was no way she was staying in that room with Jordan, not even if every wolf in the world howled outside the cabin. Vampires or no vampires, a woman had her pride and there was only so much she could stand.

Grace marched into the guest room and slammed the door. The thought of fuming in a dark room wasn't appealing. She might be infuriated, but she was also still unnerved, so she turned on the bedside lamp and slouched on the bed. After a moment, she lay on her side and tugged the blanket up to her shoulder.

Alone in the room, she pondered what Jordan had said. As much as she didn't want to admit it, there was some truth to it. She had been blurting out things she normally wouldn't say, and in some ways, she didn't feel quite herself. Like, she no longer needed her glasses and had stopped wearing them altogether.

What had just happened with Jordan, or what almost happened, had been so incredibly intense. Her body had been on fire for Jordan, in a way she'd never experienced before. She was hungry for Jordan. In the low light, Jordan's outline had pulsed red. If she was honest with herself, that was not something she'd ever experienced before with anyone. She was still angry, but Grace was also confused and scared.

She squeezed her eyes shut, but there was no way she'd be able to calm down enough to actually fall asleep. In fact, she wasn't even tired. Her body seemed to come alive the moment the day transitioned to night.

❖

Jordan covered her face with her hands. She was exhausted but couldn't relax. She was about to sit on the edge of the bed, when a sharp pain shot through her midsection. She doubled over and dropped to one knee. After a few seconds, she took a shuddering breath thinking that the pain had subsided, but agony gripped her again, as if every bone in her body was breaking at once. Jordan fell onto her side and drew her knees up, gritting her teeth.

She tried to breathe through the pain, short quick breaths as if she was in labor. Her body contracted and she lost the battle to darkness. She was dreaming, or remembering, this felt like a memory. In her right hand she saw a sword and she swept it across the ground and where the blade struck gold flecks like dust swirled in the air.

A voice somewhere behind her, unseen. *All things have their origin in the sacred source, and they constantly fight to return to it the same as we fight to honor it.* Was that a voice? Or was it only inside her mind? Or was it her voice?

Nothing is static, everything is in motion, perpetually circling, from the beginning to now and back again.

Of things that existed, Jordan somehow knew this, that substances were created first. But substances could perish, all things could perish and yet time could not. Time was eternal.

She gazed up to the firmament. An infinite power source was required for an eternal cosmos that had neither a beginning nor an end. On that infinite line of time with no end she saw herself, and others like her. She spun around to see an army in formation behind her dressed in white with shields and swords of gold reflecting the brilliance of the closest star, the sun. Something or someone fell past her position, punching a hole in the clouds so that she could see the Earth far below. Was she expected to follow? Was she expected to fight?

From below, beneath the heavens, a wave of grief rose from the dark sea of humanity. She sensed their frailty, their need, their dreams of heaven.

What did any of this mean?

Pain, sharp and searing again. Jordan looked down at her palm and saw that it was covered with blood. Now she was falling and the falling would not stop. Until the light dimmed and the sword was no longer in her hand. Falling, falling, falling.

CHAPTER EIGHTEEN

Grace sensed something from the next room. She sat up in bed and listened. There was no noise, but she could hear Jordan nonetheless. It would have been impossible to explain, but she knew something was wrong. She dashed from her room and found Jordan crumpled on the floor.

"Jordan." Grace knelt beside her and tried to wake Jordan but couldn't. The expression on Jordan's face told her that she was in pain.

The phone. Where was Jordan's phone? Jordan's coat was right where they'd left it on the floor so she began to search through the pockets until she found it. Luckily, it was a flip phone and not locked, although, it had been so long since she'd used a flip phone that she had to wrack her brain to remember how to make a call. It took another minute to bring up the contacts before she hit *send*.

"Hello?" Sam answered right away.

"Sam, it's Grace." Grace tried to sound calm but was fairly sure she didn't. "Something is wrong with Jordan—"

"Are you at the cabin?"

"Yes."

"I'm on my way."

Grace stroked Jordan's forehead. She honestly didn't know what else to do. Beside her, Jordan writhed on the floor, clenching and unclenching her fists.

"Hang on, Jordan," she whispered. "Help is coming."

Jordan seemed to be fighting someone or something. Grace drew Jordan into her lap and tried to calm her. Jordan's skin was hot to the touch.

"Just hang on, Jordan." She pressed her lips to Jordan's forehead. She was sorry for getting so angry earlier. Why did she think that she knew everything? Something unexplained was definitely going on here and they'd both been caught up in it somehow.

As she held Jordan she became aware of the warm throb of Jordan's heart and the pulse point along her neck. Her own heartbeat quickened at the sight of it. Grace gently released Jordan and backed away from her, afraid that she was not in control of her own actions. In that same moment, Sam burst through the front door with her oversized medical kit.

"What happened?" Sam set the kit on the floor and knelt to examine Jordan.

"I don't know. I was in the room next door and I just...I sensed something was wrong."

Sam looked up at her.

"And then when I came in she was already on the floor and I couldn't wake her."

"She feels feverish." Sam checked Jordan's pulse. "Jordan, can you hear me?"

Sam checked Jordan's pupils. They were unresponsive to light. Every muscle in her body was tense. She moaned softly and rolled onto her side. And then all at once Jordan completely relaxed, her body went limp. Sam eased her onto her back and lifted the hem of her T-shirt. Grace leaned closer so that she could see what Sam had discovered. Black tendrils extended in a pattern from the original entry the knife had made. The pattern now stretched all the way across her torso and doubled back on itself in an arc toward Jordan's heart. Jordan wasn't wearing a bra under her shirt, and it was impossible for Grace not to notice her small firm breasts as the black tendrils spiderwebbed across her alluring, pale skin.

"Is the pattern spreading?"

"Yes, it's definitely larger than before."

"What is it?" Grace angled for a better view of the markings.

"I don't know." Sam gently explored the original wound, which seemed to be closed and healing well. "I sent off a blood sample and we haven't been able to identify what toxin, if any, the weapon was laced with."

A pattern began to reveal itself to Grace as she studied the dark marks on Jordan's body. But that seemed impossible. She sank back on her heels.

"What? What do you see?" Sam was looking at her.

"Is that…does that look like symbols to you?"

"Not symbols that I recognize." Sam followed her gaze.

"It looks like Sumerian." Grace pointed to a particular grouping. "This looks like the Cuneiform symbol for heaven, or sky."

"You can read ancient languages?" Sam looked at her with raised eyebrows.

"Not really, but I did study linguistics and I always found Cuneiform interesting." She had a crazy thought. "Do you think the weapon was cursed? That perhaps the toxin was a curse rather than a poison?"

She honestly couldn't believe she was suggesting something like that, but given how strange things had been the past couple of days it was probably best not to rule anything out. If she was beginning to accept the crazy notion that vampires existed, then why not black magic?

"Maybe you're on to something." She'd half expected Sam to laugh, but instead, she was deadly serious.

Jordan's body suddenly tensed and then relaxed again. Her eyes fluttered and she immediately began to thrash as if she was fighting off an attack.

"Hey, it's okay…calm down." Sam tried to keep Jordan from lurching off the floor. "You passed out and you should just rest for a few minutes."

Jordan blinked rapidly and slumped back to the floor.

"Help me move her to the bed." Sam took one of Jordan's arms and motioned with a tilt of her head for Grace to help her.

"I can get myself—"

But the minute she tried to stand, Jordan almost toppled backward. Grace was at her other side to catch her and with Sam's help they shuffled Jordan to the bed. She sank into the pillows, exhausted, as if she'd traveled a million miles just to cross the room. Sam brought pillows from the sofa and stacked them at the foot of the bed so that she could prop Jordan's feet up.

"What are you doing?" Jordan was more alert, but still sounded groggy.

"I'm getting your feet above your heart." Sam frowned. "You passed out, Jordan. We should loosen her belt." Sam spoke to Grace.

Grace tried to focus on the simple task of loosening Jordan's belt and not the soft brush of Jordan's warm skin against her fingers as she worked the leather strap free. Jordan covered Grace's hand with hers.

"I'm sorry about earlier." Jordan's statement was barely audible.

"So am I."

"What did I miss?" Sam asked.

Grace knew she was blushing. Her cheeks flamed.

"I was being an ass." Jordan's voice cracked as she spoke.

"What else is new." Sam smiled.

They were quiet for a moment, until Sam spoke again.

"Listen, Jordan, you really should go to a hospital and get checked out. There's no way for me to determine with only a field kit whether there's an underlying condition that caused this."

"You mean besides being stabbed?" Jordan's sense of humor had returned.

"Yeah, besides that." Sam frowned.

"I'm not going to the hospital." Jordan attempted to sit up, but Grace placed her hand on Jordan's shoulder holding her place.

"You should lie back. Don't sit up just yet." Grace tried not to sound bossy.

"I guess I'm outnumbered."

"You most definitely are." Sam squeezed Jordan's foot.

Grace walked to the kitchen to make some tea. She should be sleeping, but so should Jordan. Sam was still in the bedroom with Jordan so Grace decided to make herself useful by putting water on to boil. Normally, she wasn't someone who did well without sleep, and she felt as if she'd hardly slept in days. And yet felt more energetic than ever. What was going on? She rubbed the wound on her shoulder at the base of her neck and debated asking Sam to take a look at it.

"How is she doing?" Grace looked up as Sam joined her in the kitchen. She offered Sam a cup of tea.

"Thank you." Sam took the steaming mug and sat down at the table. "She's asleep, finally."

"Did you have any luck talking Jordan into going to the hospital?"

"Not a chance." Sam shook her head. "She's the most stubborn person I know."

"Really?"

"You have no idea." Sam sampled the tea. "How are you?"

"I was just thinking how strange it is to be here and thinking of all the small decisions I made that brought me to this place. And how it feels like I'm exactly where I'm supposed to be at this moment." She paused and shifted her gaze to Sam. "Is that a strange thing to be thinking for someone who doesn't believe in fate?"

"I don't know." Sam was thoughtful. "I've learned not to be surprised by much these days." She paused and studied her tea. "Things I thought would never happen have happened...I've seen things I never expected to see."

It seemed like there was a bigger story behind Sam's words, but she didn't offer more and Grace felt unsure about asking for details.

"Have any memories come back to you about how you arrived here?"

"No, not really." Grace shook her head. "I remembered a little bit more about the night I arrived, but there's still part of the evening I can't recall." She sipped her tea. "Perhaps it will come back to me."

They were quiet, each lost in thought.

"Do you work at a local clinic or hospital?" Grace wondered how Sam ended up in this remote spot.

"I used to work at an ER in Oakland, but I was inspired by Eli to do something different. So, for the last few years I've been working with Doctors Without Borders."

That explained the air of dashing adventurer that surrounded Sam. She'd first thought of Sam as a sun-kissed surfer girl, but she could easily picture Sam in white shirt and khaki trousers leading a team of doctors into the outback or some other off-the-grid wild place.

"That sounds like an adventure."

"Sometimes it is."

"I sense a but at the end of that statement."

"Sometimes it's scary too." Sam smiled thinly. "There are so many people in the world living on the edge. All it would take is one disaster, either natural or manmade to tip them over the brink." Sam shook her head as if trying to dislodge a memory. "Honestly, the manmade disasters are much more unsettling and more dangerous."

"You said you were inspired by Eli?"

"Eli used to work with the Unitarian Church, but now she does mission work abroad with Habitat for Humanity."

"Wow, I feel suddenly very self-centered."

"Hey, this work isn't for everyone." Sam smiled. "It's important to have folks who just keep the world moving forward too."

Maybe. But Grace couldn't help the feeling that she hadn't been pulling her weight.

Sam lingered for another half hour, but Jordan was still resting quietly so she decided to go back to her place and try to sleep a little before the night was completely lost. Grace knew that dawn was only a couple of hours away, but still she wasn't sleepy. The thought of leaving Jordan alone caused her worry so she quietly climbed onto the bed with Jordan and lay on her side watching Jordan sleep.

Grace was careful to keep a cushion of air between them. In the darkness, Jordan's skin glowed warmly, every other object in the room was cool blue. She squeezed her eyes shut, but even with her eyes closed she could still sense Jordan's warm aura the same as if they were touching.

This was so far beyond simply a sexual attraction that Grace wasn't sure what to make of it. She hadn't even slept with Jordan and yet she felt possessive and jealous of every other person or thing in Jordan's life. She wanted Jordan and knew that she would have her, one way or another. That thought seemed as certain as the knowledge that the sun would rise.

CHAPTER NINETEEN

Jordan's senses slowly returned. Normally, she was quick to fall asleep and woke easily. Not that she would describe herself as a morning person or anything, but she didn't mind waking with the sun. It had always seemed right not to waste the daylight, regardless of how late into the night she worked.

The painful episode she'd experienced the previous night came back to her as she sat at the edge of the bed. She covered her side with her hand and took a deep breath. She'd sensed at some point during the night that Grace was with her, but the other side of the bed was empty when she woke up.

Jordan ruffled through her closet for a flannel shirt and slipped it on over her T-shirt. Then she tugged on sweatpants from a nearby chair. The narrow-slatted wood floor was cold under her feet, but that didn't really bother her. The chill was invigorating.

Her coat was rumpled up on the floor. When she picked it up to drape it over a chair, the letter she'd been carrying around in her pocket fell out. It was almost as if it was asking to be read or reminding her to read it. Jordan held it in her hand as she shuffled to the kitchen. She sort of felt as if she was suffering from a hangover, but they hadn't consumed nearly enough bourbon for that to be the case.

Grace was standing near the stove when she entered the kitchen.

"Good morning." Grace turned and smiled.

"Good morning." Her voice was raspy from sleep.

"I took the liberty of making coffee. Would you like some?"

Jordan nodded as she dropped into a chair at the table. It was all so cozy having Grace in her kitchen, as if she was meant to be there or something. She felt like she was experiencing a weird twilight zone moment. She set the letter on the table and rubbed her eyes with the heels of her hands in an attempt to loosen the cobwebs from her brain. Jordan opened her eyes just as Grace reached in front of her with a cup of coffee. The vanilla scent of Grace's skin and hair invaded her senses. She figured it was just the soap and shampoo from her own bathroom collection, but it smelled somehow different, in a good way, on Grace.

"How are you feeling?" Grace studied her as she sampled the coffee.

"Okay, I think." She tried to smile but was pretty sure she wasn't very convincing.

"I made French toast, but then realized there wasn't any syrup."

"There should be some honey in the pantry."

"That might work." Grace opened the door of the small pantry cabinet and searched the shelves for a minute before she found the glass jar of honey. She brought two plates of food and the honey to the table. And then took a seat across from Jordan.

"Thank you." Jordan realized that she was starving. The burger she'd eaten the night before was long gone. She had no idea what time it was. She figured based on the angle of the sun that it was late morning. The vintage wall clock over the stove was perpetually stuck at eleven because she never remembered to change the battery. There was also some strange comfort in the fact that when she was in the cabin time stood still.

Grace sipped her coffee. She took a couple of small bites, but mostly watched Jordan eat.

"When did Sam leave?" Jordan asked after swallowing a few mouthfuls of food.

"Early. I'm not sure what time. I lay down with you for a little while, but you were sleeping so soundly and I just…couldn't." It seemed as if Grace wanted to say more, but chose not to. "What's this?" Grace picked up the letter.

"It was delivered to my apartment, but I haven't opened it." The moment the words left her lips the wax seal broke apart on its own and the folded paper eased open. She'd carried it in her pocket for hours so she'd probably broken the seal, but that still seemed eerily timed.

Grace glanced at Jordan as if she was asking permission.

"Feel free to open it." At this point, why keep secrets? Grace currently knew more about her simply from proximity than anyone else, except for Sam and Eli.

Grace set her coffee cup aside and gave the letter her full attention. She unfolded the heavy paper and studied it for a few seconds.

"It's written in Latin." Grace glanced up at Jordan.

"It is?" Jordan polished off the last bite of her French toast and leaned across the table for a better look at the document Grace held in her hand. Sure enough, it was in some language that she couldn't read, written in perfect script just like her name on the front of the sealed message. "Too bad I don't read Latin." Her statement was laced with sarcasm. Just what she needed, one more cryptic clue that made no sense.

"I can read it if you like?" Grace offered.

"You can read Latin?" Grace continued to surprise her.

"I'm not a scholar or anything, but I think I can translate this." She returned her attention to the letter.

"I just noticed you're not wearing your glasses."

"Yeah, funny thing…I don't seem to need them any longer." Grace didn't take her eyes from the paper as she spoke.

This news didn't surprise Jordan. It meant that Grace's transition was happening and time was running out to stop it. She was annoyed with herself and her weakened state.

"This first line, *mors est vita pons,* means *the bridge to life is death.*" Grace paused. "This second line is almost a repeat of the first, *the gateway to life is death.*"

Jordan waited for Grace to continue. So far, the message didn't make much sense.

"*The ancient time when your breath was light, and how now you dream of heaven.*" Grace paused again and tilted her head. "This last part is curious."

"What does it say?" Was that what her vision had been about? A dream of heaven? What were the odds that she'd get a message in Latin and at the same time have a beautiful houseguest who just happened to be able to read it?

"*Ascende ad locum, vos qui estis ab angelis.*"

"Which means?"

Grace set the paper aside and met her gaze.

"It means, *ascend to your rightful place, you who are descended from angels.*"

A chill ran up her arms. She stared silently at Grace. "I don't know what that means." But deep down, there was a feeling that she did know. At least the dreaming about heaven part. She'd been having crazy dreams about flying and about clouds and about falling. And Kith had said something about the descendants of angels, hadn't she? Jordan pinched the bridge of her nose and squeezed her eyes shut. After a few seconds, she looked up and met Grace's gaze. "Is the letter signed?"

"Only with the letter K."

"Kith."

"Who?"

"The woman you saw at the gate. Her name is Kith." Jordan stood. She couldn't talk about this any longer. She needed a minute alone to think. "I'm going to take a shower."

Grace still held the letter in her hand as she watched Jordan practically bolt from the table.

"Hey…" Jordan paused in the doorway to her room and looked back. "Thank you for translating the letter."

Grace nodded. She laid the creased paper on the table and held her coffee in both hands.

Jordan nodded. She wanted to say, *I've said all I can say right now*, but she didn't. She only thought it and then headed for the bathroom to take a shower. She was sure Grace had a million questions, but if she did, she held her tongue.

Jordan swept her T-shirt off and stared at herself in the bathroom mirror. The pattern from the wound in her side had spread across her ribs, up and around her breast and was now traveling down the center of her chest very close to her heart. She tried to look down at it because the image in the mirror was reversed, but she couldn't get a good view of the upper portion. The pattern looked like a beautifully intricate black line tattoo, except that it wasn't. What did it mean? What would happen when the poison, or curse or whatever it was reached her heart? Should she contact the Guild and ask for assistance? No, that seemed ill-advised given the bits of information she'd gotten from Miller. Based on what he said she'd been set up by the Guild. It didn't seem that he had any reason to lie to her about that. Right now, the Guild was the last place she would look for help. They clearly wanted her dead, or worse than dead, cursed.

On some level she'd known that the Guild used vampires as informants, but not as foot soldiers or assassins. Jordan braced her hands on the edge of the sink and allowed her head to hang down, stretching the tense muscles in her neck. She rolled her head from side-to-side before she reached to turn the water on. She drew the shower curtain around the rim of the tub and set the shower head at a higher position so that she could stand under it.

❖

A half hour later, Jordan was dressed and finger combing her damp hair off her forehead. She found Grace still in the kitchen. The dishes had been cleared and washed and she was sitting quietly, finishing a cup of coffee.

"Um, I was thinking maybe we should drive into Manchester and pick up a few things." Jordan shoved her hands in her pockets. She was feeling better, but still not quite herself.

"Like syrup." Grace smiled.

"Yes, syrup and maybe something for dinner. I'm sorry that you've been stranded here and I wasn't exactly stocked for company."

"Well, I did sort of show up without an invitation."

"Still…"

Grace studied Jordan after she placed her empty cup in the sink. Jordan looked a bit more revived than she had an hour ago. Jordan was wearing a western-style plaid shirt with faded jeans and boots. Her stance signaled relaxed strength and calm. Even still, her eyes were shadowed and Grace could sense Jordan's worry as if it were her own, which was an interesting thing to notice.

"Are we going to talk about the letter?" She hadn't wanted to press Jordan, but it seemed wise to talk about it.

"I don't know what to say." Jordan exhaled. "I don't know what it means, and I don't know why it was given to me. Can we just not talk about it for now?"

"Okay." She could see the tension on Jordan's face and decided to let it go.

"Thank you." Jordan seemed relieved by the reprieve.

"Let me just use the restroom and grab a sweater and I'll be ready." She brushed past Jordan and could literally feel the heat from her body even though she made no contact.

Jordan nodded and her eyes followed Grace. She knew that even though she wasn't looking directly at Jordan. The volume had been turned up on all her senses. She felt like she could smell things, hear things, and sense things at a level she'd never been aware of before. It was more than a little unsettling to see a bird on the porch railing and be able to hear its heartbeat from inside the cabin.

She searched in her open suitcase for a cardigan and slipped it on over her blouse. Grace wasn't cold, but the damp coastal fog made her feel as if it was prudent to wear layers. As they stepped outside, she realized she hadn't really experienced anything in the surrounding area except Jordan's property. She had no memory of her journey from the city. She was looking forward to getting a better idea of where they were.

"Is this your car?" That seemed like a dumb question the moment she'd uttered it.

"Yeah. I picked it up down in the city last night."

"I like Jeeps." Grace smiled as she climbed in. This was a particularly intimidating vehicle, with oversized off-road tires, additional lights across the front of the roof, a winch, and a matte black paint job. If there was a zombie apocalypse, then this was the car to have.

Jordan waited until she was settled and then put the car in reverse. The rutted road made the vehicle feel like a boat being tossed at sea. She had to hold onto the handle near the door to stabilize herself.

"Sorry about the rough ride."

Grace couldn't help laughing.

"Um…I didn't mean that the way it sounded."

"Oh, no worries. I didn't read anything into it." But she completely had read into it. Everything Jordan said sounded sexual, even when Jordan clearly didn't mean for it to. Maybe it was all from Grace's perspective, but she was incredibly and perpetually turned on around Jordan. She wondered if Jordan could sense that.

Grace tried to redirect her thoughts to take in their surroundings. The landscape was beautiful. Jordan was driving away from the coast through a thick grove of eucalyptus trees and the scent was so strong that it was almost overpowering. It had a camphoraceous, woody, somewhat sweet scent with a trace of mint. She wasn't sure if she'd ever smelled these trees in the wild, they certainly didn't grow anywhere near Atlanta.

They finally reached the end of the dirt lane and turned right onto a paved road. Grace took a deep breath and relaxed her grip on the handle. She felt as if she'd been tossed about on a stormy sea. After a few miles they turned onto another highway from which she could see the ocean in the distance. This two-lane highway eventually drew closer to the cliffs and followed the coastline south.

"It's so beautiful here." The marine layer hovered just beyond the cliffs and she got the feeling that if the heavy fog bank retreated the sky would be blue. Every so often the fog thinned and a patch of blue peeked through.

"This part of California is pretty unique." Jordan was looking out at the horizon as she talked. "I've driven the Pacific Coast Highway all the way from San Francisco to Portland and this area has some of the best views." She paused. "I mean, there are some really great spots on the Oregon coast too, but this is a stretch of untamed beauty, from here all the way up the lost coast."

The lost coast was aptly named. Grace felt a bit lost. She almost felt as if she was having an out-of-body experience. Shouldn't she be worried about getting home? Shouldn't she be concerned about falling behind on her work? Shouldn't she more urgently want to reach out to her friends in Atlanta? Frankly, she just didn't care about any of it. That was so out of character.

A dairy farm swept past her window as if she'd just traveled back in time. The aging farmhouse from the turn of the century was surrounded by weathered outbuildings and farm equipment. Past the house on a grassy hillside, a line of well-fed cows curved across the pasture toward the barn. On the other side of the road, far from the highway, she could see horses in the distance. It was so strange to see the world so clearly without the aid of glasses. Grace felt sort of naked without them, but she really didn't need them any longer. Perhaps that should also have caused her some alarm, but it didn't. She knew that she was changing, just as Jordan had predicted she would, Grace just hadn't known exactly what that meant. It was becoming harder to deny that perhaps Jordan had been telling her the truth from the beginning.

As more open spaces swept past her window, she marveled at how little she actually knew of California. She hadn't traveled extensively here, basically only visiting larger urban centers, and she'd had no concept that most of the state was quite rural. The coastline was beautifully and wildly undeveloped, unlike the Eastern Seaboard.

A Welcome to Manchester sign told her they'd arrived in town. Although, this *town* seemed to be not much more than a few blocks along one main street. Grace saw a diner, a small organic market, a coffee shop, and a hardware store. She'd climbed out of the Jeep and was standing on the sidewalk in front of the market when Jordan's phone rang.

"Sorry, I should take this."

Grace nodded and relaxed, taking in the scene of the sleepy, coastal village. She overheard bits of the conversation, even though she wasn't trying to. Jordan was talking to Sam and even though Jordan didn't have Sam on speaker mode, she could hear both sides of the conversation which was mostly about how Jordan was feeling today. Grace walked down the sidewalk toward the hardware store to give Jordan a bit more privacy. After a few minutes, Jordan walked in her direction.

"That was Sam checking in." Jordan shoved her phone in her pocket as Grace walked with her back toward the market. "I was thinking we could get some real food for the cabin."

"That sounds like a good idea."

"Oh, before we go inside…would you like to call anyone in Atlanta and let them know you're okay? Cell service is pretty good here." Jordan offered Grace the phone from her pocket.

"Yeah, I suppose that sounds like a good idea." Luckily, she knew Natalie's number by heart. That was probably the only number aside from her parents' number that she could actually remember. She'd become completely dependent on her contacts in her phone. It took a moment for Natalie to pick up. She realized it was lunchtime on the East Coast so Natalie was probably out running errands. She did sound a bit frazzled when she answered. It was lucky that Natalie even picked up at all since she wouldn't recognize the number, but maybe she assumed it was a potential client.

"Hello?"

"Hi, Natalie, it's me." She took a breath. "I lost my cell phone."

"Oh no, did something happen in San Francisco?" She heard a car door slam on Natalie's end. "When did you get back? Did you meet anyone interesting?" Per usual, Natalie asked multiple questions at once without giving her time to answer.

"I'm actually still here. This client interview is taking more time than I anticipated so I changed my flight." Grace glanced over at Jordan, who definitely qualified as someone interesting, but she wasn't about to mention that to Natalie. "I wanted to call and let you know that I'm delayed and that if you tried to call me I won't get the message."

"That is *so* annoying...I'm so sorry for you. What a pain." Natalie paused. "Wait, who's phone is this?"

"Um, a friend, I just borrowed it to give you a call." Grace shielded the receiver with her hand and tried to whisper emphatically. "And do not leave a message for me on this phone."

"Yes, ma'am. You're so bossy. Whoever your *friend* is, she must be pretty cute."

"I'm smiling, but that doesn't mean you're right."

Natalie laughed. It was so nice to have a normal conversation after the last forty-eight hours of ultimate weirdness.

"Whatever you say, hon."

"I'll call you when I get home. Love you."

"Love you too. And I can't wait to hear all the details." Natalie clicked off.

Jordan tried not to eavesdrop while Grace talked to her friend, but it was hard not to. She accepted the phone from Grace. She was hyperaware of the tingling sensation that traveled up her arm as her fingers brushed Grace's.

"Thank you."

"You didn't really say much to your friend." Not that Jordan was someone who overshared either, but she was a little surprised by the brevity of Grace's call.

"What was I going to say? That I'm still in California because I was bitten by a vampire?" Grace's questions were laced with sarcasm, but in a playful way, as if she was actually starting to believe it herself. In which case, Jordan wished Grace would take it all more seriously. Time wasn't on their side.

So why wasn't she more urgently searching for Grace's sire? That was an interesting question. Because she wasn't quite herself, that's why.

"I guess that's true. Hardly anyone would believe that story." Jordan held the door of the market open for Grace.

"I'm in it and I barely believe it."

Jordan wished so badly that she'd met Grace under different circumstances. She loosened a tiny shopping cart from the queue of carts at the front of the store and walked beside Grace through the produce department. This is what it would feel like to have a normal life, to have a partner, and to have a job that wasn't the one she currently had. The lovely mundane act of shopping seemed worth savoring. She enjoyed watching Grace hold various fruits up to sniff them or test their freshness. She was quite beautiful, and Jordan allowed herself a few moments to just enjoy the view.

Thinking of her work reminded her that Sorcha hadn't called after the incident. In fact, her phone had been deafeningly silent as far as the Guild was concerned. Did they assume she was dead? Maybe they did. She'd taken out the vampire they'd hired to kill her. That's assuming what Miller told her was true and that all of it was a setup. And probably they also assumed Miller was dead. Someone had left him for dead under the overpass for sure. Maybe she could use her perceived death to her advantage.

"Hey, where'd you go?"

Jordan realized Grace was watching her as she rolled an orange in her hand.

"Sorry, I was just thinking about...things."

"How about we pretend everything is normal and just think about food." Grace placed her hand next to Jordan's on the handle of the cart as they continued down the aisle. "You know, I'm actually a decent cook. I'd love to make you something. I haven't actually seen you eat anything green since we met."

Jordan laughed. "Hey, I'm pretty sure there was one leaf of lettuce on that burger I had yesterday."

"Since I didn't witness it myself I'll have to take your word for it."

Grace looped her arm through Jordan's as if they were a couple, as if they were on a date. It was such casual contact, but the affection implied by the small gesture made Jordan's heart hurt. It occurred to her that she was lonely. Yes, she had great friends in Eli and Sam, but not the intimacy of a lover. She wondered how empty her life was because she'd never had that. And now the person she might like to try it with was soon to be a vampire. The situation was beyond ironic, it was just plain sad.

But this was what she did, what she was good at, tracking demons. There was still time, and if anything, she was stubborn enough not to give up. She could still fix this, and then she'd retire for real and maybe even ask Grace out on a real date.

A nice, homecooked meal still sounded like a good idea. A decent meal might actually improve her stamina and then they could drive down to the city. It would actually be easier to track her sire if Grace was with her. Any reaction Grace had to a vampire would be the certainty she'd need to stop Grace's transition.

"I keep losing you." Grace had placed a few items in the cart and she hadn't even noticed.

"I'm sorry." She had to stop saying that. "I promise to be less distracted."

"Good, because a less secure woman might start to take it personally."

"Noted." Jordan smiled. She really enjoyed Grace's sense of humor.

"Now, back to food." Grace searched the shelves. "How do you feel about chicken with tortellini? How about zucchini? I could make a vegetable-based sauce. Not the fanciest meal, but savory and warm and fairly quick to prepare."

"That actually sounds really good." She smiled at Grace as she followed along with the cart.

❖

Jordan watched Grace put the finishing touches on their very late lunch. She couldn't remember the last time, if ever, she simply lounged at the table and watched someone cook. She had a memory of her grandfather in the kitchen, but that was more about serving something basic to sustain them. Grace made it look like an art form, the way she stirred and sampled, then dashed a bit more of various spices into her sauce. She even carried a spoonful over for Jordan to sample. Satisfied with Jordan's reaction, Grace set two steaming plates of food in front of them and then sat down across from her. Grace seemed quite pleased with herself. Jordan figured it was hard to cook in someone else's kitchen with limited tools and supplies, but Grace had managed to pull it off without getting flustered.

"This looks amazing. Thank you."

"You're very welcome." Grace smiled. "This is the most normal thing I've done in two days." She laughed at her own comment.

"I suppose my life is rarely normal…so, things not being normal is kinda normal for me…if that makes sense." She sampled a bite of the chicken and pasta together. It was delicious.

They were quiet for a few minutes as they ate, although, she was aware that Grace kept watching her. It didn't make her uncomfortable, but she did notice the attention.

"Can I ask you something?"

"Sure." Jordan hoped it was something she could answer.

"I was just thinking about how I don't really know you. I mean, we haven't really gotten a chance for get-to-know-you sort of conversation."

"True."

"I wanted to know about your family. Do you have siblings?"

"No, just me. Do you have siblings?" Jordan realized that she probably wasn't very good at this sort of conversation because she so rarely participated in basic social activities. And hardly ever participated in first dates, or any dates. Small talk was not in her wheelhouse.

"I'm an only child too." Grace took a bite of food. After a moment, she continued. "I think you mentioned that this place belonged to your grandparents. Did your parents live here too?

"I don't remember my parents." She reminded herself that Grace was a writer and probably loved to ask questions.

"You don't remember them?" Grace scrunched her eyebrows a little.

"I came to live with my grandfather when I was really young, like four years old…It was just me and him."

"Did he know you were a demon hunter?"

"Yes, he basically trained me. He did the same work for a long time. Until it physically became too much for him." She didn't want to say that he was killed on the job, or that his advanced age probably contributed to his death. Her grandfather wanted to go out fighting and he got his wish. Jordan took a deep breath. Why not just share for real? "You know, that job the other night, the one where I got stabbed? That was supposed to be my last job. I told the Guild I was leaving."

"Does that make you more suspicious about what happened?"

"Yes." But she didn't elaborate. She didn't go on to say that she had considered that Grace might also be part of some larger plan, unbeknownst to Grace.

She wondered if Grace considered it strange that she didn't have more to say about her parents, but it always seemed that there were more pressing dangers to focus on. That was definitely true from her grandfather's perspective and by association, hers.

They were silent as they continued to eat. Jordan had just shared a lot more than she normally did and was grateful for a break in the questioning. But she could see the questions queuing up based on Grace's expression. Grace was studying her from across the table.

"Do you really believe in God?" Grace's expression was serious.

"Wow, you really are a writer aren't you? I can tell you love the interview process."

Grace laughed. "Yes, I suppose that's true."

"I do believe in God, but maybe not exactly the God your father preaches about."

"That sort of confined God has always puzzled me. Why would the creator of everything exist on a cloud at the edge of the cosmos?"

"I guess I've always assumed that language has its limits. At the time, that was the best description anyone could come up with." Jordan had almost cleaned her plate. She took a beat to focus on the conversation rather than the food. "How can we describe the unknowable?"

"We can't."

"Exactly."

"What about the existence of evil in the world? Do you believe it actually has a physical presence?" Grace wasn't being sarcastic the way she'd been when she'd first talked about her beliefs when Eli was there. She seemed to sincerely want to know Jordan's opinion.

"If you're asking me if there are evil creatures in the world then, yes, they exist." Jordan sipped her water and considered how best to articulate her thoughts. "I believe evil is the drive to control, to dominate, and to consume."

"Is evil merely blind selfishness then?"

"Maybe."

"Greed is a powerful force in the world." Grace seemed to agree with her on that point.

"And it always has been." Jordan wasn't sure how she knew that, she just did.

"I believe that nothing is more fundamental to human relations than one group deciding who has a place at the table. As members of the queer community we know that from firsthand experience. True goodness, true equity is expanding that table."

"You talk like a theologian." Jordan relaxed in her chair. She loved how smart Grace was, and thoughtful. She didn't mind someone having a different opinion than hers. And she wasn't intimidated by it either. She appreciated it when someone could make a reasoned argument in support of their belief. In her opinion, people didn't talk enough about these sorts of things. People spent way too much time pointing fingers and creating false narratives—us vs. them.

"I don't consider myself to be a theologian, but I was certainly raised by one. I definitely learned to debate with my father about it." Grace hadn't finished her food.

Grace didn't seem to have the same appetite that Jordan did, but that could also be a symptom of her transition.

"Jesus, as he was reported...or invented...by the author of the Gospel of Mark definitely painted Christ as the poster boy for commensality." Grace continued. "He was feasting with tax collectors and prostitutes and sinners of all flavors."

"To feed someone, to share a meal with them, is to make peace with them don't you think?" She considered that was also what they had just done. She and Grace didn't share the same beliefs and soon would be on opposite sides, but they'd shared food and were taking the time to listen to each other. It wasn't that Grace was a demon yet and she couldn't help thinking of how much, or how little, of Grace would remain if she couldn't stop her transition. The thought sank into her stomach like a stone. "Small things, seemingly insignificant acts of kindness keep evil at bay." She paused and met Grace's direct gaze. "That's what I believe."

"I think that is something we can agree on."

Jordan laughed. "Well, at least that's something."

Grace had a mischievous grin.

"What?" Jordan was afraid of what their next discussion might entail.

"Nothing." Grace stood. "I'm just smiling because I also have dessert."

"That's a very good reason to smile."

Jordan watched Grace serve two slices of apple pie onto plates. She'd seen the pie as they checked out at the market but had completely forgotten it. A fruit pie was a pleasant surprise. This almost felt like a normal day, except that it wasn't.

CHAPTER TWENTY

Grace wasn't convinced that finding Thea would solve anything, but she found herself agreeing to drive down to the city with Jordan despite her doubts which seemed to come and go. Each time she noticed something that Jordan had mentioned exhibit itself she would pause and notice. Then her brain would take over and she'd reason that it was all in her head. But how could that be true? Take her sudden twenty-twenty vision for example, she hadn't imagined that. She'd had a very real need for eyeglasses two days ago and now she had no need for them at all. That was an empirical fact, which was hard to ignore.

They were only about twenty miles from the city, on the freeway, when Jordan's phone rang.

"Hello?" Jordan's expression grew serious. "Yes…Yes, thank you." There was a moment of silence. "Please tell him I'll be there in about forty minutes to pick him up."

Grace looked over at Jordan as she hung up, waiting for an explanation.

"That was the hospital where Eli and I dropped off Miller. He's being discharged and I think we should go pick him up."

"Who's Miller?" She wasn't sure she'd heard about him.

"He was with me the night I was attacked. He might be able to help us out."

They rode in silence for a little while as the freeway found its way through various communities in Marin County, and the Marin Headlands, until the view opened up on the other side of the tunnel of the Golden Gate Bridge. Grace knew that the color was for safety—international orange—but it was also a beautiful contrast against the blue green of the bay to the east and the infinite Pacific to the west. This bridge truly was a gateway.

"Are we going to talk about the letter?" Grace had dropped it at the time, but she hadn't forgotten about it.

"What else is there to talk about." Jordan glanced over her shoulder and changed lanes. She wasn't looking at Grace as she spoke. "I assume at some point it will make sense, but right now it's nothing more than a riddle."

"I guess so." She was quiet for a minute. "Descended from angels sounds like pretty serious stuff."

"Are you joking right now?"

"No, that's what the letter said."

"I know, but you don't even believe in God and now you believe in angels?" Sarcasm was an unusual tone for Jordan.

"Not really." She had not shared her ghostly encounter with Jordan. The longer she waited to talk about it, the less real it seemed. Perhaps she'd imagined the entire thing.

"That's what I thought." Jordan smiled. "Let's just deal with one crisis at a time. Right now, we need to find your sire."

"That sounds so creepy."

"I suppose that does sound weird if you've never heard it before."

"It makes me sound like a prized horse or something." She frowned and crossed her arms.

Jordan laughed and for a moment the mood lightened, but she had a feeling the lightness would be fleeting.

Jordan parked in the patient loading zone near the main hospital entrance. Grace tried to relax, but being back in the city made her uneasy. She was unsure of the exact source of the unsettled feeling she was having. Probably it was as simple as not knowing what had really happened that night in the hotel. The thought of trying to track down Thea, who was essentially a stranger she'd met in a bar, was not appealing.

After a little while, Jordan stepped through the sliding glass doors behind a man being pushed by an orderly in a wheelchair. Once they were clear of the door, the orderly set the brake on the chair and the man, who she assumed was Miller, stood up. His arm was in a sling, but not a cast. He had some bruises on his face and seemed a little shaky on his feet, but at least he was walking on his own. Grace didn't know what he normally looked like so she wasn't sure if he looked good or bad. If she'd seen him on the street she'd probably just have assumed he'd had a wild night on the town with too much to drink. He almost looked as if he'd been in a bar fight.

Jordan opened the rear door of the Jeep and he climbed in.

"Hi." He nodded in greeting to Grace.

"Grace, this is Miller." Jordan half rotated in the driver's seat. "Miller, this is Grace."

"It's nice to meet you." She partially turned in her seat so that she could make eye contact.

He nodded again.

"How are you feeling?" she asked.

"Like I got hit by a truck." He grimaced as he adjusted his arm in the sling.

"I filled Miller in while we waited on his discharge papers." Jordan maneuvered through the chaotic hospital parking lot. "He's going to go with us."

"Are you sure you're well enough—"

"I'm fine." He cut her off. He didn't sound angry, but there was definitely an edge to his statement.

"I figured we'd go back to the hotel where you stayed and try to retrace your steps." Jordan merged into traffic on the busy street. "Or do you think we should also pay Michael Lucas a visit?"

"No, I don't think that's necessary." Grace shook her head. "Whatever happened to me definitely happened after I returned to the hotel. I'm certain of that."

"Okay, to the hotel then."

Grace nodded but she still wasn't completely sure why she'd agreed to this plan. Was she just humoring Jordan because she was really starting to care about her, or deep down did she believe Thea held the key to her current condition? It was hard to know for sure.

She stared out the window as the city swept past. There was an unusual number of unhoused people camped on the sidewalks of this particular neighborhood. She'd read that San Francisco had a real housing crisis but she hadn't realized it was this bad. And somehow, she hadn't noticed it when she traveled from the airport to the hotel. Maybe the taxi driver had chosen a more charming route.

After circling the block, Jordan managed to find street parking not too far from the hotel.

"Stay with the car." Jordan spoke to Miller. "We'll go do a bit of reconnaissance and come back for you when we need you."

Miller seemed happy to sit and wait. He relaxed against the headrest.

"What do you expect to find here?" she asked as she fell in step with Jordan on the sidewalk.

"I don't know yet. Just follow my lead."

"You don't honestly think Thea just hangs out at this hotel bar all day, do you?" Jordan's stride was long and she struggled to keep up.

"Vampires used to be human, and humans are creatures of habit. They like to return to familiar places." Jordan paused near the front of the hotel and surveyed the surrounding area. "I can see why this was a good spot."

"What do you mean?"

"Well, this is the older part of downtown so these midrise buildings and narrow alleyways offer good shadows."

"Oh, right, because of how vampires burst into flame in the sun." She couldn't help the sarcasm.

Jordan frowned at her.

"Nothing is that simple."

"I'm sorry. Can you just explain it to me?" She honestly wanted to know.

"Vampires have a sensitivity to sunlight, but it's not a burst into flames sort of thing. It's not as dramatic as the movies make it seem. Older vampires evolve and adapt and have a higher tolerance. Younger vampires have a harder time so they tend to keep to areas with plenty of opportunity for shade or even underground spaces. Like there." Jordan pointed. "A multistory parking garage is perfect. Basement parking is even better."

"What makes you think Thea is younger?" She followed as Jordan started toward the garage.

"Because she's still feeding on humans." Jordan looked at her with a serious expression. "Older vampires usually have capital, means, they can afford to buy blood from other sources. They've learned not to draw attention to themselves by feeding on humans. Like everything else in the world, those without money struggle to get by."

They stood in front of the gaping dark entrance to the concrete garage. Grace didn't like parking garages under normal circumstances and avoided them whenever possible. The parking garages in Atlanta were rife with smash-and-grab thefts and even muggings.

"We're not going in there are we?"

"No, I'm going and you're staying here." Jordan used the key fob to lock and unlock the car to get Miller's attention since he was almost a block away. He climbed out of the car and walked toward them. "You wait here with Miller."

Grace hated to be told what to do and she didn't want Jordan taking risks on her behalf.

"Why are you so stubborn?" Grace braced her hands on her hips. "I can help you."

"How? You don't even believe any of this stuff is real. The last person I need as backup is an unbeliever." Jordan probably hadn't meant the comment to sound as harsh as it did, but the words stung just the same. She must have noticed because she turned to Grace and softened her tone. "Hey, I'm not mad at you. I just need to focus right now. This is my world, not yours. So, just let me handle it. I'm trying to keep you safe."

Grace nodded and tried to understand. She wanted to keep Jordan safe too and wasn't sure exactly how to do that.

"What's up?" Miller joined them.

"I think this might be a staging area for that hotel bar over there." Jordan tipped her head in the direction of the hotel. "Stay here with Grace while I take a look."

"You got it." He smiled thinly at Grace.

Grace watched as Jordan was swallowed by shadows as she entered the garage. Her long dark coat caught the breeze and fanned out making her look like a caped superhero going into battle. Grace didn't like this one bit, no, not at all. She didn't want to go looking for trouble in a damp, dark parking garage. And she didn't want Jordan doing it either.

Beside her, Miller lit a cigarette and offered her a drag. She gladly accepted.

CHAPTER TWENTY-ONE

Jordan felt the temperature drop inside the cool concrete space. The parking lot on the entry level was full to capacity. She cut through the central walkway and took the stairs down to the lower level. At the landing, she deployed the retractable sword then stood quietly and listened.

She closed her eyes and allowed her other senses to take over. The ever-present low hum of traffic in the city was the first thing she heard. Buses at street level, cars, and a siren in the distance. Jordan passed through the high-level noise, allowing it to drop away to what lay beneath, sounds more subtle and difficult to discern. The scuttling sound of some small creature, a plastic bag carried by the wind, but still she heard no other traces of anyone on this level. Jordan opened her eyes and walked slowly away from the stairway. Headlights blinded her for a moment and she stepped between two parked cars to let the vehicle pass, careful to keep the sword hidden from view by her long coat.

As she searched the dark corners of the structure she thought of Grace. What course of action would she take if she was unable to stop Grace's transition? She'd never been faced with that choice before. Everything in her world had been so ordered to fall on one side of the line or the other and crossing that line, in her mind, meant chaos. Once the boundary was breached between demon and human then what came next? She'd never understood individuals who could exist comfortably within the gray zone. Without a moral compass of right and wrong, who was she? And what had her entire life been about? To give in now would be to say it had all been for nothing.

After following the ramp down to one more level, she sensed movement. She stopped in the circle of light and waited. The sound of footsteps made her rotate, and after a few seconds the figure of a young man, thin and dressed in a black T-shirt and jeans, appeared several feet away from her.

"I'm looking for Thea." Jordan allowed the overhead bulb to flash across the sword as a warning.

"She's not here." He froze and sized her up.

Jordan hoped he'd make a move. He circled at the edge of the circle of light from the bulb. She rotated, facing him as he moved, but hyperaware that a second vampire lurked somewhere in the shadows behind her.

Grace wasn't very good at waiting under the best of circumstances, which this was not. Beside her, Miller smoked a second cigarette. He seemed oblivious to her plight of worry.

"Are we really just going to stand out here and let her do this alone?"

Miller gave her a side-eyed look. He exhaled smoke, dropped the butt, and smashed it with his shoe before he spoke.

"No. Now that you mention it, I don't think we are."

"Good." She took a deep breath and they stepped into the darkened interior.

"Just stay close and if I tell you to stay behind me, don't argue."

"Got it." What about her personality made him think she'd argue? That made her smile. Probably everything.

"What's funny?"

"Nothing."

They walked slowly. Grace kept looking side to side and pivoting to check over her shoulder. She didn't feel much safer with Miller and his injured arm than she did if she'd been by herself in a parking garage. Once again, she thought to herself, wasn't this the stupid thing that people always did in movies? Walk into a dimly lit urban parking garage for no good reason?

The sound of clanging metal caused her to stop in her tracks. *Jordan?*

"What is that noise?" It sounded as if it was coming up the stairwell from one of the levels beneath them.

"It sounds like a fight." Miller started toward the stairs.

He stepped in front of Grace, but before they even reached the stairway, he was yanked into the darkness. Grace pulled up short, surprised and afraid.

"Miller?" She heard muffled noises from the darkness but couldn't see anything. Why weren't there more fucking lights in this garage? And then, as she backed away, she noticed that several bulbs had been broken. Shards of glass crunched under her feet. Someone wanted the space to be even darker than it normally would have been. Jordan's statement about vampires and shadows came back to her with sudden clarity.

"Miller?" She urgently whispered his name. She took another step back and bumped into something. Grace flinched and rotated quickly to see that it was Thea.

"It's Grace, right?"

Thea looked as beautiful as she had that night in the bar. It was so strange to see her in this environment. She seemed out of place. And even still, Grace had a hard time accepting that Thea was a vampire. Was that really possible? Absently, she covered the bite at her neck with her palm. Jordan had said she'd know her sire based on her own body's reaction, but she felt nothing. Other than the creepy vibe of bumping into someone in a scary parking garage and losing Miller in the dark. Both of those things conjured a very normal feeling of unease without the garnish of vampires.

"Hello, Thea." She had backed away and now made a move to go around Thea and back toward the light of the garage entrance about a hundred yards away. So close, and yet so far.

"What's your hurry?" Thea mirrored her steps, blocking her exit.

"Look, I just need to find my friend and then I'll be on my way."

"Why so jumpy?" Thea cocked her head. "You're one of us now."

"I don't think I'll ever be one of you." Bite or no bite, vampire or not, she had no intention of hanging out in scary parking garages.

Where was Jordan? She was concerned for Miller and for Jordan, both of whom were in this situation because of her. This was all her fault.

"We could be friends, you and I." Thea stepped closer and trailed her index finger down the front of Grace's blouse. "I could help you… adjust."

She took a step back, but Thea closed the space between them. And then someone else, a man, joined them from the shadows wiping blood from his mouth with the back of his hand. Her heart dropped into her stomach. She feared something terrible had happened to Miller. She was so stubborn and impatient. She should have stayed outside with him. He'd been in no condition to protect himself, let alone her.

Grace's mind raced as she glanced toward the exit. If she ran, could she make it before they caught her? She made a quick move in that direction, but the man jumped in front of her. He was faster than she was. Now they both circled her position, and with each step they closed in.

"Get away from her."

The sound of Jordan's voice was like a beacon of light in the darkness. Relief and fear fought for dominance in her system. She could see that Jordan held a sword in one hand, red with blood. Thea practically hissed at the sight of it.

Jordan didn't look at her, she was laser-focused on Thea.

"Jordan, it's not her."

Jordan allowed her gaze to rest on Grace just for an instant. Jordan was unhurt despite the blood on the sword blade, but where was Miller? It was as if she could read Jordan's thoughts as their eyes met. *Hadn't she told Miller to stay with Grace? Hadn't she told both of them to wait outside?*

"Fucking step away from her now." Jordan pointed at Thea and then the man, with the sword. "I'm not going to ask you twice."

"And what if we don't?" The guy was built like a linebacker.

He probably wasn't used to backing down. Based on her expression and body language, neither was Jordan. Jordan motioned with her hand for him to make a move and Grace held her breath, *please don't take chances on my account.* She wanted to scream at Jordan to stop.

He grinned and rolled his neck and shoulders as if he was loosening up to enter a boxing ring. Jordan held the sword out in front of her, forcing him to keep his distance. Despite his size, he was lightning fast. He deflected the sword with a sweep of his hand and tried to strike Jordan with his fist. She was almost as fast and was able to dodge the blow. She scraped the tip of the steel blade against the floor. The sound clearly aggravated Thea and the man. They both grimaced and covered their ears. Jordan took advantage of the brief opening to shove Thea away from Grace and reposition herself. The elevator bay was at her back.

"Stay behind me." Jordan put herself between Grace and the two vampires.

Grace felt utterly useless.

"A hunter defending a vampire." Thea tried to regain her composure. "How poetically ironic."

"You might save her now, but not for long." The man grinned.

"Shut up." Jordan hadn't replied, but Grace couldn't help herself. The two vampires were so infuriatingly smug and sure of themselves. It made Grace's blood boil.

"You can't fight who you've become, Grace." Thea's tone was almost taunting.

"That's enough from you." Jordan was in motion almost before Grace realized it.

With one powerful arc of the sword, she removed Thea's head from her shoulders. Grace gasped and with wide eyes watched as Thea's body turned to dust before her separated head even hit the ground. Grace's heart pounded in her chest. She felt suddenly lightheaded. Meanwhile, Jordan was all business. She barely paused after dispatching Thea before she turned on the man, but he was faster than Jordan and now he was angry. He barreled into Jordan with his shoulder and the two of them tumbled across the concrete. The sword skidded loudly a few feet away. The sound of steel on metal had rattled him just enough for Jordan to roll out of reach and reclaim the weapon. But she was barely stable on her feet when he threw a wild punch that sent her careening into a parked car. She half rolled and half slid off the hood of it.

The man was on Jordan in an instant. He roughly jerked her up by the front of her coat and butted her with his head. Blood issued from her nose immediately. Jordan braced an elbow against his throat and with her other hand drew something from her pocket that Grace couldn't quite make out. It was a small vial of some kind.

Jordan smashed the glass vial against his forehead. It sizzled and smoked like an acid burn.

"Fucking hell." He cursed and covered his eyes with his forearm. One fist still clenched Jordan's coat. He shoved her backward so hard that she practically flew through the air and bounced off one of the concrete pilons.

Grace knew that Jordan wasn't at full strength. She was scared, but instinct took over. She ran at the huge fellow and jumped onto his back. She held on with one arm and began hitting him as hard as he could with her fist. He shook her off like she was nothing. She landed painfully on the ground, almost knocking the wind out of her. Then, from nowhere she heard a shot. The gun's discharge echoed through the concrete structure. Miller limped from the shadows, his shirt was saturated with blood and his injured arm hung useless at his side. He fired again, and again. The man registered the impacts, but was unbelievably still standing. Grace watched from the ground as Miller emptied his weapon. Rage pulsed off the vampire as he faced off with Miller, which gave Jordan the opening she needed. She sprang from a flanking position, using the hood of a parked car as a launching pad, and with one powerful downward strike took off his head with her sword. Jordan landed, crouched on one knee as he turned to a cloud of dust and was gone.

Miller swayed on his feet and then fell backward. Jordan, with blood still on her face, rushed to his side.

"Hey, man…you're okay. I've got you." Jordan pressed her palm to his neck which was bleeding profusely.

"We got him." He sputtered and coughed.

"Yeah, we got them both." Jordan focused on his face.

He took a shuddering breath and reached for Jordan's hand.

"Listen, I didn't know you well, but I know you now. I see you. You were there when I needed you most. You did good, Miller."

"How bad is it?" His eyes were heavy lidded, his words barely audible.

"Not that bad." Jordan lied. Miller was clearly bleeding out from his wounds. A pool of dark red spread beneath him on the concrete.

"Make it right, Jordan." As he finished the thought, his eyes lost focus.

"Miller?" Jordan pressed her fingers to the pulse point on the uninjured side of his neck.

Grace was kneeling on the other side of him and she covered her mouth with her hand. It was obvious that Miller was dead. The horrific intensity of what she'd just witnessed made her suddenly sick. Or was it the sight and smell of so much blood? She lurched to her feet afraid that she was going to be ill. Grace stumbled a few feet away and braced against the cool concrete wall at the edge of the elevator.

After a moment, she looked over to see Jordan dragging Miller toward the wall. She left him, propped up against the concrete block wall in the shadows, but took his weapon. She tucked it into her belt and then retrieved her sword, retracted it, and tucked it inside her coat.

"Come on. We can't stay here." Jordan tugged Grace by the arm toward the garage exit.

"But what about Miller?"

"He's beyond caring now. He'd want us to get the hell out of here."

"Those people…those people turned to dust." She still couldn't believe what she'd seen with her own eyes.

"Yeah, that's what happens to vampires when you cut their heads off."

"I think I'm going to be sick." They were walking at a quick pace down the sidewalk toward Jordan's car. Random pedestrians kept looking at them. Probably because Jordan looked like a wounded gothic hero with blood on her face.

"No, you're not."

"Yes, I am." Grace pulled away and heaved what little was in her stomach into a nearby garbage can. As soon as she stopped throwing up, Jordan again pulled her toward the Jeep.

Once in the car, Jordan sped away. She zigzagged through street after street, putting distance between the parking garage and them. Finally, she pulled over to the curb and killed the engine. Grace's head was swimming.

"Here, drink this." Jordan held a bottle of water out to her.

She took several long sips and then let her head relax against the headrest. Had she imagined the entire thing? No, that was impossible. Her senses were returning, her pulse slowing. She rotated to look at Jordan.

"You're hurt." She touched Jordan's face.

"I'm fine." Jordan looked at herself in the rearview mirror. She searched in the console for a handful of napkins. She soaked them with water and wiped at the blood on her face. An ugly bruise had also started to appear on her cheek.

Grace felt tears welling up and she was helpless to stop them.

"Hey, you're okay. Everything is going to be okay." Jordan reached for her across the console.

"I didn't believe you." Her words were muffled against Jordan's chest.

"I know."

"You were telling me the truth." The statement came out raspy because her throat was choked with emotion.

"Yeah, I was."

"I'm so sorry." She needed Jordan's arms around her. She needed to be held.

"I've got you. Everything is going to be alright." Jordan tightened her embrace and kissed Grace's hair.

After a little while, she started driving again. They were quiet, each lost in their own thoughts, at least that's where Jordan's head was. And then her mind began to wander. She blinked and tried to focus, but her vision was fuzzy, and she felt suddenly very tired.

Grace was looking out the window when she sensed the car slide off the edge of the pavement. She glanced over at Jordan, who looked heavy-lidded, as if she was about to nod off at any second. Grace grabbed the wheel from the passenger seat and righted the trajectory.

"Jordan!" Grace continued to steer from her seat. "Jordan, pull over and let me drive."

"I'm okay." Jordan's response was muffled.

"No, you're not. Pull over."

Jordan finally relented and eased onto the shoulder of the highway. Cars zoomed by. Every time a truck passed the Jeep registered the turbulence, moving back and forth just a little from the wind of the passing vehicle.

Grace jumped out, waited for a break in traffic, and then opened the driver's side door. She walked with Jordan back to the other side of the car and helped her climb in. It was as if Jordan was having something like a diabetic crash. One minute she was fine and lucid and the next minute she wasn't. The sudden change worried Grace.

She hurried back to the driver's side and got in. After another minute or so, she pulled out into traffic and continued north. Beside her, Jordan slumped in the seat with her eyes closed.

CHAPTER TWENTY-TWO

Jordan straightened in her seat. She'd started to rebound about a half hour after Grace took over driving. It was as if she'd expended too much energy and her system had crashed. Whatever was happening to her, it was sapping her stamina.

She suggested they stop at a roadside café on the way back to her cabin. She was rattled and Grace definitely seemed shaken up, and more than a little overwhelmed. She thought that a break and some food was in order, but she didn't want to stop until they were well outside the city. Valley Ford was a small community along Highway 1 about an hour north of San Francisco. Grace parked in front of the diner that advertised burgers and soft serve.

"You're sure you feel up to stopping?" Grace seemed concerned.

"I'm feeling better. Thank you."

As they entered the diner a young woman directed them to sit at any open table. It was midafternoon, between lunch and dinner so the place was nearly empty.

"Want to sit in a booth?"

Grace nodded.

"I just need a minute." Grace's wounded expression made Jordan's heart ache. "Will you order a coffee for me?"

She slid into the booth as Grace walked toward the restroom. The woman who'd first greeted them came over to take a drink order. She was probably in her late teens or early twenties with long dark hair. She was chewing gum and seemed completely bored. She hardly looked at Jordan as she took the coffee order. What would she have noticed if she had? She'd left her coat in the car so now she just looked like a regular person, she hoped. Was the recent trauma written all over her face? Hopefully, she was still good at hiding her true feelings. Although, with Grace around she wasn't so sure.

The coffee arrived just before Grace returned from the restroom. Her hair was damp in front as if she'd washed her face. She wondered if Grace had been crying. Grace slid into the bench seat across from Jordan.

"Would you like to order anything else?" The young woman returned after Grace got settled.

"Do you have chocolate cream pie?" asked Grace.

"Yes."

"I'll take a slice, thank you."

"Anything else for you?" The young woman looked at Jordan.

"No, I'm good with coffee."

"She'll have pie also." Grace ordered for her.

Grace's expression was serious as she reached for three packs of sugar, ripped the tiny packages, and dumped them in her coffee without making eye contact with Jordan.

After a few minutes, the pie arrived. She watched as Grace immediately took a large bite. A tiny dollop of whipped cream was on Grace's top lip. She dabbed at it with her napkin.

"I thought you drank your coffee with nothing in it?" asked Jordan.

"Not any longer. Since there are vampires and God knows what else and the end is obviously near, I figured now is the time to indulge. More sugar, more dessert, and more...well, more of all of it."

"We'll figure this out. Everything is going to be okay."

"You are a terrible liar, Jordan Price."

"Isn't that a good thing?"

"Not at the moment." Grace stirred her coffee. "Right now, when you tell me everything will be okay I really need you to be convincing."

"Hey, I told you I'd figure this out and I will." She reached across the table and touched Grace's hand.

"But Thea wasn't the vampire who bit me, so now we're back to square one, right?" Grace's mood was a bit crestfallen.

It was true that Thea had been Jordan's primary lead and now she wasn't sure what path to take next. Perhaps Eli had some insights for her. Maybe Eli had deciphered the markings on the back of her apartment door. Maybe she'd have more thoughts about the cryptic messages Jordan had been getting. And then there was the letter. After they got back to her cabin she'd head over to Eli's place for a brainstorming session. There was no way she was giving up. The threat to Grace just now had confirmed to her that she had feelings for Grace. Not just feelings but an intense desire to keep her safe, to hold her, to love her. She glanced out the window for fear that Grace would see too much.

"What are you thinking?"

"Nothing." She tried to sound convincing. She looked back at Grace and smiled.

"I don't believe you."

Jordan laughed. "I wouldn't believe me either." She sipped her coffee but hadn't touched the pie. Her stomach was all in knots, plus, her ego was a bit bruised from almost getting her ass kicked. That was unusual. Whatever was happening to her, it was sapping her strength and causing her to doubt herself. Two things that could easily be deadly for a hunter.

"When you found me...when you...there was blood on your sword already."

"There were other vampires on the lower level." She'd bested the two young vampires easily and then she'd heard the scuffle above her. She'd known immediately that Grace was in danger. Simply remembering the moment made her heart thump in her chest. She clenched the front of her shirt with her fist and took a deep breath.

"Are you alright?" Grace was worried.

"I'm fine."

"I don't believe that either."

Jordan smiled thinly. She decided to sample the pie. Maybe a few bites would give her a sugar boost.

"How do you not scream from the rooftops about all of this?" Grace had finished half her dessert. She slid the plate aside and braced her arms on the edge of the table.

"All of what?"

"Vampires…demons…whatever else you know but aren't sharing."

"To what end?" Jordan grew serious. "People see what they want to see. If they knew about all of this what good would it do? They would just live in fear." She paused. "Plus, look how long it took for me to convince you."

"I feel bad about that."

"Don't."

"Jordan, I'm sorry." Grace hesitated. "I'm sorry I didn't listen to you. I'm sorry for Miller. It was my fault—"

"Miller was doing his job. He knew the risks."

"But we just left him there."

"Death comes for us all." Jordan took the last swig of her coffee. "Let the dead bury the dead. Isn't that the verse?"

"I know you're hurting, Jordan. I know…and I see you for who you truly are."

The sincerity and power of Grace's statement caught her by surprise. A knot rose in her throat and she choked it down. She looked away from Grace because meeting her gaze directly was too painful.

"We should get going." She left a few bills on the table and stood up.

She couldn't talk about anything else at the moment. Jordan needed something mundane to focus her attention on, like driving. But she could tell from the look on Grace's face that she wasn't going to let things go, she wasn't going to allow Jordan to hide any longer.

The first thing Grace wanted to do when they returned to the cabin was take a shower. She wanted to wash everything away, at least symbolically. Jordan tossed her coat over a chair and swept her fingers through her hair. Exhaustion was evident on her face.

"Come with me." She took Jordan's hand and lead her toward the bath.

Jordan allowed herself to be pulled along. She stood with her arms at her sides and watched as Grace adjusted the water temperature. Grace faced Jordan and began to unbutton her shirt.

"I really need to be close to you right now. Is this okay?" she asked.

Jordan nodded.

Grace helped Jordan gently tug her undershirt off over her head. Neither of them spoke, not in words anyway. She felt as if Jordan's expression spoke volumes.

"Does it hurt?" She tenderly traced the dark threads of the pattern across Jordan's chest with her fingers.

Jordan shook her head.

"What about this?" She explored the bruise across Jordan's ribs where she'd been thrown into the pylon.

"A little."

Jordan winced when Grace touched the purple abrasion across her cheek.

She worked Jordan's belt and jeans free and pushed them down over her hips until they pooled around her ankles. Jordan stepped out of them and then she stood watching Grace as she undressed. The last garment was Jordan's Y-front briefs. Grace hooked her fingers inside the waist of them and slid them down and off.

"I don't know if this is a good idea," Jordan whispered.

"Tell me to stop and I will." But she wasn't sure she could.

"I don't want you to stop." Jordan brushed her fingers along Grace's cheek.

"I want to be with you, Jordan." She covered Jordan's lips with hers. She wanted Jordan, but she needed it to be Jordan's choice.

She climbed into the warm spray of the shower and after a few seconds, Jordan joined her. Grace dipped her head under the water to soak her hair and swept it away from her face so that she could fully focus on Jordan. She drew Jordan close until she was also standing under the spray. Jordan closed her eyes as Grace ran her fingers through Jordan's hair. She took some shampoo in her hand and massaged it gently into Jordan's hair. She felt Jordan's hands at her hips and then at the small of her back. Jordan's eyes were still closed as her hand drifted up Grace's back. Jordan's small breasts were pressed against hers and the curve of her stomach touched Jordan's sculpted abs. Suds ran down between them making Jordan's skin warm and slick against hers. She took a moment to work soap across Jordan's hand where her knuckles were red and scuffed from her earlier ordeal.

Jordan had passively allowed Grace to attend to her in the shower, but as Grace touched and explored Jordan's body, she sensed a shift in Jordan. Jordan's hands on her hips felt more insistent, holding her tightly against Jordan's body.

Jordan rotated Grace so that Jordan was behind her. Jordan moved her hair aside and kissed her neck, lingering over the marks that had now changed her life forever. Jordan pressed against her until she was afraid they would both topple through the flimsy curtain onto the floor.

She turned the water off, rotated in Jordan's arms, and drew her down into a searing kiss.

Breaking the kiss, she breathlessly reached for a towel. Barely taking time to dry off as she crossed the room, she tumbled backward onto the bed. She lay on top of the covers, legs open, an invitation for Jordan to join her. Her limbs were on fire. She caressed her breast with her fingers and watched Jordan finish toweling off as if in slow motion.

Jordan tried to slow her breathing; her heart was pounding so fast she feared it might break through her aching ribs. She tossed the towel aside and crawled onto the bed. She knelt between Grace's shapely thighs and bent to feather kisses up each one, taking her time, taking in the tantalizing view of Grace's sex. She sensed that was where Grace wanted her, so she teased with her tongue everywhere else. Grace moaned and closed her eyes.

It had been a very long time since Jordan had been with a woman and certainly even longer with a woman she cared for. This, whatever this was, felt different. Did she truly believe she could have it all—possess Grace and save her and save herself all at the same time? Doubts began to seep in from the edges of her mind. Grace must have sensed her momentary hesitation because when she glanced up Grace was looking at her intently, the certainty in her gaze unwavering.

Jordan wanted to slip inside, to bury herself in Grace, and allow Grace to consume her whole and aching as she was. She sensed Grace tighten around her fingers as she hovered above her, thrusting inside her. She focused on Grace's face and waited for the crest of the wave to break.

"Don't stop." Grace sunk her fingernails into Jordan's lower back. "Don't stop."

She wasn't close enough, Jordan couldn't get close enough, so she shifted so that she could also ride Grace's thigh as she came, as she arched against Jordan's hand. She found Grace's mouth and covered it with hers, swallowing her cries.

At the last moment, Grace's fingers found her sex and slipped inside. She sensed her own release as Grace climaxed, the inescapable breaking down of all the walls that she'd so carefully constructed. She was breaking open and breaking out. She was no longer in hiding.

She rode the wave of ecstasy with Grace until it crested again, washing her ashore, splendidly spent. She collapsed on top of Grace and Grace held her close.

"I've got you this time," Grace whispered.

And Jordan knew that it was true.

CHAPTER TWENTY-THREE

For a long time, they held each other. Grace assumed Jordan was asleep, nestled against her shoulder. Jordan hadn't moved in some time and her breathing was slow and steady. She was half propped up on a pillow. She'd tugged a blanket over their entwined bodies and at some point after that, Jordan had drifted off. But Grace was awake. She was awake like she'd never been before. She lightly caressed Jordan's shoulder above the edge of the blanket and watched the light from the window shift lower on the wall and dim. It was summer so the sun wouldn't actually set until around nine, but it was definitely later in the afternoon.

Grace didn't want the day to be over. She didn't want to face what was to come, but she didn't want to go back to her old life either. How could she? She felt changed. She *was* changed.

Beside her, Jordan began to stir. She brushed a clump of hair off Jordan's forehead and Jordan sleepily smiled up at her.

"Hey." Jordan rolled away from Grace onto her back and rubbed her face with her hands. "What time is it?"

"Don't know and don't care." And she meant it.

Jordan reached for her and pulled her on top. Jordan held Grace's face in her hands and kissed her tenderly. The sensation of Jordan's firm body beneath hers made her want to have Jordan again. Jordan lying in her arms, her body curled against Grace's as she slept, had been nothing but an extended tease.

"You're so beautiful." Jordan kissed her lightly again.

"You are making it very hard for me to want to leave this bed." She brushed her fingers along Jordan's cheek careful to avoid the bruise.

"I want you in my bed. Now, tomorrow, the day after tomorrow—"

"Be careful, I might actually accept that invitation." She smiled. Jordan's expression grew more serious.

She rested her head on Jordan's shoulder as Jordan's strong arms encircled her. Had she cast a spell on Jordan or was it the other way around? She had no way of knowing for sure, nor did she care. All she knew with certainty was that she wanted more of Jordan. And she would have her, her life depended on it. That thought scared her a little and she attempted to pull away.

"What's wrong?" Jordan held onto her, blocking her escape.

"Nothing." She feared she was no better at keeping things from Jordan than Jordan was from her. But luckily, Jordan didn't press her for more.

They were quiet for a little while, until Jordan spoke.

"I'd still like to go talk to Eli. Would you like to come with me?" Jordan shifted beneath her so that Grace could see her face.

"Yes, I'd like to join you if you don't mind."

"We could pick up some food in Manchester on our way over."

Grace was feeling suddenly hungry. Vampire slaying and great sex obviously worked up an appetite.

Jordan propped on her elbow and watched Grace get out of bed. Grace had the most incredible ass. Grace was gorgeous. Her eyes were dreamy, her breasts were perfect, but her legs—she couldn't tear her gaze away from Grace's legs and her shapely ass. Grace was standing at the side of the bed when Jordan reached for her hand. She slid to the edge of the bed in a seated position and drew Grace back so that Grace was standing between her legs.

Grace caressed Jordan's face and kissed her. She slid her hand between Grace's thighs, to the place between her legs and stroked gently with her fingers.

"You're so wet," she whispered against Grace's mouth.

"It's your fault." Grace opened her legs a bit more for Jordan so that she could slip two fingers inside.

"Grace…"

"I don't think I can stand while you're doing that." Grace clung to Jordan.

Heat surged through her body and her heart began to drum in her ears. She was going to come with Grace and Grace hadn't even touched her. She swiveled with Grace in her arms until Grace was on her back in bed again. Jordan took Grace's nipple into her mouth as she thrust inside Grace. And still, she wanted more of Grace. She covered Grace's breast with her hand as she slid down. She lifted Grace's sex up to her mouth and tasted her. Grace's fingers were in her hair, holding on as she cried out.

She pressed her center against Grace's sex until her shuddering subsided. Then she trailed kisses up Grace's body, over the gentle curve of her lower stomach, around each nipple, up the elegant curve of her neck until she reached Grace's mouth. She kissed her unhurriedly as the red orange rays of the sinking sun painted the room in hues of amber.

CHAPTER TWENTY-FOUR

Grace retrieved her discarded cardigan from a nearby chair. Fresh from the shower, again, her hair was still damp. She pressed it between the folded towel in an attempt to wring more water from her still wet hair.

There was a sharp pain in her lower abdomen. She pressed her fingers to the spot. She'd have assumed it was cramps, but it was nowhere near that date in her cycle. Maybe it was the result of too much sex. Was there even such a thing? She was sure she didn't know because she'd never had the opportunity to find out.

Ah, there it was again. Was it hunger pains? She'd hardly eaten much more than dessert throughout the day. She shrugged it off and hung the towel on a hook near the door. When she entered the kitchen, Jordan was hunched over lacing her boots. She didn't look up. For a moment, Grace stood and watched her from a few feet away. She could see the blood pulsing through Jordan's body as a warm red glow. Everything else in the room was cast in cool blue. Her eyes lost focus and other senses took over. A craving so intense that she had to brace her feet further apart to keep from falling.

Somehow, she crossed the space to Jordan without feeling herself move. She claimed a fist full of Jordan's hair and forced Jordan to look at her. She sensed Jordan relax, her arms drooped to her lap, the task of tying her boot forgotten. Jordan's lips were moving, but all Grace could hear was the throb of Jordan's heart. She forced Jordan's head at a sharp angle exposing the pulse point at the base of her throat.

She was herself, but not herself. She thought of nothing but tasting Jordan, of possessing her, of devouring her.

"Grace."

The utterance of her name was small and far away. Grace bent down. She could smell Jordan's skin and feel the warmth of blood pulsing just beneath the surface on her face. She closed her eyes.

"Grace!"

Then louder.

"GRACE! STOP!"

Jordan launched from the chair, breaking Grace's hold with a blow to her arm. Grace stumbled backward and blinked. Jordan grabbed her arms just before she fell. What had just happened?

Jordan shoved Grace against the wall and held her there until she was certain that Grace could see her. The hunger, the urge to feed had finally truly arrived. If it happened around anyone else they'd probably be dead right now and Grace would have made the final transition. Jordan regretted that she'd given in to her attraction. Desire had clouded her judgment. She'd let her guard down. Grace blinked and tears trailed down her cheeks.

"Jordan?"

"You're okay now." She sensed Grace's fear. Jordan drew Grace into her arms.

"I couldn't stop myself." Grace's words were muffled against her shoulder. "I felt so out of control."

"I know."

"I don't want this."

"We still have time." She stroked the back of Grace's hair.

"I almost hurt you just now."

"We're not going to let that happen, okay?" She held Grace at arm's length so that she could see her face. Grace nodded.

But Jordan worried time was running out. She had no real leads and no real answers. All she had were a handful of cryptic clues.

"Let's get to Eli's. Maybe she'll have some answers for us." Her hand was at Grace's elbow as they walked toward the door.

CHAPTER TWENTY-FIVE

The sun was setting by the time they arrived at Eli's. Sam's truck was in the driveway too. The one-story stucco house was almost a hundred years old and in the style of the old Spanish missions, with a whitewashed arched gate and an arched stone doorway to match.

Jordan knocked but no one answered. She knocked again. Still no one came to the door. She heard a strange clanging sound from somewhere in the house and turned to look at Grace. Grace gave her a questioning look. The noise sounded again. And at almost the same moment a flurry of tiny dark wings passed overhead. She checked, but the door was locked.

Given all the strange things that had been happening, she didn't want to take any chances. Jordan searched under a stack of stones at the edge of the front stoop and returned with Eli's spare key. Grace followed her inside.

"Eli?" Jordan didn't want to shout. "Sam?"

No one was on the main level of the house, and nothing looked disturbed. There, the sound again, it was coming from below their feet.

"It sounds like it's coming from the basement." She spoke to Grace in a hushed voice.

Grace nodded and followed her toward the basement entry just off the kitchen.

"No, you stay here." She held up her hand to stop Grace.

"I'm not letting you go by yourself."

She didn't have time to argue. She opened the door. The clanking sound was louder. It sounded like metal against metal. The ancient basement, which had probably been a root cellar, had a hard, compacted dirt floor and narrow wooden slat stairs. Jordan descended slowly, trying to be as quiet as possible. She peered past the main floorboards which created the ceiling for the subterranean space.

Jordan froze. Eli was chained and in a cage. *What was this fresh hell?*

"Eli!" Jordan hurried down the remaining steps.

"Jordan, what are you doing here?" Sam came from the shadows on the other side of the cellar.

"What's going on?" Why was Eli in a cage? What was Sam doing? Why hadn't she released Eli?

Without waiting for an answer, Jordan started to work the latch of the cage door to open it. She wasn't going to stand by while her friend was clearly in trouble.

"Stop!" Sam jerked her arm away.

Eli dropped to her knees and groaned.

"What's going on? Why are you just standing there?" Jordan's brain couldn't compute the scene. Nothing made sense.

"Stop." A tear slid down Sam's cheek. Her hand was still on Jordan's arm and her shouted command had become a sad plea.

Eli jerked at the chains around each arm as she writhed on the dirt floor behind the bars of the cage. Jordan took a step back. Instinctively, she put her arm protectively in front of Grace as she backed away. Grace was beside her, staring at the scene unfolding in front of them.

Eli turned away from them, lurched forward, and then tossed herself back to the floor. Eli's body was transforming as she watched. A terrible cracking sound echoed off the stone walls as Eli's bones broke and restructured themselves. Her skin stretched and brown fur appeared through the rips and tears of her clothing as her form grew in size and shape. In a matter of several painful moments, Eli had ceased to exist, and in her place, snarling, jerking, and writhing against the chains was a werewolf.

Jordan staggered backward in shock. She looked over at Sam.

"Why didn't you tell me?" Jordan felt betrayed.

"I wanted to…Eli wanted to…but…"

"You thought I'd kill her if I knew."

Sam reached for Jordan, but she jerked her arm away.

"You should have told me anyway." Angry tears threatened, they gathered in a lump in her throat making her words sound raspy and hoarse.

"Eli wasn't mugged. She was bitten."

"Why didn't you tell me?" Her question sounded more like a plea.

"Because everything is black and white to you. You see only the demon." Sam looked over at Eli.

When Sam made direct eye contact, the wolf that Eli had become lunged for Sam. Eli strained against the chains which had been mounted to the stone walls on either side. Obviously, a double safety, chains and the cage, constructed to keep Eli from escaping.

"I don't see the demon. I only see Eli and her suffering." Sam curled her fingers around the bars.

Instinctively, Jordan reached for Sam and pulled her back from the cage. The moment she touched Sam, Eli became ferocious and the fury of her focus was clearly on Jordan.

"She's jealous." Grace spoke softly.

Jordan looked at Grace and then back at Eli. Grace was right. Eli had become incensed when Jordan had touched Sam.

"I love her. I always have." Sam's statement sounded like a confession. Sam was looking at Eli as she spoke.

Suddenly, Jordan couldn't breathe. She had to leave. She rotated toward the stairs.

"Jordan, don't leave…I'm sorry." Sam reached for her.

"Don't!" She glared at Sam. She turned and ran up the narrow steps.

She slammed the front door and strode to her Jeep as the full moon began to show itself. She backed out of the driveway too fast, and the huge off-road tires threw rocks into the night. *Fuck, fuck, fuck.*

An angry tear spilled over and ran down her cheek. She swiped at it with her sleeve. Eli was a fucking werewolf and Sam was in love with her. The raw betrayal of trust was like a knife in the heart, making it hard to breathe. She was truly alone in the world. Her grandfather had always told her that hunters could only trust themselves, but she hadn't believed him. She'd had Sam and Eli, friends she was willing to die for. Friends she believed were willing to die for her. But now she'd discovered the truth. She was an outsider.

The realization messed with her head. It made her doubt everything. *Everything.*

Jordan had intuitively driven toward the cliffs. She screeched to a stop near the boat launch next the marina. For a few minutes, she rested her forehead on her arm against the steering wheel. Then she climbed out and walked toward the moonlit, churning sea. The full moon on the eve of her forty-second birthday left her feeling empty even as it lit her path along the deserted shoreline.

CHAPTER TWENTY-SIX

Grace sat at the kitchen table and waited as Sam filled two mugs with hot water. Sam dropped in tea bags and then carried them to the table. Grace was in shock. She stared at the pattern on the side of the tea cup and allowed her eyes to lose focus. Eli was supposed to help Jordan, she was ultimately supposed to help Grace too, but Eli couldn't even help herself. What a tragedy. On top of which, Eli was a werewolf.

If someone had told Grace a week ago that they'd seen a werewolf, or a vampire for that matter, she'd have laughed in their face. She wasn't laughing now. She was distraught. And she had no idea where Jordan had gone or where to reach her or even if she should try.

"Hey, are you alright?" Sam touched her hand that she hadn't even realized was resting on the cool wood surface of the table.

"Yes." But she knew she wasn't, not really.

"At least you're not dating a werewolf."

The absurdity of Sam's statement made Grace smile.

"I'm a vampire in love with a demon hunter and you're a human in love with a werewolf. I suppose every relationship has challenges."

"You're in love with Jordan?" Sam's expression was serious.

"I think I am." Grace braced her chin on her hand. "Talk about wrong place, wrong time."

"Maybe everything will work out."

"Sam, you're as bad a liar as Jordan is." She sipped her tea.

Sam laughed. "I suppose I am." She paused. "But who has time for anything but honesty at this point." She frowned into her teacup. "I should have told Jordan. I should have trusted her, but I was afraid."

"How did it happen?"

"Eli was doing a vision quest up in the Sierras. You know, that's where you go out into the desert or the wilderness alone to fast and in Eli's case, get clarity…some people even have visions." Sam took a sip of her tea. "I left her out there for three days. I was supposed to go back and pick her up. There was a full moon that week and Eli thought it would only add to her experience."

Grace couldn't imagine camping alone in the wilderness. That sounded like a terrible idea. She'd have been too terrified to have a vision, except for the vision of a ride back to the city.

"The minute I pulled up to the campsite in my truck I knew something wasn't right." Sam continued. "Everything was shredded. There were these big slashes in the tent and there was debris from Eli's gear everywhere. I ran to the tent afraid of what I'd find and there was Eli…bruised, with scrapes all over, naked, and asleep. She had this gripped in her hand." Sam twirled a piece of horn that hung from a leather cord around her neck. "We assume she killed a deer during her first transformation."

"But to be a werewolf she'd have to have been bitten first, right?"

"Yes, she was on a construction project for Habitat for Humanity down in Brazil when she was attacked and bitten. She'd have been killed, but the men in the village had been tracking the animal so they were prepared. They did kill it, but not before it bit Eli, but they ultimately saved her life. She didn't even tell me what really happened until much later. I think she thought she'd been bitten by a regular wolf."

"As if that isn't scary enough." Grace couldn't imagine that either. "So, now what happens?"

"Well, after the first transition in the Sierras we decided we had to try and do damage control." Sam took a deep breath. "I mean, this only happens once a month during the full moon. It's manageable as long as we are careful. The rest of the time, she's Eli, she's herself. I think that's why I didn't tell Jordan."

Grace wondered what Jordan was thinking at the moment. Her two closest friends had kept a huge secret from her. She must be feeling very alone right now.

"I stupidly thought we could keep it a secret. But secrets don't stay hidden forever, and the ones that do just fester."

"Secrets are a different sort of cage."

"Yes, they are." Sam met her gaze and Grace could hear Sam's heart thumping from across the table, steady and strong.

She worried that another episode might be looming for her and she wanted to be at a minimum safe distance from everyone she knew. But Jordan had taken off without her and it was too far to walk.

"Do you think you could give me a ride back to Jordan's place?"

"Sure."

"Can I borrow a blanket?"

Sam gave her a curious look.

"I think it would be safer for you if I rode in the back of the pickup truck."

"Oh." Sam seemed a little surprised, but didn't argue. After a moment, she returned with a fleece blanket from the bedroom and handed it to Grace. A howl seeped up the stairs from the cellar. "The drive will probably do me good."

CHAPTER TWENTY-SEVEN

Jordan loved the ocean, even at night. The waves never cared how long you watched, they never cared who you were. She stood at the edge of the surf and was reminded of the righteousness of who she was, who she had been, but who she feared she could no longer be.

She gazed at the horizon, hoping to find something worth waiting for.

As the water washed ashore, a bioluminescence in the shallow surf surrounded her bare feet. She'd left her boots farther up the dune, preferring to feel the chilly, coarse sand beneath her feet.

"There are those who watch and those who are awake." Kith spoke from a few feet away. She was staring out at the darkness too.

Jordan hadn't even noticed her presence until she spoke. She took a few steps back.

"There's no need to fear me, cousin."

Cousin?

"For ages the army of spirits, once so near, have been receding." Kith looked up at the moon. "The spirits are gone even from their last citadel in the sky" She turned to Jordan. "No one believes in the glories of the heavens any longer."

"Angels." Jordan somehow felt calm standing so near this ancient vampire. Clearly, Kith had answers and Jordan wanted to hear them, even if it killed her to do so.

"Yes, angels." Kith smiled. She really was beautiful, and the moonlight only added to the eerie scene of revelation. "You are descended from Gabriel, the warrior, I am descended from Uriel, the messenger." She paused. "And Grace is descended from Ariel, the lioness of God."

"But how—"

"Tomorrow you will ascend and the Guild fears if you do that you will be a champion for the righteous. You will put an end to their status quo."

Jordan sensed that Kith was telling her the truth even though she didn't completely understand it. And what little she did understand raised many more questions. She'd suspected that Grace was somehow part of a larger plan, but Kith's revelation surprised her.

"The Guild struck a deal with the vampire clans long ago. Why do you think crime rates are so high? Why do you think housing prices have forced more people into homelessness? Humans are controlled like cattle and humanity doesn't even see it."

"Why? What does the Guild gain?"

"Certain members of the Guild leadership inject small samples of vampire blood in return for longevity." Kith's expression grew serious. "They've been doing it for so long that it's almost become an addiction, it is an addiction. Sorcha can no longer live without it."

How could Jordan not know that the Guild colluded with vampires to this extent? How had she not seen it? Because she didn't want to see it. She was happy to be an instrument of justice. Jordan was the hammer the Guild wielded to form the outcome that fit their designs

"And they think if I turn into whatever…that I'll ruin all their plans…and that's why they wanted me dead?"

"It's not quite that simple." Kith turned to face her. "The Guild, like humanity, cannot see beyond their own selfish needs." She paused. "Yes, your ascension would threaten the Guild, but more than that, it will threaten humanity's misuse of the Earth for the sake of wealth."

Memories, flashbacks, aching moments of sadness surged in Jordan's chest. Were these memories things that she'd experienced or someone else? Imagining a different way, a different future, seemed grim and valiant at the same time. She wasn't sure she was up to the challenge.

"The Earth is sick. There is salt in the groundwater, the animal kingdom has been pushed to the brink of existence…there are micro-plastics in the clouds." Kith placed her hand on Jordan's shoulder. "The Earth needs its champion."

"I'm not that person any longer." She felt defeated by life. She cared for Grace and earlier tonight, Grace, or the vampire inside Grace, had tried to kill her. Then she'd discovered her two closest friends in the world had kept a terrible secret from her. Like a door closing, she was shutting down, she doubted everything.

"Doubt is a good thing." It was as if Kith read her thoughts. She probably could. "Doubt breeds introspection, and introspection leads to truth."

"But you are a vampire."

Kith laughed.

"Yes, I am a vampire. I am also myself. I am your kin. I am the person you need right now."

"I'm supposed to kill you on sight. I'm expected to kill Grace as well."

"And yet, you haven't. Because deep down inside, buried in the deepest recesses of your psyche you know I am telling you the truth. And you also know that you need Grace."

Kith held out something wrapped in a cloth to her. She took it and unwrapped the object. The folded fabric contained a leather sheaf. Jordan gripped the handle and withdrew the blade. It was the weapon the vampire had used to stab her.

"The spike of Caiaphas." She was almost afraid to hold it. This instrument had pierced her side and inflicted the poison that sapped her strength. It vibrated with religious significance. Why would Kith give the ancient relic to her? Certainly, Kith could wield it if she wanted.

"Use it well."

"What am I to do with this?" She looked at Kith, the blade glinted in the light of the moon.

"That will reveal itself in time."

"You have too much faith in me." She slid the blade back into the sheath and put the belt around her waist.

For a moment, the only sound between them was the advance and retreat of the waves.

"I sired Grace, for you."

Jordan's heart almost leapt from her chest. Rage surged in her system. Without hesitation, she grasped the ancient weapon again, pulled it free from its case, and assumed an attack stance. She could so easily tear Kith's head from her shoulders with the blade. Kith had given Jordan the means for her own demise. Jordan could end it all right now. She could kill Kith and free Grace.

Jordan's strength returned in a flash, fueled by righteous anger. She swung the weapon at Kith, but Kith was too fast. Kith grasped Jordan's wrist and twisted at a painful angle so that Jordan was forced to drop to her knees. She glared up at Kith.

"I sired Grace for you because you need her. You need the immortality that she possesses now to awaken the immortal within yourself. By joining you will awaken the immortal in you both."

"I don't believe you." She tried to break free, but Kith held her in place. If she sensed any real threat from Jordan she didn't consider it worthy of defense, which only further angered Jordan. Her head pounded and she felt her body temperature rise, despite the cool night air.

"*Solve et coagula*, to dissolve and combine, is one of the most fundamental principles of alchemy. It is a process of distilling the essences of different things, to coax them to combine and copulate so that something new is created." Kith looked down at Jordan and her gaze pinned Jordan in place. "Something new and complex comes from the elements the world has worked so hard to keep separated."

"The letter?" She had to ask.

"Was not meant for you."

Grace alone had been able to translate the letter. It seemed so clear now.

Kith's grip on her was paralyzing. She struggled to breathe. And then as suddenly as she had appeared, Kith was gone…gone into the silent darkness. But Jordan sensed Kith's presence still. She lurched to her feet and spun around, searching the darkness for Kith. As she rotated, her feet sloshed in the shallow, frigid surf.

She felt abandoned, she felt lost.

Being lost is so close to being found.

She heard Kith's voice inside her head.

I brought you Grace, because only love can truly conquer all.

"Love ends." She thought of Eli and Sam. In the end, they hadn't trusted her or loved her enough to tell her the truth.

You say love ends, but what if it doesn't?

Jordan dropped the spike to her side. She was shaken and an ache was building in her gut. She gripped her heart as she doubled over in pain. She didn't look up, but she heard a flurry of wings pass just above her. She felt the wind from their passing as she collapsed to the ground. She slid the knife back in the case and stared up at the moon.

Something was happening to her. The rage she'd felt ebbed, cooled by the shallow surf. Her heart ached and her muscles relaxed. She knew that she could no longer move. Silently, she waited for the end to come. At least now she had some of the answers she'd been so desperately seeking. She wished she could see Grace one more time. She wanted Grace to know that none of this was her fault. She wanted Grace to know that she loved her.

Moonlight painted a broad stroke of light across the sea. She watched the shape of it shift and change with the undulating waves.

CHAPTER TWENTY-EIGHT

Grace had hoped to find Jordan when she arrived at the cabin, but the place was empty. Luckily, Jordan had turned the porch light on earlier when they'd departed so she wasn't in complete darkness upon her return.

The door was unlocked. She stepped inside.

"Jordan?" Not that she expected an answer. The Jeep was nowhere on the property so Jordan was still out.

"She'll be back." Sam followed Grace inside.

"You're right, I'm sure." But Grace secretly worried that the next time she saw Jordan it would be under worse circumstances, either for herself or for Jordan.

"Do you want me to stay with you?" Sam was sweet to offer.

"No, thank you." Grace handed Sam the fleece blanket that had been draped around her shoulders for the ride in the open truck bed. Her hair was probably quite windblown, and she made a feeble attempt to tame it. "I know that Eli needs you right now."

"There's not much I can do until sunrise except keep watch and keep her safe." There was worry in Sam's statement.

"Eli is lucky to have you." She hugged Sam.

"And Jordan is lucky to have you." Sam returned the embrace.

The urge she'd had earlier had calmed so she felt safe making physical contact with Sam, although she was hyperaware of the warmth of Sam's skin. Grace was having so many new sensations, and some were more unsettling than others.

She stood in the open door and waved to Sam as she drove away.

Back inside, Grace wandered from room to room unsure of what exactly she was looking for. She couldn't relax. It had been the same the night before. She initially felt sleepy with nightfall, but as the darkness deepened Grace began to feel more and more awake.

When she reached Jordan's bedroom she flipped on the light and again found nothing but the sound of an owl in the distance.

Grace went to the mirror in the bathroom. She filled the sink and splashed cold water on her face. She leaned closer. The color of her hair had shifted to auburn, with red highlights. She straightened and studied herself. She looked down at her chest then covered her breasts with her palms. Was she imagining it or had her breasts become firmer. She had another thought. She unzipped her jeans and checked her thigh. She'd struggled to erase a small bit of cellulite and now miraculously it was gone. Her thighs had also become firmer with absolutely no exercise. She frowned at herself in the mirror. All those hours at the gym were a complete waste of time.

She might have been happy if she hadn't known the reason. She was changing. She had changed.

Grace left her jeans in a pile and returned to Jordan's room to borrow a pair of well-worn sweatpants. She tugged on a T-shirt and got in bed. Grace wasn't sleepy, but she wanted the illusion of rest, of comfort.

She wondered what it would feel like to be a vampire.

Maybe she could stave off her desire to feed the same way Eli had done. She could hunt for a deer and feed without harming anyone, at least without harming a human. Even the thought of catching an animal and feeding off its life blood was beyond anything she could imagine. She squeezed her eyes shut and sank into the pillows.

Jordan, where are you?

A flurry of wings caught her attention. It sounded so loud inside her head, but she realized it was nothing more than a moth attracted to the bedside lamp.

She sank lower under the covers and tried to call up sensations of the afternoon she'd spent in bed with Jordan.

❖

Jordan managed to crawl farther up the beach and now lay in the sand just beyond the reach of the surf. She wondered if everything in her life had been a lie?

Kith spoke of angels. The old world.

Deep time was measured in units that humbled the human existence. Deep time was measured in epochs and eons, instead of hours, days, and years.

The inheritance and legacy that Kith spoke of stretched for a million years past and a million years to come. Was that what Jordan had seen in her dreams? She'd seen an army in white behind her, stretched in a line as far as she could see. Like the moon's glow painted on the surface of the ocean.

Once the pain subsided, a sense of calm came over her.

What was a demon hunter really?

Had Miller and so many others died for nothing?

Could she kill Grace if called upon to do so? Or Eli?

What did it matter any longer? The Guild was compromised. The work she'd always considered a calling was nothing more than keeping an imaginary balance sheet for a ruling party who'd sold them all out for some tainted fountain of youth. Who was qualified to decide on which side of the ledger someone's soul resided? Certainly not the Guild and certainly not Jordan.

She'd been so arrogant, so sure of her absolute rightness. She felt ashamed.

Maybe souls were much more complex than she'd been taught to believe. To view individuals as demon or not, lost or found, maybe that was all too simplistic.

Jordan lay unmoving as everything seemed to move around her. The retreat and surge of the sea, the firmament above, and time. She was in a waking dream, apart from her body but confined in it at the same time. She could sense the movement of the Earth and the creep of tectonic plates beneath its surface. The Earth cried out to her or perhaps it was the collective voice of the creatures of the earth. In any case, sadness overwhelmed her and she rolled onto her side and pulled her knees to her chest. She listened until she could no longer remain in that altered state.

Exhausted, she allowed sleep to come finally. The dark sky above was her blanket.

CHAPTER TWENTY-NINE

Grace could not sleep. She'd kept a vigil on the front porch waiting for Jordan. She'd carried a blanket out to the front steps with her as the air cooled and the night sounds began their chorus, but still Jordan didn't return. After a while, she was unsure of exactly how long she'd lingered on the porch, but her fingers were numb from the chill and her back was stiff. Grace wandered into the kitchen with the blanket still draped around her shoulders.

The letter still rested on the table. She picked it up and read it again.

The bridge to life is death.

The gateway to life is death.

The ancient time when your breath was light, and how now you dream of heaven.

The first two lines of the letter said the same thing. Hadn't Jordan told her that she would ultimately die when she became a vampire? That seemed like an eerie coincidence. The last line was still a puzzle. She let out a long sigh and dropped the letter to the table.

Grace draped the blanket on the bed, slipped into her jeans, and retrieved the jacket she'd first borrowed from Jordan. She'd decided she could no longer sit and wait, plus, she was wide-awake so Grace decided to go for a walk. This time she didn't even bother to carry a flashlight. The full moon was all the light she needed. Seeing it reminded her of Eli's transformation. Eli was a werewolf. Shouldn't she be more freaked out about that revelation? But somehow, she wasn't. Had creatures always existed in the world and she'd been too blind to see them? Now that she knew of this hidden world there would be no way to unknow it.

The sound of waves crashing at the base of the cliff was a constant reminder of how close she was to the ocean. Grace turned inland, following a deer trail through the tall grass. All the plant life around her pulsed blue, sometimes blue-green. The night was beautiful and if she hadn't been so worried about Jordan she might actually have been able to enjoy it.

Grace had been looking up at the trees, and when she glanced ahead she saw something cast a warm red glow amongst the gnarled trunks of the ancient cypress trees. The deer took a step, then two, then the doe froze. Grace felt a connection between herself and the animal as she held its gaze. After a moment, she slowly approached the animal and it still didn't run away from her. Tentatively, Grace reached out and touched the deer. It remained frozen, its gaze fixed on hers. Had she entranced the animal without trying to? The artery along its neck glowed hotly and Grace was overcome with hunger. No. Hunger was not a strong enough word for the urge that threatened to send her into a frenzy. What she was experiencing was more like a ravenous craving, a craving for blood. How could she know that? She'd never tasted blood before. Even rare meat repulsed her. But right now, she wanted nothing more than to sink her teeth into the doe and drink her fill. Grace refocused on her fingers against the doe's fir. Her nails had miraculously grown longer. It was as if she was seeing someone else's hand attached to her body. She jerked her hand back. She'd broken her gaze at the same time. The deer twitched and then darted away. A sharp pain in her stomach caused Grace to wince. She covered her abdomen with her palm and applied pressure.

She sensed something else.

Grace jerked her head up and pivoted to face the direction of the Pacific. *Jordan?* Something was terribly wrong. She could feel it. Dread overshadowed her desire to feed. She started back toward the cliffs at a brisk pace.

When she reached the cliff trail she scanned the white-capped waves beneath her. She couldn't actually see the beach from the trail so she left the trail and walked along the cliff's edge. As she slowly studied the beach, a faint spot of warmth began to take shape. It was faint, but somehow Grace knew it was Jordan.

She searched for a trail to the base of the rocky shore. Finally, she found a rough, dirt path that looked as if it led down to the beach.

In some places Grace had to use her hands as well as her feet to keep from sliding on the steep route. Looking up, she could see the overlook she'd just descended. The cliff looked as if it was being slowly reclaimed by the surf and that at any moment the earth might break away and bury her.

Grace glanced down the shore. The red-orange glow she'd seen earlier seemed to fade every time the surf advanced. Jordan must be in the water, but she wasn't moving.

Grace returned her attention to the climb. She scrambled down the last few feet of the rough trail. She lost her footing at the very end, falling backward into the soft sand. She dusted off and ran toward the now fading red beacon.

"Jordan!" Grace waded into the cold water. Every urgent step splashed salt water into the wind and into her face. Jordan was unconscious and slowly being carried out to sea in the shallow surf. "Jordan!" She brushed hair away from Jordan's forehead and lifted her head above the water line. "Jordan, wake up!"

The water that surrounded Jordan's body seemed to glow with some sort of bioluminescence. Grace had never seen anything like that before and it only seemed to be happening around Jordan and nowhere else.

Grace needed to get Jordan out of the water. Her body temperature had cooled so that her outline was barely warm at all. The red Grace had seen from above was barely visible. She hoisted Jordan up, placing a hand under each shoulder, and struggled to drag her unresponsive body backward. But Jordan was too heavy and every time the surf ebbed the water sucked them farther out. Grace waited for a moment. She held Jordan's shoulders above the water. Her head lolled to one side.

Grace had an idea. The next time a wave washed ashore, she tugged Jordan quickly as the wave lifted her body. Then she stopped and waited for the next wave. The progress was slow, but eventually she was able to drag Jordan just beyond the water's reach. Grace knelt beside Jordan and stroked her face.

"Jordan, please wake up." She pressed her lips to Jordan's. They felt cool against her skin. "I don't know what to do. Please help me." She whispered the words against Jordan's slightly parted lips. Was that a prayer? Was she praying now?

Remember.

It was as if the word had been whispered inside her head. *Remember.*

Grace rocked back on her heels as a vision returned to her. That night at the hotel. She saw the woman, Kith, above her, smiling. *Kith was her sire.* That's the response she'd had to her when she saw her from the window. Grace had wanted to go to Kith that night, but Jordan's episode had stopped her. And then when she'd looked up, Kith was gone.

Remember.

Grace closed her eyes. She could see Kith use a blade to make a small cut in her arm that Grace had tasted. The memory came back in a deluge of sensations and with it, the craving returned, making it hard for her to think. She squeezed her eyes shut as she lurched to her feet and walked away from Jordan. She wanted to save Jordan, not hurt her.

And then it became clear to her. White hot, like a flash of lightning.

The letter that only she could translate wasn't meant for Jordan. It was meant for her.

Grace rotated slowly and looked at Jordan.

The gateway to life is death.

Maybe that was true for both of them.

She returned to Jordan and knelt beside her. She ripped Jordan's shirt open and covered Jordan's heart with her hand. The dark lines of the poisoned curse had spread and now closed around her heart. Moonlight glistened on Jordan's damp skin. Her breathing was shallow and slow. The faint pink hue of the sunrise appeared at the cliff's edge. Time was running out. Somehow, Grace knew that and knew what she had to do.

"This is the only sacred ground I care about." She held her hand on Jordan's heart and then covered her own heart with her other hand. She bent down and whispered to Jordan. "I want you to know, I am a believer. I believe in you."

"Grace…" Jordan whispered her name.

"Jordan, I'm here." She stroked Jordan's forehead.

Jordan was so weak. Her eyes were barely open and her gaze seemed unfocused. Grace was unsure if Jordan was really looking at her. She sensed Jordan's fingers squeeze her arm.

"Do it."

"Jordan, I—"

"Do it, save yourself…save yourself for me…"

Overhead, Grace heard the frenzied passing of winged creatures. She didn't look up but instead focused intently on the sheath hanging from the belt around Jordan's waist. The hunger returned. The intensity of it threatened to overwhelm Grace, but she fought against it, fought to remain lucid, to remain in control.

Jordan's body was limp in her arms. Grace was losing her; she could feel it.

"Jordan, I love you." If this was going to be the end of everything, then she wanted to say the words aloud, even if she was the only one to hear them.

She drew close to Jordan, kissed her lightly, and then sank her teeth into the pulse point along Jordan's neck. Grace was becoming something else. The moment she tasted Jordan she knew that she could never be who she was before. Jordan's essence filled Grace's senses, her fight, her fear, her bravery, her love…yes, love. Like an event horizon, Grace knew there was no escape, no return, she could only move forward. The strength needed to break free was beyond her grasp. Tears streamed down Grace's cheeks. Jordan loved her. Jordan's essence, her lifeforce, told Grace everything she needed to know.

Remember.

There it was again. The whispered command. Kith's voice inside her head broke the trance and Grace forced herself to release Jordan. She withdrew the ancient dagger from the sheath. It was hot in her hand, but she didn't release it. She cut her arm as Kith had done in her recently recovered memory of that night. She covered Jordan's mouth with her arm. After a moment, Jordan stirred. She didn't open her eyes, but she reached for Grace's arm. Grace removed her arm when Jordan's eyes fluttered. Grace had ceased to notice time. The moon had fully given way to the sunrise. The cold surf was upon them again. As if to remind Grace of the endless sea and all the waters of the Earth, a closed system, like time eternal.

Jordan blinked. As her eyes gained focus, she saw Grace above her. The sun had breached the horizon. It was her birthday and she wasn't dead, but she also wasn't quite herself either. She was unsure of the exact time and as she'd collapsed on the beach, she'd had an urgent need to see Grace. She wanted Grace to know everything was okay. Jordan was at peace with her fate, and she wanted Grace to be at peace also. But now Grace was here, and so was she.

"Grace." She raised up and drew Grace into her arms. "I was afraid I wouldn't see you again."

"Jordan, I know you wanted to save me from this, but—"

Her words were choked by emotion. She wrapped her arms around Jordan's neck and Jordan kissed her. As their bodies came together in the embrace, Jordan felt changed. She had the sensation of floating. She was alive and Grace was in her arms. She felt invincible. Love had been stronger than the poison in her system. Only when she heard the unmistakable sound of wings did she open her eyes to discover that this time, the wings were theirs. Without realizing it, she'd taken flight and was holding Grace in her arms as they hovered several feet above the surf.

The immortal within Grace had awakened the immortal within her. Everything Kith had told her had been the truth. For the first time in a long time, Jordan felt truly alive.

Grace's eyes were closed as she clung to Jordan's neck.

"Grace, open your eyes."

Grace looked at her. Flecks of red were evident. Grace had transformed and so had she. And she wasn't afraid of it any longer.

"I only meant to save you."

"Don't look down." Jordan smiled as they continued to rise above the cliffs.

"We have wings!" The expression of surprise on Grace's face made Jordan smile.

"I have wings, thanks to you."

"Jordan, I no longer need to see wings to believe in heaven." Grace relaxed in her arms. "I only need you."

Jordan kissed her. It was a strange sensation. She simply thought of flying and her wings did the rest, effortlessly as if she'd always had the power to fly but had forgotten.

"I want you to know that I'm a believer too." Jordan allowed her wings to still and guided them softly back to the sandy beach. "I believe in us."

Once they were on the ground her wings retracted and withdrew from sight, as did Grace's. She somehow knew they would return when she needed them. Grace took off her jacket and draped it around Jordan's shoulders. She'd closed the snaps at the front of her shirt, but it was still wet. She bent to pick up the knife that protruded from the sand. Jordan wiped the narrow blade against her trousers and slid it into the sheath. She held out her hand to Grace and they walked along the beach back toward where she'd left her car the previous night.

She not only felt changed, Jordan felt new. She felt whole.

Before they traveled very far, Kith descended from above and stood in front of them. Her wings were white with golden highlights at the edge of each feather.

Jordan didn't know what to expect from Kith and protectively shifted in front of Grace. Just hours earlier, she'd tried to kill Kith for what she'd done to Grace. Now she realized she owed Kith a debt of gratitude. She braced for what might happen next, unsure of how to read Kith's serious expression. But then Kith smiled and opened her arms to embrace them.

Jordan and Grace hugged Kith. The three of them held each other for a moment. Then Kith turned her focus to Grace, she held Grace's face in her hands and gently kissed her forehead. Then she turned to focus on Jordan.

"I have so much to tell you. Now that you have become your true selves." Kith smiled.

"Thank you." Those words sounded so inadequate, but she didn't know what else to say.

"You are both my family now." Kith held onto each of them, her fingers were cool in Jordan's hand. "We will make a difference together."

"The power of the trinity, the power of three." Grace's expression brightened. "I finally get it now."

Jordan couldn't help smiling. What had seemed like the end, was in truth, just the beginning.

Chapter Thirty

S am and Eli were waiting for them when Jordan parked in
front of the cabin. She'd been so angry with Eli and now she
realized that her anger, her resistance was the thing that held her back.
Her inability to accept the idea that people could be more than one
thing at a time, that not everything was as absolute as she'd believed.
Eli could be her friend, a generous person, and a werewolf. It seemed
so simple to just offer empathy and forgiveness rather than judgment.

As they approached the steps. Eli stood and she could see that
Eli was expecting the worst from her, which made her heart ache. She
climbed the steps and drew Eli into a hug. After a few seconds, Eli
returned the embrace.

"I'm sorry." Jordan sincerely meant it.

"I'm the one who's sorry." Eli pulled away to look at her. "I
should have told you the truth."

"I know that you didn't because you thought I couldn't handle
it." A sense of peace washed over Jordan. "I should have judged less
and listened more."

"Jordan…" Eli's words were choked by emotion.

"I was harsh when I should have been empathetic." Jordan
needed to say more, a simple apology wasn't enough. She knew that
now. "All I really knew was the hunt." Jordan averted her eyes and
looked down at the floor.

"I forgive you, Jordan. Can you forgive me?" Eli placed her
hand on Jordan's shoulder.

Jordan looked up, smiled, and embraced Eli.

"You seem so…different." Sam joined them.

"I'm not the only one." She extended her hand to Grace, and she joined them in the small huddle on the porch. Grace smiled.

She'd wanted to save Grace, but in the end, Grace had to save her. It all seemed so clear to Jordan now that she felt foolish to not have seen it sooner. The journey she and Grace had taken had surely been one that they needed to do together. Kith had seen to that. And for that, Jordan was grateful.

"Want to see something cool?" Jordan's question was playful. She handed her jacket to Grace and flexed her arms and shoulders. Huge white wings spread behind her. Sam and Eli regarded her with wide eyed expressions. "I can fly."

"Holy shit." Eli stared at the massive expanse of her wings.

"How did this happen? What exactly did happen?" Sam asked.

"Let's go inside, and we'll tell you everything." Jordan no longer wanted secrets in her life. She wanted to share her life with the people she loved. She retracted her wings and climbed the steps to the porch.

At the threshold, Grace held back as the others entered the cabin. Jordan glanced back, she realized that Grace had crossed the consecrated boundary only because she'd been holding her hand when they arrived. But Grace could no longer enter without an invitation.

"Please come in, Grace." She extended her hand to Grace. Their fingers entwined.

Grace smiled. Once inside, she pressed Grace's fingers to her lips and kissed them.

Grace couldn't take her eyes off Jordan. She'd known Jordan in the most intimate sense of the word and now could hardly bear any separation between them. Everything in the room was amplified. The emotions of those gathered, the sound of heartbeats, the lack of her own. She'd died on that beach and been reborn in Jordan's arms.

She had so many questions, but Kith had promised to return and answer them all. She watched the three friends embrace and reconnect, she felt apart from them, but connected at the same time through Jordan.

After a moment, Jordan reached for her and drew her into a group hug.

CHAPTER THIRTY-ONE

Grace thought of the conversation she'd had with Natalie. She'd known it would be easier for Natalie to believe in love at first sight than for her to believe that Grace had become a vampire with wings—that she was descended from angels. In the end, she'd told Natalie about meeting Jordan and that she was going to stay in California for a while, *maybe forever*. That last part she kept for herself.

All the things she'd worried about before her transition now seemed so small and insignificant. She was learning to see the world in a new way, and Kith was helping her understand who she was. Jordan was concerned with the bigger forces at work in the world and now, so was she. It felt transformative to be part of something larger than herself. Not that she'd dreamed of literary fame as a writer or anything, but even the act of stepping away from her work had made her see how insignificant it was in the scheme of eternity.

Kith had become part of their circle. Kith had become an ally and a friend. She was helping Jordan understand who she'd become. The creature Jordan had assumed was a foe had become her mentor, and Grace's too for that matter. The three of them had an intense connection. Kith was the family Jordan no longer had. And for her, Kith was a patient teacher.

Changing the scale of time and place gave Grace many things to think about.

For now, she was focused on Jordan, focused on supporting her. Changing the world began the moment Jordan ascended, but there was something that needed to be dealt with first. They'd parked several blocks from the glassy high-rise offices of the Guild. Jordan's fingers were entwined with hers as they walked along the sidewalk toward the sleek building.

"Wait here." Jordan stopped near the entrance.

"I'd prefer to go with you." Grace didn't want Jordan to go alone.

"This is something I really need to do for myself."

Grace nodded. She kissed Jordan on the cheek.

Jordan glanced back at Grace as she entered the building. Grace was beautiful and she could no longer imagine her life without Grace in it. They had been through a lifetime of change together in such a short time.

Jordan grimaced as she rode the elevator to the top floor, just as she'd done so many times before. The moment the doors swished open, she strode toward Sorcha's office. Jordan's long dark coat billowed as she briskly walked toward the double doors. She didn't wait to be ushered in. She slipped her fingertips into the seam of the doors and forced them apart. Alarms sounded and red lights flashed as Jordan passed through the entryway and kicked the next set of doors open. A surge of adrenaline snaked through her system, but she wasn't afraid, she was focused.

Sorcha was behind the oversized desk at the far end of the room. She slowly stood. She looked as if she'd seen a ghost.

"Hi, Sorcha, I came by to inform you that despite your best efforts, I'm not dead." Jordan stood in front of the desk. She shucked her coat off and it pooled on the floor. She flexed her arms and shoulders. Broad, brilliant white wings filled the space in front of the desk.

Sorcha sank to her chair, dumbfounded.

Jordan drew the spike of Caiaphas from the sheath at her waist and stabbed it into the surface of the desk.

"The Guild is finished." Jordan paused. "You are finished."

"You don't have the power to make that decision."

"I think I just did. You should never have confused authority with virtue." Standing in front of Sorcha now, Jordan wished she'd acted sooner. But everything had happened in its own time, as it was supposed to. If things had been revealed to her sooner she'd probably not have been ready to accept them.

Jordan knew that there was an alarm under the desk that allowed Sorcha to call for assistance. She'd no doubt activated it the second Jordan kicked the door down.

"I've already dispatched someone to terminate your girlfriend, the vampire." Clearly a stall tactic. She knew it was a bluff, but it still angered Jordan.

She heard loud footsteps behind her and as if in slow motion, the discharge of a weapon. Jordan's wings reacted as a defense, deflecting the bullets so that they ricocheted around the room. A lamp shattered and tumbled off a nearby table. Framed prints broke apart and fell to the floor. Some of the bullets inevitably struck her attackers who fell behind her with a loud thump. Jordan never took her eyes off Sorcha. And when Sorcha pulled the firearm from her desk Jordan was upon her in an instant. She swooped across the desk and thrust the dagger into Sorcha's chest.

Sorcha tried to speak, but only her lips moved. No sound was uttered.

"This is for Miller." Jordan's words were hushed but stern. "And for me."

She kept her fingers around the knife until she was certain Sorcha was dead. She wiped the blade and returned it to its case. Then she remembered what Kith had said about Sorcha micro dosing the blood of vampires. Just to be safe, she withdrew the sword that she carried on her other hip, extended the blade and relieved Sorcha of her head.

Jordan loathed violence, but sometimes it was necessary. She looked at the carnage around the room and then turned toward the wall of glass and the city beyond. She took a deep breath and smiled.

❖

A loud crash caused Grace to flinch. Up the block from where she stood, shards of glass rained down on the sidewalk. No one was standing on the spot where the chair landed, it was late and way past regular business hours. Hardly anyone was about in the financial district. A man across the street in a business suit looked up. Grace followed his gaze.

Jordan's outline descended from above. Her wings were outstretched as she glided to the ground near Grace.

"Jordan, what—"

"Did I ever tell you how much I hate elevators?" Jordan rolled her shoulders, and her wings withdrew from sight.

"No. I guess we still have a lot to learn about each other." Grace slipped her arm through Jordan's as they began to walk away from the building.

"Luckily, we have an eternity." Jordan smiled.

"How did it go with your former boss?"

"She…Let's just say that she was surprised to see me."

"I'm going to need a bit more than that." Grace squeezed Jordan's arm.

"The Guild is finished." Jordan grew serious. "This is the beginning of something…better."

Grace wasn't worried. She'd been touched by eternity and all the elements of time and self had been stripped away. She was truly aware of her soul in the world and she knew whatever came next would be wonderful because she knew she'd be with Jordan.

Jordan could see the questions in Grace's eyes. She stopped walking and gave Grace her full attention. Grace had saved her in every way that a person could be saved. When it mattered most, Grace had believed, and that belief had saved them both. Jordan held Grace's face in her hands and tenderly kissed her.

"I love you, Grace Jameson."

"I love you too." Grace smiled.

Jordan realized that in her heart there was an empty chamber waiting to be filled. Grace had filled it. Her life had been nothing when compared to the immeasurable expanse of time eternal and still, deep down, without realizing it, she'd held out hope there really was more to her existence than administering judgment wherever the Guild directed. She didn't want to be that person any longer. She didn't want to see everything in stark black and white. The Earth was vibrant and alive and she and Grace were part of the fabric of it all.

Jordan knew she'd drifted for a moment.

"What now?"

She allowed her gaze to refocus on Grace as she held her.

"I have someone I want you to meet." Jordan smiled. "His name is Hero."

Jordan had broken through the surface of the dark sea. All her concerns had become nothing more than shadows cast against a wall. Because now she knew with certainty that she'd dreamt of heaven because heaven was real and she was holding it in her arms.

The end

About the Author

Missouri Vaun spent a large part of her childhood in southern Mississippi, before attending high school in North Carolina and college in Tennessee. Strong connections to her roots in the rural south have been a grounding force throughout her life. Vaun is a two-time Goldie Award winner. She and her wife currently live in northern California.

Books Available from Bold Strokes Books

And Then There Was One by Michele Castleman. Plagued by strange memories and drowning in the guilt she tried to leave behind, Lyla Smith escapes her small Ohio town to work as a nanny and becomes trapped with an unknown killer. (978-1-63679-688-8)

Digging for Destiny by Jenna Jarvis. The war between nations forces Litz to make a choice. Her country, career, and family, or the chance of making a better world with the woman she can't forget. (978-1-63679-575-1)

Hot Hires by Nan Campbell, Alaina Erdell, Jesse J. Thoma. In these three romance novellas, when business turns to pleasure, romance ignites. (978-1-63679-651-2)

McCall by Patricia Evans. Sam and Sara found love on the water, but can they build a future amid the ghosts of the past that surround them on dry land? (978-1-63679-769-4)

One and Done by Fredrick Smith. One day can lead to a night of passion…and possibly a chance at love. (978-1-63679-564-5)

Promises to Protect by Jo Hemmingwood. Park ranger Maxine Ward's commitment to protect Tree City is put to the test when social worker Skylar Austen takes a special interest in the commune and in Max. (978-1-63679-626-0)

Sacred Ground by Missouri Vaun. Jordan Price, a conflicted demon hunter, falls for Grace Jameson who has no idea she's been bitten by a vampire. (978-1-63679-485-3)

The Land of Death and Devil's Club by Bailey Bridgewater. Special Liaison to the FBI Louisa Linebach may have defied all odds by identifying the bodies of three missing men in the Kenai Peninsula, but she won't be satisfied until the man she's sure is responsible for their murders is behind bars. (978-1-63679-659-8)

When You Smile by Melissa Brayden. Taryn Ross never thought the babysitter she once crushed on would show up as a grad student at the same university she attends. (978-1-63679-671-0)

A Heart Divided by Angie Williams. Emma is the most beautiful woman Jackson has ever seen, but being a veteran of the Confederate army that killed her husband isn't the only thing keeping them apart. (978-1-63679-537-9)

Adrift by Sam Ledel. Two women whose lives are anchored by guilt and obligation find romance amidst the tumultuous Prohibition movement in 1920s California. (978-1-63679-577-5)

Cabin Fever by Tagan Shepard. The longer Morgan and Shelby are stranded together, the more their feelings grow, but is it real, or just cabin fever? (978-1-63679-632-1)

Clean Kill by Anne Laughlin. When someone starts killing people she knows in the recovery world, former detective Nicky Sullivan must race to stop the killer and keep herself from being arrested for the crimes. (978-1-63679-634-5)

Only a Bridesmaid by Haley Donnell. A fake bridesmaid, a socially anxious bride, and an unexpected love—what could go wrong? (978-1-63679-642-0)

Primal Hunt by L.L. Raand. Anya, a young wolf warrior, finds herself paired with Rafe, one of the most powerful Vampires in the Americas, in an erotic union of blood and sex. (978-1-63679-561-4)

Puzzles Can Be Deadly by David S. Pederson. Skip loves a good puzzle. Little does he know that a simple phone call will lead him and his boyfriend Henry to the deadliest puzzle he's ever encountered. (978-1-63679-615-4)

Snake Charming by Genevieve McCluer. Playgirl vampire Freddie is on the run and a chance encounter with lamia Phoebe makes them both realize that they may have found the love they'd given up on. (978-1-63679-628-4)

Spirits and Sirens by Kelly and Tana Fireside. When rumored ghost whisperer Elena Murphy and very skeptical assistant fire chief Allison Jones have to work together to solve a 70-year-old mystery, sparks fly—will it be enough to melt the ice between them and let love ignite? (978-1-63679-607-9)

A Case for Discretion by Ashley Moore. Will Gwen, a prominent Atlanta attorney, choose Etta, the law student she's clandestinely dating, or is her political future too important to sacrifice? (978-1-63679-617-8)

Aubrey McFadden Is Never Getting Married by Georgia Beers. Aubrey McFadden is never getting married, but she does have five weddings to attend, and she'll be avoiding Monica Wallace, the woman who ruined her happily ever after, at every single one. (978-1-63679-613-0)

Flowers for Dead Girls by Abigail Collins. Isla might be just the right kind of girl to bring Astra out of her shell—and maybe more. The only problem? She's dead. (978-1-63679-584-3)

Good Bones by Aurora Rey. Designer and contractor Logan Barrow can give Kathleen Kenney the house of her dreams, but can she convince the cynical romance writer to take a chance on love? (978-1-63679-589-8)

Leather, Lace, and Locs by Anne Shade. Three friends, each on their own path in life, with one obstacle…finding room in their busy lives for a love that will give them their happily ever afters. (978-1-63679-529-4)

Rainbow Overalls by Maggie Fortuna. Arriving in Vermont for her first year of college, an introverted bookworm forms a friendship with an outgoing artist and finds what comes after the classic coming out story: a being out story. (978-1-63679-606-2)

Revisiting Summer Nights by Ashley Bartlett. PJ Addison and Wylie Parsons have been called back to film the most recent Dangerous Summer Nights installment. Only this time they're not in love and it's going to stay that way. (978-1-63679-551-5)

The Broken Lines of Us by Shia Woods. Charlie Dawson returns to the city she left behind and she meets an unexpected stranger on her first night back, discovering that coming home might not be as hard as she thought. (978-1-63679-585-0)

Triad Magic by 'Nathan Burgoine. Face-to-face against forces set in motion hundreds of years ago, Luc, Anders, and Curtis—vampire, demon, and wizard—must draw on the power of blood, soul, and magic to stop a killer. (978-1-63679-505-8)

All This Time by Sage Donnell. Erin and Jodi share a complicated past, but a very different present. Will they ever be able to make a future together work? (978-1-63679-622-2)

Crossing Bridges by Chelsey Lynford. When a one-night stand between a snowboard instructor and a business executive becomes more, one has to overcome her past, while the other must let go of her planned future. (978-1-63679-646-8)

Dancing Toward Stardust by Julia Underwood. Age has nothing to do with becoming the person you were meant to be, taking a chance, and finding love. (978-1-63679-588-1)

Evacuation to Love by CA Popovich. As a hurricane rips through Florida, so too are Joanne and Shanna's lives upended. It'll take a force of nature to show them the love it takes to rebuild. (978-1-63679-493-8)

Lean in to Love by Catherine Lane. Will badly behaving celebrities, erotic sex tapes, and steamy scandals prevent Rory and Ellis from leaning in to love? (978-1-63679-582-9)

Searching for Someday by Renee Roman. For loner Rayne Thomas, her only goal for working out is to build her confidence, but Maggie Flanders has another idea, and neither are prepared for the outcome. (978-1-63679-568-3)

The Romance Lovers Book Club by MA Binfield and Toni Logan. After their book club reads a romance about an American tourist falling in love with an English princess, Harper and her best friend, Alice, book an impulsive trip to London hoping they'll each fall for the women of their dreams. (978-1-63679-501-0)

Truly Home by J.J. Hale. Ruth and Olivia discover home is more than a four-letter word. (978-1-63679-579-9)

View from the Top by Morgan Adams. When it comes to love, sometimes the higher you climb, the harder you fall. (978-1-63679-604-8)